NOT THE ONES DEAD

DANA STABENOW

"Kate Shugak is the answer if you are looking for something unique in the crowded field of crime fiction."
Michael Connelly

"For those who like series, mysteries, rich, idiosyncratic settings, engaging characters, strong women and hot sex on occasion, let me recommend Dana Stabenow."
Diana Gabaldon

"A darkly compelling view of life in the Alaskan Bush, well laced with lots of gallows humor. Her characters are very believable, the story lines are always suspenseful, and every now and then she lets a truly vile villain be eaten by a grizzly. Who could ask for more?" **Sharon Penman**

"One of the strongest voices in crime fiction." *Seattle Times*

"Cleverly conceived and crisply written thrillers that provide a provocative glimpse of life as it is lived, and justice as it is served, on America's last frontier." *San Diego Union-Tribune*

"When I'm casting about for an antidote to sugary female sleuths... Kate Shugak, the Aleut private investigator in Dana Stabenow's Alaskan mysteries, invariably comes to mind." *New York Times*

"Stabenow is blessed with a rich prose style and a fine eye for detail. An outstanding series." *Washington Post*

"Excellent... No one writes more vividly about the hardships and rewards of living in the unforgiving Alaskan wilderness and the hardy but frequently flawed characters who choose to call it home. This is a richly rewarding regional series that continues to grow in power as it grows in length." *Publishers Weekly*

"A dynamite combination of atmosphere, action, and character." *Booklist*

"Full of historical mystery, stolen icons, burglaries, beatings, and general mayhem... The plot bursts with color and characters... If you have in mind a long trip anywhere, including Alaska, this is the book to put in your backpack." *Washington Times*

DANA STABENOW

NOT THE ONES DEAD

An Aries Book

First published in the UK in 2023 by Head of Zeus
This paperback edition first published in 2024 by Head of Zeus,
part of Bloomsby Publishing Plc

9 7 5 3 1 2 4 6 8

A catalogue record for this book is available from the British Library.
Library of Congress Cataloging-in-Publication Data is available.

ISBN (PB): 9781804540183
ISBN (E): 9781804540145

Typeset by Divaddict Publishing Solutions Ltd

Printed and bound in Great Britain by
CPI Group (UK) Ltd, Croydon CR0 4YY

Head of Zeus Ltd
First Floor East
5–8 Hardwick Street
London ECIR 4RG

WWW.HEADOFZEUS.COM

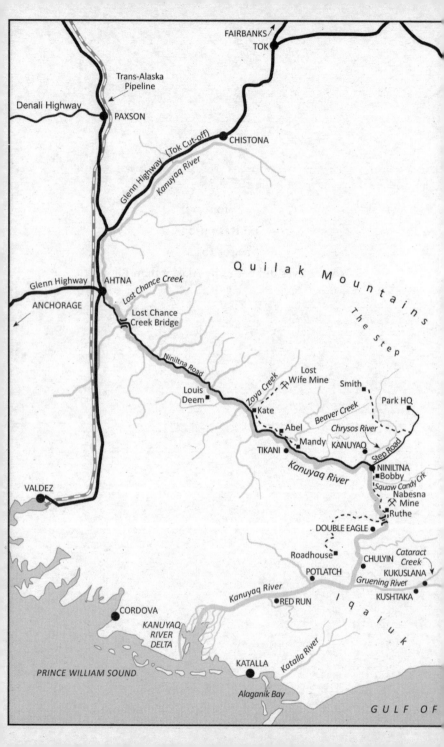

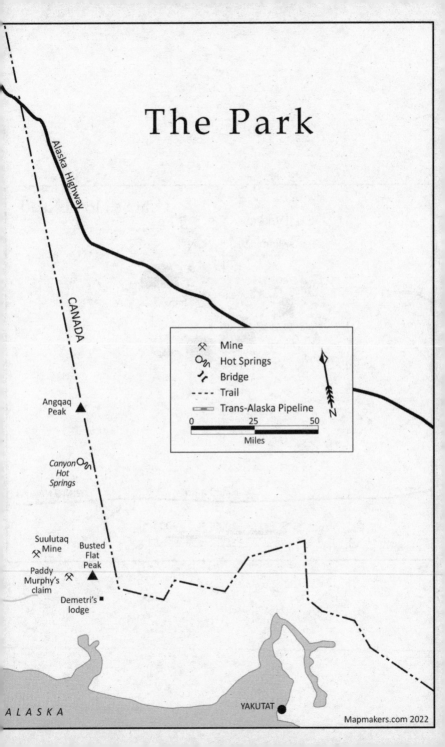

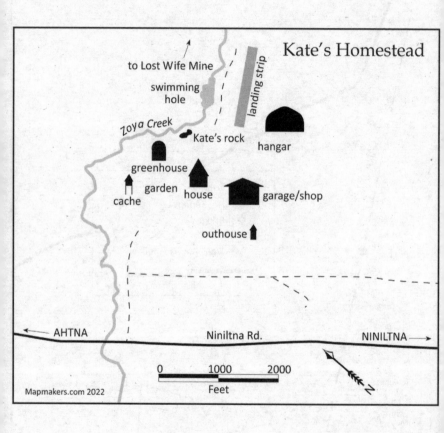

Kate's Homestead

to Lost Wife Mine

swimming hole

landing strip

Zoya Creek

Kate's rock

hangar

greenhouse

garden

house

cache

garage/shop

outhouse

AHTNA

Niniltna Rd.

NINILTNA

0   1000   2000

Feet

N

Mapmakers.com 2022

NINILTNA

AHTNA

Niniltna Road

KANUYAQ RIVER

Park HQ →

Chrysos River

Annie
Mike

Meganaks

Step Road

Herbie's

Auntie Vi   trooper   NNA
             post

school

gym

Old Sam

Bingley
Mercantile

Clear Creek

Emaa

post
office

Auntie Joy

Chugach
Air Taxi
hangar

landing strip

Riverside
Café

N

Grosdidiers

Demetri
Totemoff

0   1500   3000   4500

Roadhouse

Feet

Mapmakers.com 2022

One

TUESDAY, JUNE 1
The Park, the Niniltna road, 70 miles
southeast of Ahtna Junction

BOBBY CLARK ALWAYS WORE SHORTS TO Ahtna, January or June. It put both his prostheses on full display, which put him solidly in the category of retired military, which he was. White guys, and it was mostly whites who lived in Ahtna, the Alaska Natives having settled down the road in Ahtna Junction after the ANCSA lands distribution, would eyeball his bionic limbs, one over the knee and one under, and nod in solidarity. Some would raise a hook in salute. Some would give their own leg a significant tap. The guys with the canes and the walkers and the ones still in a chair would look envious but not to the point of going for their gun.

Over the years, he had also made it a habit to make the cop shop his first stop. He was on a first-name basis with the police chief, Kenny Hazen, and had at minimum a nodding acquaintance with the officers who worked for him. Bobby

I

was all for keeping the peace, especially when almost anywhere else in this country the color of his skin would be enough to get him shot for rolling down his window after a pull-over.

He had a wife and a daughter now, and he was going to dance with his daughter at the father–daughter dance at her high school in ten or twelve years. His first goal for any shopping trip was to come home alive.

In pursuance of that goal, he'd put the manager of the Ahtna Costco on speed dial on his cell phone. The guy had a standing invitation to drop by for a drink whenever he was in Niniltna. He'd made a point of befriending the new Fish & Game trooper stationed in Ahtna and extended the same offer, although that wasn't a stretch because Bobby had known Eddie Totemoff since he had been the star forward of the Cordova Wolverines and the Wolverines flew north for their annual grudge match with the Kanuyaq Kings.

Bobby never went empty-handed into Ahtna, either. Sometimes it was a couple of fillets of Boris Balluta's justly famous smoke fish to spread around. Other times it was a few jars of Ruthe Bauman's equally famous rhubarb chutney. Last August he'd brought in one of Dinah's raspberry slab cakes, which had been well received, but this year she was head down, ass up in a documentary the Niniltna Native Association had hired her to do on Ekaterina Shugak, which had expanded to include the four aunties. He was pretty sure she hadn't even heard him when he'd told her yesterday that he was making an Ahtna run.

After hunting and before snow it might be five pounds of

freshly ground mooseburger or a package of caribou steaks. Ahtna's mayor changed with the political winds but the city manager, a thin, tough, bleached blonde named Dolores Easter was an enduring fixture and owned a fondness for George Dickel Single Barrel 9 Year Old, with which Bobby took care to keep her well supplied.

It was fucking exhausting to be black in America.

It was fucking expensive, too. Boris didn't give away his smoke fish.

He'd left the house at eight a.m., Dinah already at work in the studio he had built for her next to the A-frame, six-year-old Katya building a Lego fire rescue helicopter on the floor next to her. He had been in stealth mode because at the first sound of the engine Katya would have burst out the door, demanding he take her along. He didn't want anyone giving her the side eye. He was probably being overly cautious, giving the advance work he'd been doing for years in Ahtna, but then he was a black man from Tennessee and he'd imbibed caution with his mother's milk. A lot of white Americans had come north following the oil rush of the seventies and eighties. Many of them had stuck around, and not for the betterment of the state, either.

Now he was on his way home again and happy to be, the back of his GMC Sierra piled as high as the cab with everything from batteries to toilet paper—learned that lesson during Covid—to a package of New York strips that had him, in his imagination, firing up the grill the second he got home, to some kind of stinky cheese Dinah liked, to tampons, which he could finally buy without turning red enough to show through his skin. Yeah, that's right, he thought when the other men in line looked askance, I got a woman, you losers should be so lucky.

All of it was tarped and roped securely to the tiedowns that lined the pickup's bed so he felt free to let the speedometer creep all the way up to forty. The gravel road had been graded and oiled the month before but it never took long for the axle-killing potholes to return. The Sierra bounced from one to the other, daylight between the surface and his tires more often than not, a billow of dust behind him large enough to look like his very own cumulous cloud. He slowed over the Last Chance bridge, sped up again, and slowed down again at the jog in the road before the Deem homestead.

Deem had been dead for over three years and people still called it the Deem homestead. Howie Katelnikof, the little weasel, and Willard Shugak had taken up residence. No Deem relative had yet appeared to turf them out. Every now and then Dan O'Brian made growling noises about acquiring the original 160-acre homestead for the Park, which invariably provoked Kate Shugak to visit the Step to instruct him in the error of his ways.

Personally, Bobby thought that was why Dan did it. He didn't blame him. There were a lot of Park rats who would do their bit to provoke a visit from Kate Shugak. Although not him, because he was a married man and a father nowadays. He grinned to himself, and then his stomach growled, loud enough to hear over the road noise. He'd meant to stop in at the Ahtna Lodge for one of Stan's fine steak sandwiches but there had been a sign on the door saying "Closed for Special Event". There had been so many black SUVs in the parking lot that the lodge had taken on the air of a General Motors dealership. When he was backing out onto the road he caught sight of a trio of men who looked ripped and were dressed in black head-to-toe like they'd taken the Johnny Cash song way too seriously. He spent the rest of the drive into Ahtna speculating on what the special event was. A conference of the local chapter of the National Funeral Directors' Association? A conclave of cocktail waitresses? In which case he should turn himself right around, but those were men he'd seen, not women, so scratch that. A *Call of Duty* RPG convention?

At that moment he caught sight of another cloud of dust billowing from the opposite direction, which resolved into a Ford SuperCrew in Rapid Red, a nice ride, although nothing compared to his Sierra in Pacific Blue Metallic. They were fast approaching and they were taking their half of the road out of the center so he swore a mild oath—well, mild for him—and pulled as far to the right as he could without driving down the bank into the Kanuyaq, which was uncomfortably near to the road on this stretch, as witnessed by many washouts over various springs since he had moved to the Park.

The oncoming red pickup didn't take the hint and move to its right. In fact it seemed to shift even more toward the center and even over to his side. "Motherfucker," he said, and checked to see that his seatbelt was fastened. It was, and a good thing, too, because that oncoming obviously dead-blind asshole was coming straight for him and he had no more room and no time to think about it and all he could do was look desperately for a section of the bank that was a little less steep with maybe some thick brush to slow him down and stop shouting profanities and save his breath and let up on the gas and hold tight to the wheel as he tried to keep the Sierra pointed in the same direction it was traveling as they plunged together over the bank at the side of the road.

He mostly succeeded. There had been a moment there when he thought she was going over but she settled back down again and the clump of alders he'd been aiming for slowed her down enough that she didn't run into the stand of cottonwood just beyond it and then into the river itself. The pickup lurched to a halt, bouncing him off the steering wheel but still upright. The airbag didn't inflate, which was either a design flaw or pure dumb luck. A quick glance over his shoulder showed him that the tarp was still secure. All in all, nothing short of miraculous. He sat there for the length of a nanosecond, marveling.

And then he heard the laughter.

He looked in the rearview mirror and saw that the red pickup had backed up to where he had gone over.

He bent over and reached for the thumbprint lock on the aluminum case bolted to the bottom of the dash on the passenger side.

Two

KATE HAD SPENT THE DAY FOUR-WHEELING the trail, hauling a trailer full of garden tools. She had her phone in her hip pocket and earbuds tuned to a playlist featuring everything from the Rascals to Springsteen to Pink, and somehow Brad Paisley had managed to sneak in there, too. She suspected that when her phone had gone missing the week before, Jim had added to her "Heavy Rotation" playlist. Brad got down, though, and he sure could pick. What she found less forgivable was the boy bands.

One day in the not-too-distant future Jim would forget his phone at the house. When it surfaced again his entire playlist would contain nothing but the soundtracks of Broadway musicals. She channeled her inner Khan to the open air. "Revenge is a dish best served cold."

A Steller's jay took the threat personally and launched himself from the branch of a nearby black spruce to beat wings into the northwest.

The trail was one she had spent years building, first blazing with an axe, trying to find the easiest way across, around, up, and down the one-hundred-sixty acres that comprised the homestead staked out by a forebear, back in the day when that kind of thing still happened. If he'd lived to see ANCSA, her father would have had land for the asking. Instead he had died young, along with her mother, and she had fallen heir to the homestead and the cabin he had built to claim it. It had tried to fall down for the entire time she'd lived in it and repairs had occupied much of her free time. Four years ago, the cabin had been replaced by a house. The house was sturdily built and had so far proved indestructible, and she had had to find something else to do to fill her off hours.

Not that there had been many of those this past year. A gang of thieves had been burglarizing empty cabins on Mat-Su Valley lakes. Area law enforcement was quoted by the *Frontiersman* as being baffled. Well, law enforcement such as it was, the denizens of the Valley as allergic to taxes as they were. Half a dozen victims had pooled funds and gone looking for a PI. They'd found Kurt Pletnikof, of Pletnikof Investigations, who tapped his silent partner to do the grunge work. Thanks a lot, buddy.

It hadn't been that onerous a job. As soon as she figured out that the lakes were all fly-in, she looked for cabins on other fly-in lakes in the area, figured out what she hoped was the next target, and with the owner's permission took up residence in one of them. It took a week, which was boring, especially for

Mutt, but Kate read half a dozen books and finally at dawn on the seventh day a blue-and-white Cessna 172 on floats came spluttering into view. It bounced four times as it landed on a calm day with no wind. Pretty much told Kate everything she needed to know about the pilot.

It taxied to the cabin third down from the one Kate and Mutt were occupying. Two men got out. They moored the plane and walked up the trail to their target. She watched with interest as they forced an entry with a crowbar. After that it was a simple matter of sneaking through the tall grass, unmooring the aircraft and pushing it out into the lake, and waiting until they noticed. When they did, Mutt took down one and Kate the other. They weren't armed, and once they were restrained, Kate sent up the flag using a satellite phone. It took until ten a.m. for the trooper to get there and the rest of the morning for him to stop giggling.

While that was wrapping up, one of her satisfied customers had passed the word and put the family of the victim of an unsolved murder in the Mat-Su on her track. That had been a much shorter but far more difficult and dangerous job and she had been lucky to escape with her life. She had made the mistake of not telling Jim all the story, momentarily forgetting that he had been an Alaska state trooper for more than two decades and that among themselves troopers were gossipier than a potluck dinner at the school gym. It didn't matter if you were still on the job or not, you were always in the loop. Jim had yelled at her for an hour and then taken her to bed and kept her there all night.

She understood. The need for reassurance was powerful. And they had been apart for three weeks.

And not that she was complaining, either, but she was just a little tired today. Hence the four-wheeler instead of two legs and a wheelbarrow.

Her homestead was a square plot of land that encompassed the aforesaid house, a shop, a garden shed, an old outhouse she hoped never to have to use again, a salmon creek, a defunct gold mine, and four hundred feet of the Niniltna road. Not to mention an airstrip, along with a hangar the size of Dubuque. Technically the airstrip and the hangar —and the plane—belonged to Jim, so she didn't count them, although it would have taken someone smarter than the two of them put together to imagine how he'd take them with him if he ever got into a snit and decided to decamp the premises. The plane, sure, he'd probably decamp in that, but the rest...

She smiled to herself. There would be no decamping. It might be the one thing she was most sure of in her life.

The homestead was in almost the exact center of a twenty-million-acre national park, a grandfathered-in piece of private property, one of many that the Park's chief ranger, Dan O'Brian, was always and eternally dreaming and scheming of reacquiring for the National Park Service. He was a true believer, was Dan, and had been heard to say many, many times that the only thing the United States had ever gotten right in 245 years was the national parks. He wouldn't die happy until every bit and piece of private property around which the Park had been created was returned home again.

In which case, Kate thought, he was doomed to die disappointed. She looked around but Mutt was off somewhere terrorizing the small mammal population. She turned off the engine and dismounted, groaning a little as she stretched out her back.

It was the first Wednesday after Memorial Day, which holiday marked the official start of planting as it usually saw in the first night temps above freezing. For the past week the sun had banished every cloud between Canada and the Bering Sea, leading to record high temperatures and an unaccustomed number of cases of sunburn across the southern half of the state. She looked east, at the Quilaks. Snow was disappearing rapidly from their peaks, and they looked a little embarrassed at the shortness of their skirts.

The range formed the eastern boundary of the Park, running along the Alaska–Canada border. The highway to Tok formed a rough guide to its northern boundary, as did the road from Ahtna to Anchorage and the Alaska Railroad to the west, and then of course the Mother of Storms, operating under the US Coast and Geodetic Survey's nom de plume of the Gulf of Alaska, formed the southern border. Glaciers descended from the Quilaks in enormous slabs of ice, between which, foothills were jostled to one side by outliers of single mountains and the occasional butte standing rebelliously apart from their mother range.

It comprised an enormous territory, larger than Maryland and Massachusetts put together, and contained the entirety of the Kanuyaq River, broad and winding, with hundreds of smaller rivers, creeks, streams, brooks, rivulets and rills feeding into it, each and every one of them with a treasure unique to itself, be it nuggets of gold hidden beneath sand and gravel or one of five species of salmon spawning above them.

She could see almost all of it today by the light of a sun hanging in an unrelenting clear sky. After the first two weeks it felt as if it were going to hang there forever, and the NOAA forecast held out no hope for rain anytime soon.

Her little piece of the Park was part hill, part vale, the hills rounded off by millennia of erosion, the vales created by the carving of glacier-fed creeks, all of it interrupted irregularly by glacial erratics, boulders as small as her ATV and as large as her house. The Homestead Act had been written originally for prospective farmers but there wasn't much in the way of farmland on Kate's parcel, or anywhere else in the Park for that matter.

Over decades of walking, hiking, slogging, and bush-whacking those acres, Kate had eventually traced the most accessible route for a path that encompassed most of it. By now it was wide enough for a four-wheeler, and avoided bogs, too-steep hills, and those boulders too big to shift. After she'd figured out the route of the trail, she began identifying small patches of ground where something might conceivably grow, and began planting. Flowers, always perennials that she'd seen come back every year elsewhere in the Park, Alaska wildflowers mostly, especially forget-me-nots, but also chocolate lilies and sedum and western columbine and Siberian iris and pink pussytoes and the diminutive purple primrose native to the state. She had stumbled over a patch of sweet-smelling moss campion near the old mine and had since successfully transplanted it to half a dozen other locations on the property. But in protected nooks, those few she could find, she also planted ruffled velvet iris and golden queen trollius and as many Himalayan poppies as she could lay hands on—the Ahtna nursery set aside a flat for her every spring. And primroses of every kind and color. It was always a gift when a late spring stroll revealed a mound of Dorothy primroses glowing with an unearthly pale yellow light.

There were all kinds of evergreens growing indigenously, of course, most of which she couldn't put a name to. They were positively promiscuous in their attempts to start shoots everywhere on any sort of ground—a gravel cutout on the creek, a rocky tor, a swamp, and, naturally, the trail itself. She pulled the ones she found on the trail and replanted them where she hoped they would form windbreaks for her other plantings. They took hold about half the time. The other half of the time, they proved too surly to thrive somewhere it wasn't their idea.

Berries, of course, although there were already plenty of blueberries, one variety that she waited to harvest until after the first freeze because there was nothing more out of this world than the taste of a blueberry the size of her thumbnail picked at the moment of maximum sugar content. It was like a tiny popsicle. Cloudberries and crowberries liked higher ground and any attempt to transplant them from Canyon Hot Springs had failed. And of course raspberries of any and every variety. The downside was the moose, who liked raspberries every bit as much as she did.

The upside, of course, was also the moose. She never had to go far to fill her freezer every fall. One halcyon September she'd bagged a bull from her front doorstep, not that anyone ever believed the story when she told it, and it was far enough in the rear view now that she barely believed it herself. But she was still grateful for the winter of good eating he had given her.

It had been the last moose she and Ekaterina had butchered out together.

A sweet, three-note descant trilled through the air. She smiled.

A half hour later the ATV trundled into the yard, just in time to meet Bobby Clark trudging in from the Niniltna road. He was limping a little, one prosthesis looking a little bloody where it met his knee, and he was covered in dust and sweat. One hand held a big-ass gun, an automatic with an equally big-ass clip.

He halted. She let the four-wheeler roll to a stop. They stared at each other for a moment.

"You look peeved," she said.

Three

WEDNESDAY, JUNE 1
The Park, Kate's homestead

WHEN THEY RETURNED FROM HAULING his Sierra back up onto the road, he consented to follow her back to the house and allowed her to soothe him with coffee and fry bread fresh out of the pan. He was just getting started on the tale, often interrupted with colorful editorial commentary, when they heard the Stationair overhead and she made him wait until Jim got there to start over.

"Hey, Bobby. Your pickup looks a little worse for wear." Jim paused inside the door. Mutt bulled in, between him and the door, and immediately pounced on Bobby, doing her best to convince him he was her greatest love in all the wide world and then some.

"Fucking WOLVES in the HOUSE, Shugak!" He did his best to fend off the wolf, who was having none of it. His face was much cleaner when she dropped back to all four feet and grinned up at him, tongue lolling out. He looked a trifle less tense, too. The unfettered adoration of 140 pounds of dog was its own stress reliever.

And his protest had sounded less emphatic than his normal bellow anyway. The day had taken its toll.

Jim walked to the kitchen, kissed Kate, went back in for a second because he knew Bobby was watching, and got a beer out of the refrigerator. He took a long, luxurious pull. "To what do we owe the honor?"

With an effort Kate refrained from rolling her eyes. Jim never forgot that Kate and Bobby had once been an item. Long ago and far away and for only a brief time, but he never forgot. In a voice as neutral as she could make it, she said, "I had to pull him out of the ditch, and he was just beginning to tell me how he got there when you got home." She refilled Bobby's mug and delivered a fresh piece of fry bread to prime the pump.

He chewed and swallowed, at first mechanically and then with more actual in-the-body enjoyment, and after a while began to talk.

At first Kate didn't know which was worse, the story itself or the way Bobby told it. His voice was flat, almost monotone, displaying no shock or even surprise. "I heard them laughing. One of them said, 'Well, that was fun,' and another, 'How many years you think we just scared off that coon?' and a third, 'Too bad we didn't kill the nigger,' and that was when I went for the HK." He nodded at the black machine gun he had insisted on carrying into the house, where Kate had insisted he put it in the gun rack over the door between the .30-06 and the pump-action shotgun. "Bottom line is they weren't taking their half out of the middle until they got close enough to see who was behind the wheel."

Jim had nothing of value to add to this conversation—no one was going to run him off the road for driving while white—so kept his mouth firmly shut.

"Assholes." Kate's tone was matter-of-fact. Accepting, even.

Yeah, Jim thought, for sure that was worse.

Bobby dredged up a wintery smile. "They are everywhere." He drained his mug and sat back. "Plates were muddy. The whole rig was covered in mud, like they'd been off-roading. They never got out because I pulled myself out of the window, sat on the sill, and showed them I was armed and what with. They took right off. I didn't get a look at their faces but I think there were four of them. I know I heard three and maybe four different voices. For as much as I could see inside the shadow of the cab they were all wearing desert camo." He pointed at his eye, which had swelled mostly shut but at least wasn't bleeding anymore. "I couldn't see too well." He shrugged and this time he sounded a little weary. "Could have been worse. Could have—"

"Don't," Kate said. "Don't you fucking dare."

Their eyes met. There was a long silence heavy with history, and not only personal history, either.

Jim let it endure for as long as he could. "So. Are you going to make class tomorrow?"

Bobby glared at him, but a one-eyed glare is by definition only half-hearted. "Jesus Christ, you are one single-minded son of a bitch."

Jim did his best to look hurt. "I'm just being a responsible chancellor."

"Yeah, you're the Booker T. Washington of the Park." Bobby sighed. "Don't worry, I'll be teaching my goddamn class."

"Good." Jim did not offer an apology but then Bobby hadn't expected one. If there was one thing Kate clearly understood about both of these men, it was that they cut no slack with each other. But then they cut no slack with themselves, either. They both thought they were Superman.

She looked at Mutt, who looked up at her. Solidarity, sister.

"And how was your day, dear?"

Jim grimaced. "Did you hear the 'chancellor' bit?"

"I did, and I want credit for not laughing out loud."

Bobby perked up a little, which was probably why she'd said it. "Me, too."

"Yeah, yeah. It's not my fault." He sounded whiny and he knew it. "My damn board hung it on me."

"You mean the governing body of your soon-to-be-august institution?"

'Yeah, them." He sounded glum. Hell, he was glum. "They said I should have a title."

"'A chancellor is the leader and chief operating officer of an academic institution,' it says here. Oooh. And the vice chancellors, the provost, the deans and the faculty all report to them." Kate looked up from her phone. "Can I be provost?"

Bobby waggled his eyebrow. "Sounds kinky."

Jim knew they were ragging on him and he knew why. Still, it was little short of miraculous how fast his idea of a vocational school in Niniltna had come together. He knew it had something to do with already having buildings in place and a bottomless pocket—his, thanks to his father's gift for investing in gold-plated stocks—but the pace of progress had been dizzying. Three months from his purchase of Herbie Topkok's house and shop he had employed a master carpenter, a master mechanic specializing in automotive repairs, a master plumber and—what he regarded as his prize catch— an electrical engineer on staff. With help from his dominatrix board, the school had created an academic year divided into thirds arranged around having August not in session so the Alaska Natives among them could go to fish camp. And they had a student body of eighteen. Six of them—he was particularly proud of this—were girls.

The master carpenter and the master mechanic had been lured from retirement, one in Anchorage and the other in Fairbanks. When the, well, the faculty—he had a hard time getting used to that word—had sat themselves down to talk about eligibility for entry into the Herbie Topkok Polytechnic Academy, the master mechanic had had an unusual idea. Jim, who didn't know any better, had thought it sounded pretty nifty and okayed it, although the master plumber—an actual plumber from Seward whose wife had left him for the high school English teacher and all he wanted was to get out of town—was skeptical. The electrical engineer, who lived in Ahtna, had not been present and later told Jim he'd thought it was a batshit crazy idea when he'd first heard about it but the students were proving him wrong every day.

What they did was get online and Google the most difficult Lego builds. They had ordered the top ten so rated, and had them same-day shipped to Kurt Pletnikof's office in Anchorage, which put a considerable dent in the monthly budget and bewildered the hell out of Kurt. Then Jim flew the, yes, the faculty plus Legos out to various and sundry villages, where Jim talked each local school into letting them hold a career day, or afternoon or hour, commandeered half a dozen tables, and invited the students to go to work. "Actually, Phil bellered out something like 'Assemblers! Assemble!'"

Phil Mason being the carpenter, and Neil Nowak, the mechanic, being the speaker.

Fascinated, Jim had said, "How did you choose?"

Neil sat back, hands laced over his considerable belly, and smiled. "The ones who sorted the pieces before they started putting things together."

Phil nodded. "And who put together teams and assigned roles. You know, 'You on the chassis, you on the engine, you on the lift.' They invariably finished first and their builds held together."

The Lego test identified potential students. Their families were soothed by the caliber of the members of the board, sometimes reinforced by personal calls. No one said no to Jim's board. The board was well pleased with the result, although Tara, one of the board members, did say of the six girls, "Well, it's a start." Jim quite agreed with her.

They had opened their doors the first of May, although he'd sweated blood filling inventories as demanded by staff. Until now he had lived in blessed ignorance of the different kinds and sizes of nails required to frame one wall. Phil Mason had been his first hire, and Phil's first class had been put to work immediately remodeling half a dozen derelict cabins in and around Niniltna, because Auntie Vi had only so many rooms in her B&B and none of the instructors wanted to live in the dorm (once Herbie's family home) with the students. Like everywhere else in Alaska, Niniltna had no long-term, low-cost housing.

Many mistakes were made by the new apprentices. All were corrected. Profanity was employed. "Yer typical jobsite," Phil said. In the end, the instructors had housing with power and running hot and cold, and only one student had dropped out. "The hell with this, I'd rather go fishing," he had said on his way out the door. The rest of them stuck because most had grown up fishing with their families and they knew how unreliable the salmon runs had become everywhere but Bristol Bay.

When the last cabin was finished someone had approached Phil with an offer for a small construction job, a remodel on a house out of town. Phil consulted Jim, who thought the notion of real-world experience was a fine idea that might lead to post-graduation jobs, so Phil and the class disappeared from campus for a week.

Applications were beginning to come in unsolicited, and Native tribes and villages and corporations—prodded, no doubt, by his board members—were beginning to take notice. And a couple of the mechanic students had indicated an interest in pursuing an A&P certificate, not surprising as airplane mechanics were the highest paid mechanics there were and prized above rubies in Alaska. So he had conned Bobby, who had been annualing his own aircraft for years, into giving them some hands-on experience beneath the cowling of his Super Cub.

"Well," he said now, drawling out the words, "as the provost has to do everything the chancellor says…"

Bobby snorted and hoisted himself to his feet. Jim and Kate both saw him sway a little but were smart enough to pretend they hadn't. "Thanks," he said to Kate.

"Any time." She gave him a look that he interpreted, correctly as *I'll keep an eye out for the assholes.*

He gave her one right back that she read as *They had their fun. They're long gone.*

Maybe. Maybe not.

Later that evening, Jim very cautiously put out a conversational pawn in the form of a question he thought he knew the answer to but wasn't certain sure. "Why isn't the Park like everywhere else?"

She didn't pretend not to understand. "Because of the aunties."

He waited.

"Because of local leaders. Sometimes they're cranky, and sometimes they're scary, and sometimes they're loving, and sometimes they just listen to you with all their ears, and sometimes they cast a shadow so large as to encompass us all. But this kind of shit they will not tolerate."

Vi, Edna, Joy, and Balasha, and the chief of the tribe, Ekaterina. "Three of them are dead."

"Others will take their places." She saw his look and shook her head, a faint smile crossing her face. "Wait and see."

Four

FRIDAY, JULY 1
Niniltna

AFTER THE DRIEST JUNE ON RECORD Niniltna looked a little crisped around the edges. The Park's chief ranger, Dan O'Brian, had declared a burn ban within its borders and it was that rare government edict that most Park rats were happy to oblige. At the end of June there had been a brief blaze when Yuri Andreev was sharpening a shovel and the grinder threw a shower of sparks into a clump of dead grass, but Yuri lived just down the hill from the airstrip and the entire village had responded with buckets and boots to stamp it out before it spread. There were comments from Auntie Vi, freely spoken, at volume, and in public. Immediately after which, Yuri returned to the *Terra Jean* where it was anchored in Amartuq Creek and had his nets in the water for every opener for the rest of the summer. The aunties made sure to keep that object lesson at the front and center of the Park's attention. Dan said he might as well put Auntie Vi on retainer and be done with it.

Jim was bringing the 206 around to land to the south, but he and Kate both were casting wary glances at the southern horizon, from which an increasingly thick band of cloud, black against the blue of the sky upon which it was encroaching, was making its inexorable way north. "It's going to rain on the Fourth," Kate said.

"From the looks of that I'd say it's going to rain all month."

Mutt thrust her snout in between them and wuffed what sounded like agreement. "Yeah, you would know," Kate said, and Jim chuckled.

They landed without incident in spite of the many small planes lined up on each side of the runway. Jim found an empty space between a Piper Tri-Pacer that had seen long and hard service and a snazzy Beechcraft Bonanza. He shut everything down and they got out to walk the Cessna tail-first into the tiedown. "The holiday weekenders flooding in a day early."

"Good we came this morning. Let's try to get out of here by noon before this turns into an air show."

"I heard that. You got the list?"

Kate patted her back pocket and felt the outline of a crumpled piece of paper. "Yes."

"Okay, you hit the store and I'll check the mail."

"Deal. If you see Auntie Vi, duck."

"If I see Auntie Vi, I will run."

"Good enough." Kate grabbed a canvas shopping bag out of the plane and she and Mutt checked for incoming before crossing the runway. She waved at George Perry, who was standing in front of his hangar talking to his mechanic, and trotted down the hill. If she moved fast enough they shouldn't spot her from the Niniltna Native Association offices. There was a trail behind the trooper post, now closed, that went the back way to Bingley's and they sidled down it with finesse and dispatch. Every step raised puffs of dust and the alders drooped tiredly overhead. It hadn't rained since April. The land itself was thirsty.

They came out at the back of the store and circled around to the front. The main street, never named, was a continuation of the road from Ahtna. Buildings old and new formed an irregular line, some with small gardens that were withering in place. She saw a raspberry patch covered with green leaves and pink blooms. Someone had been hauling water from the river, which was just beyond and down from the far side of the street. Vehicles had been parked everywhere, on the street and off it. Further down, in front of the Riverside Cafe, she saw two big white camper vans. One of them had a vanity plate. She squinted but it was too far away to read.

Some people waved. More people didn't. Lots of strangers in town.

She felt a sting in her left buttock and jumped. "Hey!" She looked down at Mutt, who gave her an admonitory glance. "Put your teeth away, dammit, I'm going." She pulled the list out of her pocket and went inside.

It was crowded with people, the only one of whom she recognized was Cindy Bingley behind the counter. Cindy looked uncommonly grim for someone who was about to have her best weekend of sales for the year. "Cindy."

"Kate." Cindy glowered down the first aisle at someone Kate couldn't see.

"Please tell me you have half-and-half." They hadn't for over a month. Frigging Covid and supply chain issues made a lot of popular items fall off the truck in Ahtna and never make it down the road to Niniltna. Not that the truck made it down the road that often anyway, but it was hard to justify even a quick flight to Ahtna for a half gallon of half-and-half.

"In the cooler."

Kate got a basket and started filling it. She wanted to make cowboy caviar for their staycation on the Fourth. At home she had all the canned items the recipe called for, and by a miracle, here were avocados, green peppers, red onions, and even cilantro, although it looked as limp as the alders along the trail. She looked up. "Yes!" There was one lone jalapeño and she snatched at it in fear someone would reach over her shoulder and beat her to it.

"Whatsth that?"

She looked down to see a three-foot-high human, bright blue eyes staring up at her from beneath a mop of white-blond hair. It was wearing a pair of blue jean coveralls over a white short-sleeved tee and sneakers. She couldn't tell if it was male or female. It was clutching a package of Red Vines in one hand. "A jalapeño pepper."

The human made a face. "Pepperth. Ugh."

"Are you dissing my cooking?"

The human grinned, showing a gap where its two front teeth had once been. "Yeth."

27

"Hulduh!" A thin, elderly woman in a cotton housedress and white-strapped sandals hustled down the aisle and grabbed Hulduh by the arm. She shoved the child behind her, glaring.

Involuntarily Kate looked behind her to see what the threat was. When she looked back the woman was herding the child toward the door.

"Was it something I said?"

No one answered. She shrugged and put the pepper in the basket and went to the register. "Who was that?"

"Assholes." Cindy rang up her items without further commentary. Kate came outside to find Jim waiting for her. Impossibly the street seemed even more crowded than when she had gone inside, and then she realized that the two vans she'd seen parked in front of the Riverside had moved up the street. The old woman was pushing Hulduh, protesting, into one of the vans, which was filled with more children who looked and dressed just like him or her—Kate had no idea what gender was assigned to the name Hulduh—in varying age and size, with identical corn-silk hair, and skin so white they looked albino, but with pale blue eyes.

A man in his forties who bore a strong resemblance to the old woman came around the end of the van, followed by another man dressed in desert camo. He wore a sidearm in a holster. The first man nodded at him and he stopped, spread his feet and clasped his hands over his belt. He had a cap pulled low over his eyes and he stared unsmiling over Kate's head.

She must have left the house that morning without washing off the "Unclean" written on her forehead.

The first man looked at Jim. "Hello."

"Hello. Brought the family into the Park for the Fourth?"

"Oh no. We bought property in the area. Having some work done on it before we move in and thought we'd take in the sights."

"Welcome," Kate said, keeping a wary eye on the crazy lady who was now glaring at her from inside the van.

"You're a local, then?" the man said to Jim.

"Yes."

"How long?"

"Some years now. I'm Jim Chopin, and this my partner Kate Shugak."

The man shook Jim's hand. He didn't appear to see Kate's. "Cisco Barre."

"Barr? Any relation to the Alaska Barrs?"

"'Fraid not. Barre with an e. Well, I expect we'll see you around."

Barre with an e had yet to acknowledge Kate's existence and Jim was done being civil. "You know, I don't think we will."

"Cisco! Get in and let's get out of this place." The old woman's voice was high and cracked but it expected to be obeyed immediately and it was.

The man named Cisco gave Jim a nod that was either imperturbable or oblivious and walked around the front of the van to climb into the driver's seat. The vehicle started with a nearly soundless purr and moved off down the street, stirring up the dust. The guard dropped his hands and walked away.

Kate nudged Jim. "Check out the plates."

It took a moment before the red mist cleared from his eyes and he could focus. "Yahweh1."

The second van went by, also filled with what were obviously Hulduh's siblings. It, too, bore a brand-new Alaskan plate, this one reading "Yahweh2."

He felt her hand grip his arm. "Jim. Look."

The guard in the camo followed the second van in a bright red SuperCrew. There were three other men dressed just like him inside.

"Do you think—"

"Don't you?"

The SuperCrew's plate was also a vanity plate but it was muddy and Kate couldn't read anything past the first letter, Y.

Probably "Yahweh3."

Five

DAN O'BRIAN HAD LONG SUSPECTED THAT the first chief ranger had selected the site for Park headquarters in the hope that no one would ever be able to find it.

Dan would have liked to have explained to him, at length, how well that hadn't worked out.

The Step was a long, broad plateau that interrupted the fall of the Quilak Mountain range about halfway down before it subsided into rolling foothills and a serpentine river valley. A runway had been bulldozed right down the center of the plateau with a surface that felt like a rumble strip on landing. A clump of prefabricated buildings between the airstrip and the backing massif, some of which dated back to before World War II, resembled a sullen lineup of defendants in a magistrate's court the day after an all-night binge. They should have been razed and replaced already, but trying to get money for the National Park Service out of Congress for inessentials like office space and housing had for the last forty years been a task that made the twelve labors of Hercules look like a snap by comparison.

So the pre-war buildings remained, and Dan, the current chief ranger, had done his best by them, fixing roof leaks and burst pipes and electrical wiring long past code. He had managed to connect the Step to Niniltna with a dirt road that had a surface that was even worse than the airstrip. Traversing it in winter was impossible for any vehicle with less torque and traction than a Sno-Cat. In summer four-wheel drive and a very high ground clearance were both mandatory. Even then, arriving at your destination without a flat wasn't a given. This year the drought of early summer had given way to an almost continual downpour beginning the Fourth of July weekend, which had proved particularly problematic to the surface of the alleged Step road.

And yet. Somehow people managed to arrive at the front door of Park HQ anyway.

But not the couple facing him on his laptop this afternoon.

He was sitting in the dingy room that passed for a mess hall, redolent of the smells of deep-fried fat and baked rhubarb, lunch that day having been fried chicken, potato salad, and rhubarb upside-down cake. They finally had a group of interns who didn't run when they saw a bag of flour.

Harry and Marge Bachman, the couple on the screen, were both white and in their thirties, both residents of Anchorage. They were avid backcountry hikers, not professionals but dedicated and informed amateurs. They had married the same year he took the job of chief ranger and they had celebrated their honeymoon by hiking Busted Flat Peak, located in that part of the Park so extremely southeast it was almost in Canada. The origin of its name had been lost to history but if you knew it was there, it had one of the few actually discernible trails leading in switchbacks up the south face of a three-thousand-foot peak which emerged on a flat, mesa-like top.

Dan had never been certain that three thousand feet constituted an actual peak in a Park where the next lowest peak was five thousand feet high and the highest peak was eighteen thousand feet. Anqak, the highest peak in the Quilaks, was known locally as Big Bump. It was shorter than Denali by three thousand feet but graded a harder technical climb. It was reserved for only the most extreme climbers who had the added intestinal fortitude to face the required Middle Finger at the Roadhouse following every successful summit.

Busted Flat Peak, you should excuse the expression, was a walk in the Park by comparison, and Harry and Marge had returned every year on their anniversary to hike it again. Harry was a geologist with the state Department of Natural Resources and Marge was a biologist with the Department of Fish and Game. They were nice people, always registered their climb on the Park website, always packed enough food and water, always carried a med kit, always carried an emergency beacon and never once had to trigger it, always observed any burn ban in effect even at three thousand feet, and not one time had Dan or any of his interns ever found so much as a scrap of trash following one of their stays. A reputable air taxi flew them in from Anchorage, landing them on one of the hundreds of no-name fly-in lakes in Alaska, and they never failed to meet it when it landed to pick them up again. If only half of the hikers who came into the Park were half as informed and responsible, Dan could run the place by himself.

Harry and Marge were on Zoom, on different screens, talking to him from their respective laptops and, from the background, different rooms. Marge was indignant but trying not to take it out on Dan. Harry was flat pissed off. "We've been hiking that trail every year since... well, hell, Dan, you know since when! What call did those assholes have to run us off? The Park's public land; it belongs to all of us!"

Well, Dan thought, to those of us who can afford an air charter. Which isn't all of us, not by a long shot. "Did they identify themselves?"

"They said they were security for local landowners." Harry leaned in, so that Dan could experience the full effect of the red rage that had suffused his face. "They were armed, Dan, and not with hunting rifles, either. I'm not a gun guy but these guns were automatics. Military, you know? They looked like the AR-15s we see in the news after every mass shooting."

"Did they pull them on you?"

Harry sat back. "No," he said grudgingly.

"The fact that they were carrying them was scary enough," Marge said. "We're used to seeing hikers with hunting rifles, Dan. Heck, we're even used to some packing sidearms like

.357s to scare off bears." She swallowed. "These two guys were carrying weapons meant to kill a lot of people very quickly. And we were alone. Just the two of us."

And not armed, Dan thought, because Harry and Marge never went armed on their hikes. Which was probably just as well. Otherwise he could be dealing with the aftermath of a gunfight. "What did they look like?"

"They were wearing camo, with name tags," Harry said. He was still red-faced.

Dan suspected he was as embarrassed as he was upset by being outfaced by men who had threatened his woman. "Uniforms?"

Harry looked at Marge. Marge looked at Harry. "Uniforms?" The red in Harry's face began to fade. "Well, yes, I guess. They wore the exact same thing, anyway."

"Same boots, too. And billed caps."

"You said they had name tags. Do you remember their names?"

They both looked uncertain. "It was last names in all caps, Harry, wasn't it?" Marge looked uncertain, and Harry looked frustrated. "I don't remember the names, though."

Dan repressed a sigh. "Do you remember what they looked like, physically?"

"One was older. He did all the talking. The other guy was younger. He hung back."

"Gym rats. Like they spent all their off time lifting weights. One of the guys, the older one, his arms wouldn't even hang straight."

Marge nodded. "Bulky. Like young Schwarzeneggers but without the charm."

"Blond? Brunet? Redhead? White? Black? Indigenous?"

"They looked white. Their hair was covered by their caps."

"Did the caps have some kind of logo?"

Marge brightened a little. "Yes. Um." She thought. "Not a logo, exactly, but some weird name made of letters and numbers."

"J649." Harry was definite, and flushed again when both Marge and Dan looked surprised. "The big guy, the talker, he got into my face."

"Dan?"

"Yeah?"

"I know this won't seem as important to you as it does to us, and no reason it should, but this is the first time in ten years that we haven't celebrated our anniversary on Busted Flat Peak." Despite her best efforts a single tear escaped and left a silvery trail down her cheek. "I really resent those yahoos scaring us off."

When Dan had promised to investigate, after everyone had signed off and he'd carried his laptop back to his office, he sat back in his chair and swiveled around to look at the view, which was, as always, spectacular, be it cloudy or bright.

What bothered him most about Harry and Marge's complaint was that it wasn't the first.

Dan understood full well the delicacy necessary to work with locals instead of unilaterally enraging them, which often led to gunfire. He sat in on Niniltna Native Association meetings on request, knew most of the residents residing over the twenty million acres of the Park by sight, and their kids and grandkids, too. The one permanent representative of the federal government between Ahtna and the Canadian border, he'd officiated at more local weddings than Kate Shugak and he'd certainly drunk the mourners at every memorial under the table. In short, he was as much one of them as any Outsider could be. He had tried his best to extend that relationship and reputation to every citizen of Alaska who visited or had business in the Park. Like the Bachmans.

He swiveled back around to face his desk. His office was a square piece of real estate whose shape and dimensions were crowded with small cliffs of bookshelves and several separate avalanches of paperwork. He didn't quite need a sherpa to navigate from door to desk but at some point a shovel might be necessary. The kingdoms of earth might have run on oil, according to the old saw, but the kingdom of the National Park Service and the many, many departments necessary to the management of eleven separate regions, including Region 11, his own, ran on memos, regulations, permits, and the most recent Secretary of the Interior's muscle tics. There was always a form that had to be filled out and always a checklist to follow. It was no wonder the Forest Service wanted to open logging back up in Southeast. Empirical evidence received by him personally, over time served indicated that the NPS had to be running the nation out of paper all by themselves.

He pawed through paperwork until the file he wanted surfaced, a nondescript manila folder that was thinner than any of the other files but still thick enough to merit attention. By virtue of a hearty shove he cleared a space in front of his chair, ignoring the small cascade of files to the floor, and opened it.

There were four reports, to which he would add today's when he wrote it up. He didn't normally print out reports but after the third one of these he had started a physical file. He opened his laptop, spent half an hour summarizing the interview, and sent the report to print. The printer, an elderly specimen for which HP was about to stop making cartridges was in the hall. He had to wait a while before it got the message and he heard the wheezing chug-a-chug that told him it was soldiering on one more time. He fought his way out of the office, retrieved the report, and returned to his chair.

Over the past two months five different groups, including Marge and Harry Bachman, had hiked the trail to the top of Busted Flat Peak and overnighted at the cabin the Park Service had built in a nook just below the edge three years before. The Bachmans, he remembered, had at first given this innovation the side eye, until Herb pointed out they wouldn't have to pack in a tent for the first time in seven years. Marge, still dubious, nevertheless went along and they filled out the online form and made their annual trip. He'd joined them for a drink at Fletcher's in Anchorage when he'd been there on business and it turned out they had been delighted with the little cabin made of rough-cut logs harvested from the Park itself and put together by that year's group of interns under the supervision of an NPS carpenter. There were four bunks separated by a central table, a counter for cooking, and, luxury of luxuries, a tiny wood stove and a wood bin the interns kept filled in season.

He swiveled again to admire the view outside his window. Termination dust had made its annual appearance on the peaks of the Quilak Mountains the week before. A little more snow and they would begin to look a little less like geographical features and more like the coniform cones of an ozarkodinid, slowly opening its jaw to snatch up anyone or anything unwary enough to come within reach of its teeth. They didn't discriminate, either, as the flight crew of the small jet in January had learned too late to do them any good.

The Quilaks descended into foothills that rolled south-southwest all the way to the Gulf of Alaska, including the one on Busted Flat Peak. Dan had hiked up to the cabin himself, a privilege, one of the few he arrogated to his position. He had curled up in his Alpinlite on his Thermarest and listened to a brief shower patter on the roof that night with immense satisfaction, and coffee on the narrow porch the next morning had been a religious experience. Marmots whistled from below, eagles shrieked from above, porcupines rattled from the nearest berry patch, and every now and then a grizzly rolypolyed by, although not often because it was too far from the nearest salmon stream.

If it wasn't Eden itself, it was near as dammit as advertised. The cabin had never been empty, not a single night in season, and there was a waiting list in case people were so careless as to have died before being able to take advantage of their reservation. Hikers in summer, hunters in fall, plus a few intrepid adventurers in the winter hoofed it up on cleats or snowshoes. A couple of mountain bikers had made the attempt the year before. Dan had never known if the bikes made it all the way to the top or were abandoned halfway. At least their owners hadn't yelled for help or been reported missing by family members.

Breakup was about the only time the cabin was ever empty, and even then it was only a few nights a month. Over the past two years Covid had only accelerated traffic to the cabin, and to the entire Park and all the other parks, forests, and refuges in Alaska for that matter. People had decided that if they couldn't get on a plane then they'd get out into the open air, of which there was plenty in Alaska.

This August had seen the usual visitors, and as usual there was nothing usual about them. A Girl Scout troop, a group of orienteers practicing for the annual Heaven Trail Run they held in the Park, a small nonprofit corporate board on an extremely rural retreat, a book club—all women—that he would have liked very much to have insinuated himself into, but they told him he couldn't come because he hadn't read the book, Andy Hall's *Denali's Howl*. It was on his own to-read list but that, he thought, might be inappropriate to the occasion. He had hoped the ladies didn't frighten themselves into falling off the mountain, although that was one group he'd be okay mounting a rescue effort for. Gratitude was a fine thing and he would have been fully prepared to take advantage of it should it have been offered.

Interspersed between the groups there were the singles and the couples and regulars like the Bachmans.

Which was why he took their complaint seriously. He opened his laptop and clicked on the Zoom recording and ran through it again. After two plus years of virtual meetings he hated Zoom with the fire of a thousand suns but he had to admit that, on occasion, it came in handy.

The Bachmans had been confronted by the two self-proclaimed security guys halfway from the trail head at the lake landing to the cabin on top of Busted Flat Peak. At the beginning of the steep part, the two men had materialized out of the brush. Harry was talking.

"They said they were acting for their employer, who had bought a lodge in the area."

"Demetri Totemoff's lodge?" Dan's voice from off-screen.

"They didn't specify. Is that right, Dan? Is it private land?"

"Are we never going to be able to go back to Busted Flat?"

Dan could hear the steam in his voice when he answered. "It is not private land, not where the trail is, Harry, and Marge, yes, you are going to be able to go back to the cabin. I will get this sorted out, don't you worry. Furthermore, I owe you a night. You pick it, I'll book it."

He closed the laptop and looked up. One entire wall of his office was covered by a map of the Park, floor to ceiling and corner to corner, tacked right to the Sheetrock. The smaller pulldown he had had since he took the job had finally begun to tatter into illegibility and he'd replaced it last year with this one, which was of larger scale and much higher resolution but

DANA STABENOW

on which Dan had labored mightily to color in all the various pieces the Park didn't own. He resented all of them, in spite of the fact that the map was in fact mostly green, indicating twenty million acres' worth of federal lands in the stewardship of the National Park Service, himself its chief steward. The Kanuyaq Mine, Niniltna, Ahtna, Cordova, the villages and cabins along the river were red specks within the green. Blue parcels indicated Native lands granted by ANCSA and ANILCA, most of them choice lots also on the river, the main highway for Park rats in summer after it thawed and winter after it froze, not so much during breakup.

Many of them had been homesteads once upon a time, with their parcels grandfathered in as the Park had been created around them. There were a lot of mining claims, too, small operations, each of them usually backed up with enough firepower to launch the third invasion of Iraq. You really didn't want to land on their airstrips without an invitation, and even then, things could get dicey when they saw the NPS decal on the side.

And of course there was the big mine, the Suulutaq, the largest copper and gold deposit in the world. It occupied a big, shit-brown splotch southeast of Niniltna, about halfway to the coast. Its status changed with whoever was in the White House, although the Supreme Court had handed down a verdict that excluded the EPA from the mix once and for all. Maybe. The Park rats had mixed feelings about that.

So did Dan. Yeah, that's what we do on this planet, he thought, we pull stuff out. We pull stuff out of the ground and we pull stuff out of the water and that's why there's no more kings in the Kanuyaq, and no more oil in Prudhoe Bay, and why no more king crab in the Gulf, and, you know, fuck the noise in your own head, O'Brian. You can only do what you can do.

His eyes traveled south and a little more east, where there was another splotch of red. It represented Demetri Totemoff's lodge. Or it had.

Demetri had been one of the first of the Park's Covid casualties. Before he'd died he'd managed to get himself tangled up with some half-assed environmental group and he was not much missed by Park rats, and evidently not much by his wife and family, either. The lodge had been sold immediately and the last anyone had seen of Alina she was boarding a plane for Anchorage. The kids were grown and gone, and one supposed that she had joined them wherever they were, but no one really knew because she hadn't sent so much as a postcard.

Between Covid and business as more than usual, Dan hadn't had time to drop by the lodge and introduce himself to the new owner. Now he was wondering just how big a mistake that might have been, because the five reports of harassment by assholes purporting to be defending the borders of their employer's private property were marked by a group of pinheads clustered between Demetri's lodge and Busted Flat Peak.

The month before, he'd heard from a group of three young men, one of whom had been diagnosed with terminal cancer.

They had known each other since kindergarten and a trip up Busted Flat Peak was their way of celebrating their lifelong friendship and of saying goodbye. Just like the Bachmans, two armed men had turned them back. Dan had heard the story from one of the three, who was pretty tight-jawed about it, and who was wrecked anyway because his friend had died shortly thereafter.

Three other groups, two couples from Outside and one group of four friends from Homer, had suffered similar experiences. Not everyone who had climbed Busted Flat Peak by far, but enough to constitute a nuisance.

One would have been too many.

Dan had the map on his wall in digital format on his laptop in large scale. He opened it again, zeroed in on the southeast corner of the Park and checked to see that the Busted Flat trail did not, in fact, run across or anywhere near Demetri's lodge, which sat on a standard 160-acre plot. It did come a little close to a mining claim—he squinted—oh yeah, old Paddy Murphy's claim that was. And—he zoomed in to be sure—a little close, yeah, but it did not encroach. They had good surveyors in the National Park Service, goddammit. They didn't make amateur mistakes.

He zoomed out a little, so that the screen covered the area in question, and sent it to print.

He was going to pay the lodge a little visit, introduce himself, and introduce them to the realities of national parks in general and this one in particular. And he was going to enjoy himself.

His phone rang. He snatched it up. "What?"

"Dan? Jeanette." One of the Rangerettes. She sounded tense. "There's a fire."

His blood went cold and he forgot everything else. "Where?"

"At the foot of Chistona Glacier."

He began to relax. "Jeanette, that's way the hell and gone from anywhere. There's no way we need to—"

"It was started by campers. They aren't registered, but a private pilot saw them and the fire, and phoned in from the air. They were hiking the glacier and two of them were hurt in a fall. The other two managed to evacuate one of them back to their campsite but the second one is still on the glacier. And now the fire is spreading and they're in the middle of it."

"Fuck." He dropped the copy of the map and raced out of the building.

Six

THE NINILTNA ROAD WAS THE REMNANT OF an old railbed that had supported a train that ran between the Kanuyaq copper mine and the port of Cordova. Built in the early years of the last century to carry the copper ore to southbound ships, it had seen service for thirty years before the copper ran out and the company left, pulling the tracks up behind them.

Park rats, living where the price of anything was tripled by transportation costs, had descended en masse on the tarred wooden ties left behind, before the caboose of the Kanuyaq River & Northern Railroad was over the horizon. To this day you could see the ties in decks, raised-bed gardens, creek bridges, boardwalks, docks, buried for tiedowns on airstrips, and in repairs to every log cabin still standing at least in part because of those old ties.

The Kanuyaq River & Northern Railroad also made its presence felt in the occasional fugitive railroad spike that would work its evil way to the surface of the road, there to be picked up by the tire of a passing pickup or the tread of a speeding snowmobile. Always with the pointy end up, of course.

Another remnant of the Kanuyaq River & Northwestern Railroad was a roadhouse. Originally, there had been half a dozen of them spaced along the tracks, stocked with spare rails and ties and spikes and grease and coal dumps, with crews to service the engines in case of breakdowns, which in Alaska were many, especially during the winter.

One remained. The sign over the door said "The Roadhouse" but it was known locally as Bernie's, for its owner, Bernie Koslowski. A refugee from the sixties, he had escaped over the border into Canada a step ahead of the draft board and eventually migrated into Alaska, where, by means best left unexamined, he acquired the title to the last homely roadhouse standing and proceeded to turn it into a bar. It didn't hurt that it stood just outside the borders of the Niniltna Native Association's land.

Niniltna was a predominately Alaska Native village, once a fish camp for Athabaskans and a few Eyaks, later settled by Alutiiqs, known now as Sugpiaq, who had been forced out of the Aleutian Islands when the Japanese occupied Attu and Kiska in World War II. Alcohol was the worm in the Alaskan apple, and the elders of Niniltna were determined it wouldn't chew through their people. That determination wavered from year to year with which elders were still living, and in the past three decades, the village had gone from being damp, where

47

alcohol was allowed for personal use, to dry, where no alcohol was allowed whatsoever and armed villagers met you at the airstrip to search you, your baggage, and your plane before you were allowed to set foot in the Park.

Considering the size of the Park, the multiplicity of small private holdings it contained, and that each one had its own airstrip, this prohibition naturally gave rise to a thriving population of bootleggers. It was like whack-a-mole trying to keep them out, although law enforcement, lay and secular, both gave it their best effort. Meanwhile, if you wanted to make the journey over a road that was a washboard at best in the summer and much improved by the snow that turned it into a slalom in the winter, Bernie's was there to pop a cap on an Oly or pour you a stiff one. Many Park rats so wanted, and Bernie had thrown up a dozen small cabins behind the bar for hunters, tourists, and patrons whose car keys he'd taken away.

At some point soon after he opened the doors, the aunties themselves—Vi, Edna, Balasha, and Joy—had materialized, occupied what became their designated corner, Irish coffees made to order at their elbows, there to work on the most recent quilt while receiving obeisances from Park rats one and all. After that, the success of Bernie's Roadhouse was assured, and since it was the only legal drink between Ahtna and Cordova, it was well patronized no matter how far away from everything else it was. Bernie was never told so in so many words, but he was attuned enough to the Park zeitgeist that he never applied for a package license and so never sold anything by the bottle. The Roadhouse was a bar, not a liquor store. The aunties—and Ekaterina Shugak by her silence on the subject—had spoken.

Bernie had done a lot to maintain the century-old structure as time and profits allowed. The original logs had been insulated and Sheetrocked on the inside and clad in vinyl siding outside. The original porch, made of the aforementioned railroad ties, had been disassembled and replaced with a smart new porch that was more of a small deck with a gable roof, which he was now giving some thought to enlarging into an Arctic entry. When someone came into the bar on a cold February afternoon the gale force wind it generated was enough to freeze all his regulars to their stools, not to mention him behind the bar. It was a large room fifty feet on a side with a high roof and a kitchen behind the bar where fast food was served up hot and tasty. Food always sold more booze, and booze was where he made his money.

Over the past winter he'd refinished the surface of the bar and the brass rail that ran beneath it. He'd even sprung for new stools, a renovation applauded by everyone. The tables and chairs scattered around the four square feet of dance floor would have to wait on the color of the bottom line at the end of the year. He couldn't put it off for much longer, though. Last week one of the chairs had collapsed beneath the weight of Willard Shugak. Willard had ascended from the wreckage unharmed but Howie Katelnikof, that little weasel, had made enough of a fuss that he'd scored free drinks for both of them out of it.

The previous year Bernie had replaced the ancient plywood

floor and laid down vinyl peel-and-stick tiles, and this spring he'd repainted the interior white, which doubled the ambient light in the room and might single-handedly have been responsible for a pregnancy scare, an engagement, and an elopement. It turned out that actually being able to see the object of your desire was a powerful aphrodisiac.

Of course, that depended on the object. From behind the bar Bernie cast a covert glance at Pete Kvasnikof vying with Ivar Ollestad for the attention of Allie, one of the servers. She delivered their beers with efficiency and dispatch and got out of hands' reach in short order.

"Hey," he said, when she returned to the bar. "That something I should address?"

"What?" She looked over her shoulder. "Nah. They're drinking up their fishing settlement and feeling their oats. No harm." She smiled and shrugged, and he could see the attraction. She had red hair cut short with a deliberately ragged edge over blue eyes that sparkled with fun, and filled out a very nice tee.

It was Sunday, the day before Labor Day, the second day of the three-day holiday, after which the tourists and the non-Park fishermen and hunters would finally go home and leave the Roadhouse in peace.

Peace was not in evidence tonight. The place was packed to the literal rafters, some guy in the back doing pull-ups from one of them to the counted encouragement of his friends. He recognized only about a quarter of them which always made him a little uneasy but so far everyone's credit card had cleared. He would always and ever carry a warm spot in his heart for the Suulutaq Mine, which had marched cell masts into the Park right down the Niniltna road directly to their front door, which meant almost everyone had cell service now, at least along the road.

Rafe, the temp bartender, cleared Allie's tray and refilled it immediately, then wasted a second or two watching her walk away from him. For that matter, so did Bernie, because the view was excellent. Chloe, the other server, arrived with empties and got a perfunctory smile from Rafe as he filled her new orders, but then Chloe was thin and pale with fine, dishwater blonde hair she had trained to fall in her face, obscuring her features. A baggy gray sweatshirt and too-big cargo pants completed an ensemble specifically designed to render her invisible to the males of her species.

Bernie sighed to himself. She had cause. So far as he could tell, she was the only functioning daughter of Father Smith, and the only one to remain in the Park after his arrest. She was doing the best she could, and he was helping her by giving her a job. But she was no Allie.

Beyond Chloe he saw Mark, Luke, and Peter Grosdidier perk up as Allie arrived at their table. Boris and Nathan Balluta at the table next door were also attentive. Boris, ever the dandy, leaned back a little in his chair so she would be blinded by the sartorial splendor of his deep-blue cashmere V-necked sweater with the crisp white oxford button-down collar beneath. Très chic, Bernie thought, hiding a grin. Boris' hair, too, looked very Captain Pike pompadour, but then Boris was the most ardent of *Star Trek* fans, live-action and cartoon. For a while he had attempted Burnham extensions, although shorter, which had been commemorated in everyone's Twitter and TikTok feeds until they grew out and he moved on to Mount Anson.

Never a dull moment, and Bernie went back to the storeroom for more Alaskan Amber. He'd picked up two cases—feet set, lifting with his legs: his back wasn't as young as it had been—when he heard a commotion from the bar. He set both cases down again, not without relief, to investigate.

And emerged onto a riot, albeit a small one. It appeared to be being adequately handled by a joint Grosdidier–Balluta task force. Their ire was concentrated on four men—Bernie squinted—strangers to him. Hunters, probably, as they were dressed in camo with matching caps. They had labels across their breast pockets, he guessed in case they got lost and forgot who they were. Desert camo instead of jungle, which seemed odd, but then plenty of people came to the Park in L.L. Bean from the skin out, determined to make their mark on the Boone & Crocket score charts in their hip pockets, and they were odder by far. It was no trouble at all to not take them seriously. Nevertheless, Bernie felt for the baseball bat he kept behind the bar.

They weren't going quietly and they looked collectively as if they'd spent serious time on a TRX but this wasn't the task force's first rodeo.

"Hey, you, yeah, bartender! You gonna do something about this?" one of them shouted before being overwhelmed by Park rats.

Another was less tactful. "You gonna stand by your white brothers or not, motherfucker!"

Which might have gone some way toward explaining the extra enthusiasm the task force put into his removal.

A third pawed at his back. Bernie realized he was trying to get at a belt holster, and he dropped the bat and pulled out the pump-action, pistol-grip shotgun just in time to see a black, businesslike automatic materialize in the nogoodnik's hand.

He lost no time in racking in a round. The loud Whack! Clack! brought all activity to a frozen halt for one split second, which turned out to be just long enough.

"Don't do it, Tate," one of his friends said, already dangling between Boris and Nathan, "the boss isn't going to like this as it is."

Tate's hand fell away and live action resumed. One by one they were ejected out the front door, their glide ratio suffering as they left the lift and thrust of their launchers behind to embrace the properties of drag and weight. Well, weight, anyway. Bernie couldn't see exactly what happened on the other side of the door but he was sure they didn't remain airborne long. The thuds would probably have been audible if the bar hadn't been so crowded and Pink hadn't been calling them all fucking heretics at the top of her voice. Or maybe it was hypocrites? Hard to tell. The new music playlist download was getting a lot of full-throated airtime that evening, at a volume that made the lyrics spoken or sung nearly indecipherable.

The task force, looking pleased with itself, dusted off its hands and adjourned to the bar. Luke was even bragging along with Pink about taking all the heat they could take. He gave Bernie a lopsided grin and swiped at the blood gushing from his nose.

"What was all that about, anyway?"

"They were making improper suggestions to the lady," Boris said grandly, giving Allie a little bow. Like he hadn't been planning improper suggestions himself. His left eye was rapidly swelling shut.

"Racist assholes," Mark growled. He was holding a bloodstained napkin to his mouth. "They called us—" He looked at Allie.

"I have heard the word," she said dryly.

His ears turned red. "Didn't like that she was talking to us. Said she should stick to her own kind."

Bernie pretended to be puzzled. "Human?"

"And then told us to go back where we came from," Luke said.

"Niniltna, I guess." Boris was nursing a set of bruised knuckles. Allie wrapped some ice in a bar rag and pressed it to them while the other four watched enviously.

"Well." Bernie pulled glass steins out of the freezer and set them up in a row on the bar. "Thank you for your fumigation services, gentlemen. I believe this calls for beer on me. Try this new pale ale I've been working on…"

Seven

THE TECH LORD AND HIS ARM CANDY insisted on being seated first, and changed their mind twice about where. The tech lord wanted the right seat. She pouted and he relented, grudgingly. Amber Macintosh didn't hold out a lot of hope for the length of the relationship.

Then the arm candy—what was her name? Belle? Bambi?—remembered that she had done extensive research on the Internet, which informed her that planes don't back into mountains, and demanded a seat in the last row. The tech lord regained his shotgun seat peck rights. Fortunately the other passengers, two parents, their daughter and son-in-law, were inclined to be tolerant. Peace reigned.

Amber got everyone loaded and ran down the checklist. It was partly cloudy and the forecast called for winds three miles out of the south. The high hanging over the Park for the last three days was still firmly in place. That only meant that the first big fall storm was building strength behind it in the Gulf of Alaska, but that was for later, not today, and this was her last flight of the season.

She was operating her own plane, a red-and-silver Beaver on contract to Ahtna Air, finishing up a summer of carrying air tourists on flightseeing trips to gawk at glaciers and grizzlies and ferrying others into remote lodges for hiking and fishing and sometimes even just being out of cell phone range. There was the occasional emergency medivac to break up the routine, along with the rare intrepid backcountry adventurers who wanted to be set down in the middle of nowhere with a pack and picked up again a month later when they'd had their fill of freeze-dried food and mosquito bites. She never made the mistake of bringing them back on their return trip with any other passengers, she never let any of them ride shotgun if she could help it, and she kept the windows cracked the entire trip no matter the altitude. The landings to pick them up were always interesting, though. Wheels down on a bumpy creek bed under six inches of rushing water and the prop wash kicking leaves up all over the windshield had a way of getting and keeping your attention.

But it was what she'd signed up for, and no complaints. She'd put in her one thousand hours, a third of them as a pilot instructor out of the Kasilof airstrip, bunking in a single-wide trailer and fending off the advances of her students. Most of them were middle-aged professional men who would learn enough to get their certificates, buy a slick, nearly-new Cessna somewhere Outside, and pay another, more experienced pilot to fly it up to Alaska. Which aircraft would then be parked at

Merrill or Lake Hood or Birchwood and forgotten except on Sunday afternoons when he'd drive the family and friends and colleagues he wanted to impress out to admire it after dinner. One whole percentage of the population of Alaskans had a pilot's license, or so they said. That worked out to about ten thousand pilots, or rather, people with pilot's licenses. They didn't say what percentage of those pilots had more than the ten hours in the left seat required to solo.

But hours in the air were hours in her log book, and this summer all her hours counted as pilot in command. Would she go commercial? She still wasn't sure. She liked the challenges of Bush flying—she'd picked up some charter work for cash, which was always nice—and she was only twenty-seven. Plenty of time. Besides, if she wanted to go commercial and stay in Alaska, she'd have to fly out of Bering. The biggest town in the Y-K Delta, the hub for dozens of smaller towns and villages up and down the Yukon and Kuskokwim river deltas, population seven thousand, zero available housing, and a whole bunch of politics she didn't like the sound of.

Of course, there were a lot of places in Alaska of which all those same things could be said, including Ahtna, her current base of operations, and the Park itself, which was where she spent most of her time. She could only describe it as a wonderland of mountains and glaciers, rivers and streams, all of it teeming with wildlife. Moose schooled up in snowdrifts beneath the bare branches of willow and alder, conserving their energy during the winter. In the summer they stood knee-deep in ponds, tearing up greens from the lake beds. In fall the bulls clashed over harems of cows who stood around looking bored. Small packs of wolves were always on the move, smart and experienced enough now to run when they heard the sound of an airplane engine. Bears, brown and black and cinnamon, ranged over bald knobs with a view that went on forever, if only they had the eyesight to see it. Aloft, raptors from the kestrel to bald and golden eagles vied with her for air space, along with massive flocks of southbound Canada geese and sandhill cranes.

The past two years had been a feast for the eyes, especially for someone raised in the suburbs of Los Angeles, where the Santa Monica Mountains more often than not were hidden by a brown haze and the only wildlife worthy of the name were the coyotes, who wouldn't bother coming down out of the hills if people weren't so careless of their pets. Mac inhaled a breath of fresh, clean air—admittedly mixed with a bit of gas fumes and exhaust, because she was working out of an airport, after all—before she leaned in the door and gave the safety briefing. The tech lord was nervous and trying not to show it. The family was thrilled before they'd even gotten off the ground. The arm candy was checking her lipstick in a pocket mirror. Bright red, of course. Mac hoped her sneer wasn't showing. Her parents had raised her better than that.

She settled into the left seat, worked the pedals and the yoke while checking the flaps and rudder. The engine started at a touch with a satisfying roar. There were two inbound aircraft, one of George Perry's single Otter turbos—man, that was a nice ride and would she ever like to get her hands on one of them—and a Spernak taxi flight from Anchorage. Ahtna didn't have any regularly scheduled airline flights but the runway was paved and lit and there was an automatic weather station whose forecasts were better than NOAA's.

The Otter touched down like a feather and rolled out like buttercream frosting. The Spernak flight followed with a bounce that must have had pilot and passengers peeling themselves off the ceiling. Out of curiosity she watched it roll to a stop near the rudimentary terminal building. It was a Cessna 206, nicknamed "the pregnant plane" for the luggage compartment on the belly. The instant the wheels stopped moving the pilot's door slammed back and a tall man in a Carhartt's bib overall bailed out. He was followed immediately by a woman in jeans and hoodie who slapped at him with both hands. He fended her off as best he could, holding his arms up in front of his face and backing away. She followed, still swinging with enthusiasm and sometimes even connecting.

"Who's that?" someone said behind her.

"*The Bachelor*, the Ahtna version," she said, and taxied down to the end of the runway and took off.

Eight

"I'M NOT DEAD YET."

Art Gorst Jr. hid a sigh. The old man was in a mood. Let's be real, he thought. The old man has been in a mood his whole damn life.

"Get in if you're getting in, dammit."

There was the faint sound of an approaching aircraft and Art looked up but it wasn't in sight yet. Sounded like a Beaver, whose distinctive growl even Art could recognize. He climbed into the rear seat of the Super Cub. It was a faded red with the name "The Hemorrhoid" written on the fuselage in large white script because, said Frank, flying long hours in one was what it gave you.

Frank ran the front seat back with a vicious shove and Art assumed a wide stance just in time to save his knees. With a celerity belying his eighty-seven years Frank vaulted up into the front seat and pulled it forward with another emphatic

60

shove. You have to hand it to the old bastard, Art thought. He still has the energy to get mad and stay that way.

They put on headsets and the Super Cub spluttered into life. The old man taxied in a swirl of s-curves to the end of the little dirt runway and lost no time in getting them into the air. They leveled off at five hundred feet. He didn't bother looking but Art would have been surprised if Barr Sr. had the airspeed at anything faster than 75 mph. He did like to fly low and slow. The old man was a born beachcomber and that went for inland travel as well.

They'd certainly spent their share of time in the air over the Park this past summer. At last count the old man had scouted a dozen different parcels of privately owned land within Park boundaries. So far he'd bought two. One was a homestead where the residents had refused to get vaxxed and the entire family of five had died of Covid. Their heirs were Outsiders who wanted nothing to do with a property that, to them, might as well be on the moon. He'd also bought a mining claim where the owner was retiring to head south. He'd tried for a hunting and fishing lodge that had come on the market the year before and been outbid, which Art knew still stung.

He looked at the back of Barr Sr.'s head. The old man still had hair, amazingly, but now Art could see his scalp gleaming pinkly through it. He remembered when he was a boy and Frank was still in his fifties and the last one of his generation of friends left with a full head of hair. He'd make them all remove their hats when they came in his house, while he kicked back in his La-Z-Boy, two fingers of the Macallan in a heavy Waterford tumbler in hand and a shit-eating grin on his face.

Art was in his fifties himself now and his hairline was receding like a spring tide on Cook Inlet. "Frank. No fooling, now."

Frank heard the serious note in Art's voice, and over his shoulder, Art watched Frank's hands still on the controls. "What?" The note of belligerence was clearly audible over the headset, albeit muted, encouragement enough for Art to continue.

"I'm not saying I'm a hundred percent against it, Frank. Jesus, I wouldn't dare, not with your track record."

"What, then?"

"Well, your track record, for starters."

"Meaning?"

"Meaning you and Dad made all your money—"

"You, too, now."

"Okay, and thanks for that," Art said, surprised. Frank wasn't big on compliments. "My point is the business is founded on air travel. We were the only regional airline in Alaska who stayed in business after Covid put damn near everyone else on the auction block. We got a lot of goodwill from that, and Ikiak Air is flying more routes and making more money than it ever has before. How many times have you said to me, if it ain't broke don't fix it?"

"A few, I expect."

The old man sounded amused now, and Art took courage.

"You haven't told me, and I get that you don't have to, but you never said why you want to go into making movies."

He tensed, waiting for the explosion. It didn't come. Instead, a long, slow sigh. "You been looking at the state population, Art?"

Art blinked. "What?"

"Been tanking the last three, four years."

Art was puzzled. "The boomers are aging out and moving south, yeah."

"It's more than that." The old man actually sounded sad. "We got ourselves a governor who, far as I can see, is trying to wreck everything me and your dad built up from statehood on. Okay, we cut some corners and we never shied away from making a buck, but Alaska had 50,000 people at statehood and now we got over 730,000, although it's not looking like for very much longer. Why is that?"

Art didn't answer. He didn't have to.

"I'll tell you why," Frank said, and the bitterness in his voice was painfully clear. "North Slope and Cook Inlet are about outa oil—there used to be four tankers a day outa Valdez and now there's one! Fossil fuels are on their way out anyway; you can't find a bank who'll back an oil prospect anymore. The federal government makes it so damn complicated to mine anything that people who find something they might make a buck on give up before they get started. Fishing's bad everywhere but Bristol Bay; Jesus, you can't even catch a king on the Kenai no more!"

Art sat listening behind him, thinking he was hearing the

death cry of the Alaskan old fart. Nothing Frank said was wrong. Art himself was hoping to get the last kid through college and top off his and Courtney's retirement accounts before heading out to Arizona. Not that he was ever going to say that to the old man.

And he had yet to talk himself back into Courtney's bed, anyway. He winced away from the thought.

"What do we do, Art? Do we just throw up our hands and walk away from everything we did to build this place? Or do we look around for new industries, new ways to get people here?"

"Like filmmaking." Art tried to keep his skepticism out of his voice.

"You got a better idea?"

"Tourism?"

Frank snorted. "You seen what the cruise ships have done to Southeast. I'm not sure how much more tourism the state can take, and besides, we need something year round. There's a new streaming service born every minute, all of them crying out for product. Alaska's one of the most photogenic places you can name. Jesus! Look at that!" His finger stabbed at the windscreen and Art saw the sun break through the clouds and glance off the Kanuyaq River and slide up and over the Quilak Mountains like a shower of gold. "Not just movies, Art. Television series, commercials—the greenies'll wet themselves using Alaska scenery as a backdrop for one a them doing a stand-up about saving the cross-eyed robin or what-the-fuck-ever. And all them productions will need crews. You ever sit through the end of a Marvel movie watching the names of all the hundreds of people worked on it? Talk about a cast of thousands! They'll have to build infrastructure, studios, whatnot. And all those crews'll need homes and grocery stores, and schools for their kids, and bars where they can get away from their wives. Or spouses or partners or what-the-fuck-ever they're calling themselves nowadays."

Art thought that Frank actually sounded like he knew at least a little bit about what he was talking about, but he felt honor bound to say, "Probably won't keep them here, Frank."

"Maybe, maybe not. Leastways, this fellow Maguire knows how to make movies and is interested in getting the business started."

"He's really willing to put his own money into it?"

"He says he is. And need I remind you, Art—"

Art said it with him. "None of us plays with our own money when we don't have to."

A snort of laughter. "You can be taught after all."

Nine

THE FIRST DRONE THAT DAY WAS SENT ALOFT by that little weasel and perennially aspirational grifter Howie Katelnikof. His roommate, Willard Shugak, had fallen in love with a drone he'd seen on Amazon that automatically returned to its place of launch before it fell out of the sky. By way of being a mechanical idiot savant, Willard had completely disassembled the drone in thirty minutes flat the day Howie brought it back from the post office in Niniltna. He had it reassembled in another hour with a better battery he'd ordered from Best Buy. They took it outside the old house sitting on the Deem homestead, from which they had not yet been evicted, and put it up in the air until the battery hit red on the remote, thirty minutes later than advertised.

Howie was impressed. "Dude, if your parents hadn't been boozers you woulda been right up there next to the guy in the wheelchair with the funny voice."

Willard beamed. "Let's see how far it can go, okay, Howie?"

66

"Okay." They put in a new battery and sent it up again. After some serious mental calculation and concentrated work with pencil and paper, they determined it had gone two miles before it automatically returned to the launch site. Some intense reading of the instructions informed them that FAA regulations required that recreational drones remain within line of sight, a mile or less.

Howie grumbled. "Goddamn government. Fingers into every damn thing. Getting so a man can't do nothing without Big Brother breathing over his shoulder."

Willard looked woebegone. "Can't we use it then, Howie?"

"Sure we can!" Howie slapped him on the back.

This Labor Day they had moved operations by way of four-wheelers to east and south of Niniltna. A lively sense of self-preservation kept Howie from making their camp too close to any privately owned properties. He was sure that Ranger Dan would never find them in this wide-open area, where there was nothing but willows and alders and a spring-fed pond too little to land a plane on but big enough to attract the attention of moose. "Okay, Howie, put up your drone! Time to start bagging us some retail levels of game."

Now and then Willard inconveniently retained the occasional stray bit of information. "But, Howie. We only have one tag between us. Won't Dan the ranger man be mad at us?"

"You want pancakes for breakfast tomorrow, Willard?"

Willard broke into a smile. "Pancakes. So good. Can we have hot syrup again?"

Howie grabbed Willard around the neck, having to jump to do so because Willard was about a foot and a half taller than he was, and gave Willard a noogie. Willard gave his rich chuckle and fended Howie off. Howie dropped back to his feet and held up his hand for a high five. Willard slapped it, his objection forgotten.

It is illegal to use a drone for hunting in Alaska. Willard didn't know that but Howie certainly did.

The second drone went aloft at almost the same time about fifty miles east, rising up over the village of Niniltna and buzzing briskly out over the Kanuyaq River. It carried a payload consisting of dual HD cameras and a battery life of twenty-five minutes. It didn't need a remote because it was controlled through an iPhone app.

The iPhone belonged to a *National Geographic* photographer who was putting together a series of videos of the Kanuyaq River from its source in the Quilak Mountains to its mouth on Prince William Sound. It was September and the water was low, as had been the snowpack the previous winter, and it was too early for ice. While the late silvers were few in number the shallow water of the river and its attendant streams made for excellent photography, the struggle of the long silver bodies of the fish fighting their way upstream seen clearly against the tumbled rock of the streambed. The photographer had a decked skiff with a small outboard loaded with camping equipment and supplies, including a sat phone with a data uplink so he could upload each day's footage to his server in San Francisco.

He'd picked up new batteries at the post office in Niniltna, enjoyed an excellent latte and mild flirtation with the proprietor of the Riverside Cafe, and found to his surprise and delight that the local grocery store stocked Dare cookies, those odes to Canadian institutional baking. He'd bought two packages of Lemon Crème, four Fudge Chocolate, and six Maple Crème, which, if he rationed them, might get him all the way to Cordova.

He launched the skiff after he launched the drone and drifted downriver behind it, the kicker exerting just enough power to keep the bow headed downstream. It was a perfect day for filming—enough cloud so that the sun didn't glare off the water's surface, rendering it opaque. He monitored the drone's feed on his iPhone with one hand and fed himself a Maple Crème with the other.

The weather gods had been kind and the weather had continued excellent during his stay, resulting in some spectacular shots of scenery and wildlife. Every square foot of this Park was more photogenic than Princess Diana had ever been on her best day. If the powers that be at *NatGeo* decided that his footage did not please their refined sensibilities, his 1.3 million Instagram followers would be more than happy to purchase signed stills harvested from it in sizes ranging from 8" x 10", 24" x 36", and the far more lucrative 48" x 64", more if matte, and even more than that if matted and framed.

He settled back against the cushion of the fold-up seat he

had brought along for the ride, and reached for another Maple
Crème.

The third drone was launched from a location further south
and east. It was not a drone available for purchase on Amazon,
eBay, or indeed anywhere in the public marketplace. It flew
higher, faster, and longer, and it had two cameras with a
resolution that could identify the piece of roast beef sandwich
you had for lunch stuck between your central incisor and left
canine from a thousand feet. Accompanying the two cameras
was an infrared camera and a thermal imager, along with four
directional microphones. Designed to do all of this soundlessly,
it was the very latest in snoop technology spawned by the geeks
at DARPA and was so eyes-only that it was currently being
replicated by only two criminal organizations as opposed to
all of them, although that would indubitably come in time.

For now it was being deployed exclusively by the good
guys, or so they liked to call themselves. This good guy sent it
up and retired into a small clearing in the middle of a cluster
of alders perched on the edge of a deep, narrow gorge, a feeder
creek for the broad river to the west. The stream at the bottom
looked cold and probably was. The drone's operator thought
he saw some fish jumping there, and hoped that his machine
would harvest enough intel in short enough order for him to
declare this job done in time for him to wet a line before dark.

Movement up the creek caught his attention and he touched
the controller, adjusting the flight path. He was staking out

a small rocky promontory that interrupted the otherwise straight stretch of this section of the creek. On the same side, upstream, where the cliff curved briefly inward, there was an adit, the entrance to a mine shaft. Framed in old railroad ties, the hole behind it had been dug by hand perpendicularly to the cliff's face. It looked like it had been there a long time and so it followed that the shaft behind it must have some depth. There had to be something valuable there or why bother? He was so tired of Mountain House beef stroganoff, which had comprised most of his most recent resupply. His boss was a sadistic bastard at the best of times but this was pushing it.

The square, rectangular opening disappeared into darkness, reached by a flight of crude steps made also of tar-soaked wooden ties and set irregularly into the nearly sheer side of the cliff. It was not a journey he would care to have made even once but he'd watched the old man with the wild mass of curly gray hair trot down it daily and re-emerge to trot back up it again, covered with an impenetrable layer of rock dust from the day's work. The backpack he'd worn down looked considerably fuller coming back up.

The miner didn't look his way. He never did, in spite of the fact that he'd been camping on the miner's land for over a week. Ass End, Alaska, sure wasn't Arlington, Virginia.

The miner was usually up and over the edge of the canyon and out of sight by now, but today he was met at the top by two men. The watcher felt a kick of excitement. Some action to report on at last.

The miner was easy to identify, a big man in blue-striped

mechanics overalls, stained and fraying. One of his visitors was wearing what looked like he thought lawyers wore when they got an hour outside the city limits: Eddie Bauer or Lands' End or L.L. Bean or some such combination. He had on an Australian bush hat with one of the sides turned up. He kept swatting at bugs and looking behind him nervously for nonexistent wildlife. Even a cursory glance exposed him as spectacularly out of his element.

Even through the lenses of the cameras the watcher could see that none of the man's clothing had ever come close to a mountain trail or a campsite. His eyes narrowed. They must have flown in. The miner had an airstrip, the one he'd landed on, but he hadn't heard an aircraft that morning. He toggled the controls, bringing the drone in closer. He wanted to hear the conversation if he could.

On the screen of the controller he saw that the second man was wearing camos and a ball cap. He was thin and wiry and moved awkwardly, as if too young to be fully in control of his own limbs. The watcher zoomed in on the logo and the thrill of recognition nearly brought him to his feet. Nearly. He took a breath to calm his racing heart and lower his blood pressure and goosed the drone a little closer. Even from this height the roar of the water competed with the men's voices but he pushed the drone closer and finally he could hear them speaking.

"I told your boss, I already sold to someone else." The miner. He could only see him from the back but his shoulders looked tense.

"I'm afraid he doesn't believe you, Mr. Murphy."

The miner hunched a shoulder. "I can't help what your boss does or doesn't believe. I've sold the property and I'm dragging up." The other man must have looked confused because he said impatiently, "I'm headed Outside." Another pause. "I retired, okay? I'm moving as far from Alaska as I can get and still be in the country. I'm going someplace warm." He sounded impatient to get there, too.

A silence. The man in the bush hat looked at the man in the cap, who shrugged. "Well, who bought your property then, Mr. Murphy?"

"Don't see how that's any of your business."

The man in the bush hat smiled. "I think my employer would like to make it his business."

"That's his problem." Murphy pushed his way between the two of them and set off up the trail to his cabin, which from prior reconnaissance, the watcher knew was a very old one-room building, its roof overgrown with moss and wildflowers and the occasional small evergreen of indeterminate origin. Each wall had one very small window, and there was an outhouse out back with a dangerous tilt to it.

The man in the bush hat said something to the man in the ball cap. The man in the ball cap unholstered a side arm, an automatic, had to shake it to disentangle the muzzle from the hem of his jacket, and pointed it at Murphy's retreating back.

The watcher stifled a shout of warning but it was a near thing. He checked to make sure that he was recording. He was. Recklessly, he moved the drone in closer. The device had been designed to operate almost soundlessly but nothing with moving pieces was ever completely silent.

The man in the cap fired a round.

Murphy whirled around, his face congested with anger, in the same movement slipping the backpack from his shoulders, straps gathered in one hand. It swung down and around and he let it go like a Russian shot-putter and the pack flew directly at the guy with the gun. The guy with the gun was caught completely off guard, although he did manage to get off another shot before the pack caught him square in the chest. He fell flat on his back and was still close enough to the edge of the little canyon that his head overhung the side.

The watcher wanted to cheer. Again he managed to restrain himself. Stealthy. Years of training.

Murphy, who should have taken off up the trail to his cabin, instead followed up, shoving the guy in the bush hat—who was watching all this with his mouth open—back a couple of staggering steps. Arms windmilling, he caught his balance barely in time to keep himself from going over the edge. Meanwhile Murphy landed on the ball cap guy and started wrestling with him for the gun. The grunts of the struggle were audible over the drone's microphones. Murphy got in a couple of good hits, until the guy in the bush hat found an old tree limb and brought it down on Murphy's head with a hell of a crack. It broke in half and at the same moment there was a gunshot. The man in the bush hat let out a cry and crumpled to the ground next to them.

There was another shot. Murphy's body gave a convulsive

jerk and went still. The man beneath him heaved Murphy's now dead weight to one side and staggered to his feet, his camos stained with blood. He stood, swaying, looking from one body to the other. "Fuck. Fuck, fuck, fuck. Mother*fucker*."

He stumbled a few steps away and leaned forward, hands on his knees. The watcher thought he might retch but the man straightened up and yelled at the sky instead. "What a goddam cluster fucking mess! How the fuck do I clean this one up?"

The man in the bush hat made a feeble gesture from where he lay on the ground. Not dead, then. He said something indiscernible to the pickup on the drone.

"What?"

The man in the bush hat gestured again.

The man in the cap went still for a moment, as if struck by a realization, and then began to pat his pockets. Eventually he found what he was looking for, a sat phone, and punched feverishly at the keypad.

He didn't have to wait long for an answer. "It's Bragg." His voice broke on his own name and the watcher reflected on how very young he sounded. "I got a—a situation at Murphy's place." He listened. "What do you mean?" He swiveled and looked right at the promontory where the watcher lay concealed.

Dammit. How the hell had they spotted him? The watcher swore beneath his breath and worked frantically at the controller, calling back his drone. He closed his eyes, listening for the hushed whirr of its blades slicing through the air. Every agonizing moment dragged by like an hour. The passage of time wasn't helped by the killer's shouts and oaths echoing from the walls of the canyon. It sounded like the shooter was bushwhacking in his direction.

He swore again. His mission was meant to be strictly covert. No definition of covert he'd ever seen had included hand-to-hand combat with the object of his surveillance. His boss was not going to be happy about this.

There, there it was, the hum of wings more delicate than a butterfly's. Except they seemed to be running more loudly and roughly than they had been, sounding more like a bee, and a big bee at that. Had one of those asshole's shots damaged his drone?

And then he heard the sound of a small airplane engine—no, two—approaching from different directions, momentarily drowning out the sound of the drone.

He looked up to spot them, and instead saw a second, completely unfamiliar drone hovering directly above his hiding place.

Ten

"SON OF A BITCH!" Gorst Jr. had been looking out the right-side window, gazing yearningly upon the thousands of acres of undeveloped country passing beneath. "What?" And then he caught his breath as the aircraft was yanked abruptly off course into a steep climb, and then it fell, both jerky, uncoordinated maneuvers unlike anything he had experienced in a lifetime flying with his father's best friend.

"Fuck!" A rough yaw as the nose came up and the tail came around. His head banged against the window. Blood dripped down the glass. "What the hell, Frank?"

"Did you see it?" The engine labored through a steep turn, the left wing pointing straight down at the ground before coming slowly up again.

"See what?"

"We nearly ran into a fucking drone! Some fucker's flying a—"

77

There was motion to his left. He looked in its direction and beneath the wing saw a Beaver in the air with them and way too close. "Frank!" The name was a scream. "Frank, for fuck's sake, traffic nine o'clock ascending—"

But there was no more time.

Missed the drone, he thought. Hit the Beaver.

Dimly he heard Barr Sr. bellow a curse. Still in a mood.

Not even time to feel afraid.

Eleven

"ARE YOU BEING SERIOUS WITH ME RIGHT now?"

Belle Anahonak looked indignant. "Of course I'm being serious!"

"'Microaggression,'" Van said, sounding out the word.

Belle nodded vigorously.

"I made a mistake," Van said. "I noticed it right away, I immediately apologized, and I reposted the corrected article on the website there and then. It was up for maybe five minutes at most."

"But you misidentified one Native elder for another."

"Yes. As I said, I made a mistake." Van was proud of how steady and sane her voice sounded. By comparison, but still.

"Nevertheless." Belle drew herself up into a pillar of virtue and held up her phone so she could read from the screen. "'Microaggression is a term used for commonplace daily verbal, behavioral, or environmental slights, whether

79

intentional or unintentional, that communicate hostile, derogatory, or negative attitudes toward stigmatized or culturally marginalized groups.'" She lowered her phone and looked at Van expectantly.

Van raised an eyebrow. "Wikipedia?"

Belle looked a little defensive. "So?"

Van leaned back in her chair. Her office was one small room, ground floor, at the front left-hand corner of Herbie Topkok Polytechnic Academy. One door in the back wall led to the school, the other—and the one Van was heartily regretting right now—opened onto the main street that led through Niniltna. "Again, I made a mistake, I apologized, and I corrected it immediately."

"This kind of conflation is representative of centuries of the mainstream media slighting women and people of color. I feel it is necessary to draw this microaggression"—Belle sure liked that word—"to the attention of the board of directors of the Niniltna Native Association. They may feel that taking out an ad on the *Kanuyaq Currents* website was premature."

Van nodded. "Out the door and left up the hill toward the airstrip. The NNA offices are on the right between the trooper post and the school."

"I know where it is!"

Van nodded again. "Out of curiosity, Belle, what is it you want here, exactly? Do you not want a weekly newspaper in Niniltna? Do you want one but want it run by someone else? Do you want to build some stocks, lock me into them, and have the village children pelt me with spawned-out salmon?"

NOT THE ONES DEAD

The door was brand new and on heavy-duty spring hinges so Belle's attempt to slam it behind her was a trifle anticlimactic.

Van stared at the door and thought it over. Should she be worried about this? Would there be blowback from the NNA board, most of whom had known her from childhood and one of whom was her adoptive mother?

She knew a sudden chill. Worst of all, was she in fact a microaggressor?

She understood racism but because she was white she knew her understanding would only ever be intellectual, never emotional or, for that matter, actual. No one was ever going to shoot her for sleeping in her own bed while white.

Van texted Johnny, back in the academic grind in Fairbanks.

Have you ever heard of the term microaggression?

He must have been in class because there was no immediate reply. At the thought of the tall, homely nineteen-year-old who had gone from best friend in middle school to love of her life in high school, all the tension went out of her body. She missed him.

She didn't miss the classes.

She surveyed her new domain. She had a desk and two client chairs, a brand-new MacBook loaded with the best newspaper program money could buy, a floor printer for printing out hardcopies for those Neanderthals—whoops, subscribers—who refused to give up their flip phones, and a bookshelf that took up one whole wall, crammed with Alaska histories, biographies, and reference works from *The AP Stylebook for Alaska* to the WPA's 1943 *Alaska* to a sixteen-year-old bound version of the Alaska Statutes, comprised of fourteen volumes, the up-to-date version of which could be found online on the state website. There also might have been every book printed by an Alaskan or about Alaska in the last ten years. When she had moved in, it had certainly looked like bookshelves all over the Park had been emptied into this one room as if from the back of a dump truck. She supposed it was one way to make room for new books.

The glass door was framed by two large windows, all of them looking out on Main Street. If she wanted to watch the river she'd have to go outside and go around the building. It was a very nice office, built by Topkok Polytechnic students. She hoped her term of occupancy would last longer than a month, but she wasn't really much worried. She had an in with the headmaster.

An alert popped up on her screen from the *Kanuyaq Currents* Facebook page, which she had invited all of the Park rats from Ahtna to the Kanuyaq River delta to follow. She had invited everyone to post comments and alerts to breaking news, too. She had ended by expressing a mild hope for civility and crossed her fingers. So far so good.

She had barely finished reading the alert before she was on her feet, reaching for her iPhone 13 Pro and her coat, checking first to make sure the battery pack in the right-hand pocket was present and fully charged, and the old-school reporter's notebook and half a dozen pens were in the left. Halfway out the door she went back for the spare charger. She was certain she wasn't going to be near an electrical outlet for some time.

The Roadhouse was on fire.

The Bush Telegraph had for decades been a reliably rapid first responder to any incident. When the Suulutaq Mine developers brought in cell service to the Park, marching cell towers up the road from Ahtna to Niniltna and introducing Park rats to smartphones, the Bush Telegraph had moved online with wholehearted enthusiasm. Everyone was on a dozen different Facebook pages, from 511 road conditions to the Alaska State Trooper Dispatch page to the inevitable family genealogy page to, of course, the closed pages frequented by conspiracy theorists, domestic terrorists in waiting, and tree-hugging, bunny-loving, latte-sipping lefties who prophesied an end to the American empire every time they lost an election. There were also pages posting ads for goods and services and alerts for births, deaths, and school bake sales for those people who just wanted to get on with their damn lives.

They were all on-scene that day at the Roadhouse with more arriving every moment. Van stopped behind a pickup parked haphazardly half on, half off the road and got out to trot a quarter of a mile to the scene. She had her phone out and the camera app recording before she was halfway there.

The Roadhouse was engulfed in flames, and as she arrived, the roof caved in with a deafening rending of joists and plywood. A cloud of sparks exploded into the air. The flames inside leaped ferociously skyward. Their heat lofted the sparks higher, to be caught by the stiff fall wind beginning to blow inland off the Gulf. Five of the six cabin roofs were already alight, and through the camera lens, she saw the sparks had ignited the roof of Bernie's house as well. Some of the trees at the edge of the clearing were also burning, dead brown sticks of beetle-kill just waiting for a match. The intensity of the fire and the unrelenting wind and no fire department closer than Ahtna ensured that whatever burned would keep burning until it ran out of fuel or it started raining again.

It was the only watering hole in the Park and a single destination resort for every guy on the run from an angry spouse and every woman on the prowl for a Suulutaq miner, known locally as a "ka-CHING." It was where climbers fresh off summiting Big Bump came to raise a Middle Finger in victory, and adventure tourists toasted the end of their hikes into the Quilaks, and rafters lubricated the rest of their journey down the Kanuyaq. Every local birth was celebrated, every death mourned, every wedding shivareed at the Roadhouse.

Van worked her way through the crowd to stand next to Bernie, a tall, thin man with a hairline that had already receded over the top of his head, with what remained gathered in a skinny ponytail that reached his belt. "Was anyone hurt?"

He looked at her, dazed. She repeated her question and he blinked, as if coming slowly to consciousness. "No. We got everyone out of the cabins right after the explosion."

"How about your kids?"

"Away at school."

"Enid?"

No answer, while Van remembered belatedly that the Koslowskis were on another of what they euphemistically called "breaks" from each other. "What happened?"

"It woke me up at oh dark thirty."

"What did?"

"I think it must have been the propane tank outside the kitchen exploding. Big boom, and when I got up to look out the window I could tell right away the place was gone. I got everyone out of the cabins and then got inside the bar just long enough to rescue a few things before it got too hot. By the time I got back outside, the cabins and my house were starting up." His shoulders rose and fell. "I had a go bag packed from the fire last summer sitting next to the front door of the house. I grabbed that and backed the pickup out of the garage. After that—" He closed his eyes and shook his head once.

"I'm so sorry, Bernie."

He gave a wan smile and held up a bottle of tequila, in the bottom of which rolled a white, wrinkled column of human flesh and bone. "I saved the Middle Finger."

"Priorities." She looked away, uncomfortable with the desolation she saw in his eyes. She stood there, watching with him as his livelihood burned to the ground. It was all she could think to do for him.

"Jesus."

At first Van thought someone was commenting on the fire, but then a phone dinged nearby, then another. A third, a fourth, everyone's phones were lighting off. Van looked at hers. It was another alert on the *Currents* Facebook page. She read it and fell the hair lift on the back of her neck.

There had been a midair collision over the Park.

"Where?" someone said.

"The NTSB is on their way," someone else said, reading from their screen.

"The troopers are advising people to stay away."

"How, if we don't know where it happened?"

"Oh god, Mel is flying back from Anchorage today."

"Text her."

"I just did. She's not answering."

"She's probably just out of service, Jase. Give her a minute."

"I have to go." Jason Kvasnikof shoved his way through the crowd, his face white. Other people began to follow him to their cars and there was a momentary traffic jam as F-150s and Subarus and Cherokee Chiefs began backing and filling in their haste to leave.

Van stayed where she was, as it looked as if it would take time for the roadway to clear. Bernie was still watching his life burn down before his eyes. She touched his arm. "Have you got somewhere to go, Bernie?"

The roof of one of the cabins fell in with a crash. All that remained of the Roadhouse itself was a burning shell. The heat of the coals was warm on her face. The smoke made her want to sneeze.

Next to her Bernie sighed. "I don't know. I guess I'll go into town. See if Auntie Vi has a room."

"Do you have insurance?"

His laugh was absent any humor. "Only if I can prove absolutely I didn't start the fire. And how do I do that?" His shoulders rose and fell on a sigh. "I was here, and so was the propane tank."

She had a hard time believing he would burn down his own business, but then she knew him and she wasn't an insurance agent on the hook for a large payout. "You don't have any motive." It sounded like a weak defense even to her.

"I owned a bar fifty miles from the nearest town, and Covid sure as hell didn't do my income any good, and my wife left me, and so did my kids." Bernie sounded more philosophical than bitter. He hadn't been the best of husbands, or of fathers. "I'm no lawyer but even I can see myself burning the whole place down and using the money to move somewhere my patrons don't have to drive an hour to buy a beer."

As if he could no longer bear to look at the ruin of his life, he turned away.

"Bernie, was anybody mad at you? Especially recently? Mad enough to do something like this?

He gave a half-hearted snort. "There's always somebody pissed off because I won't serve them drunk, or when I take away their keys. But as mad as this?" A crash came from behind them as the rest of the walls fell in. He shoved his hands in his pockets and looked at the ground. "The Roadhouse was a lucky place for me. I was out in the boonies. I could make up my own rules and stick to them without anyone looking over my shoulder. And the Park rats are good people, mostly. The aunties especially, and what they say goes. They loved that I wouldn't serve drunks, or pregnant women, and that I took car keys from people I didn't think should be driving. If I'd had a problem, I would have gone to them first."

Van was unfamiliar with the Roadhouse's origin story. "And they were never mad at you?" She had heard of the days when armed village elders met planes at the airport and searched them for bootleg alcohol. It was difficult to reconcile the two views.

Bernie gave a faint smile, still looking at the ground. "Well, one time Auntie Edna accused me of putting too much coffee in her Irish coffee."

"Sounds like Auntie Edna." Edna Aguilar, celebrated in song and story as she had never been in life, had never missed an opportunity to take umbrage against someone, especially if that someone had a penis. Although those without came in for their fair share, Van thought with feeling. Like every other Park rat she felt the lack of an auntie. She didn't feel the lack of Auntie Edna.

"Short pouring," she said. "All the motive anyone would ever need for arson."

Bernie just looked at her.

"Too soon?"

Twelve

MONDAY, SEPTEMBER 5, LABOR DAY
Niniltna

KATE AND MUTT PULLED UP BEFORE THE Niniltna post office. Like many rural post offices in Alaska, it was in the front room of someone's house, that house owned by the new postmaster, a dour individual by the name of Duane Jackson. In his forties, tall and very fit, he wore the uniform shirt of the Postal Service with military precision, and was mostly silent except for the necessities of conducting the business of the USPS. Bobby Clark had taken one look and said flatly, "Veteran. Sandbox."

Jackson had appeared when the previous postmaster, a large woman given to ankle-length muumuus in flowered fabrics who sold crystals and beadwork from a corner shelf in the tiny lobby in defiance of regulations, had eloped with a masseur from Ahtna. The last anyone had heard of Cheryl was a card from Gulf Shores, Alabama. On the back the message read, "Cheryl's Healing Crystals and Espresso.

Licensed Masseur by appointment only. Come visit us in our new seaside home! Discounts available for package purchases and old friends."

A USPS clerk from Anchorage had been detailed to Niniltna while they looked for someone to take Cheryl's job permanently, during which time said clerk discovered some serious discrepancies in the bookkeeping, especially concerning money orders. Many of them appeared to have been issued free of charge, possibly in exchange for cash which went unrecorded.

The pandemic had made hiring difficult everywhere, but eventually Jackson had appeared, and rumor filtered back through one of the clerks at the Ahtna bank who was a second cousin of Selina Shugak's that he'd bought the house with a VA loan, which confirmed Bobby Clark's assessment. Jackson was apparently unmarried, with no children in evidence. Park girls who went for the tall, dark, and brooding approached and were politely but firmly rebuffed. Outside the post office Jackson was seen occasionally at Bingley's buying groceries. He had a newish model Ford F-150 pickup, but then so did half the Alaskan male population.

He opened and closed the post office on time and had the mail sorted into mostly the correct boxes. So far, at least, he hadn't sent packages back before someone was able to get into town to pick them up, which was more than could have been said for Cheryl. Park rats on the whole were willing to give him a conditional pass. It wasn't the first time a hermit had found refuge in Bush Alaska and it wouldn't be the last.

NOT THE ONES DEAD

Fall had come early that year, which the Park rats mostly welcomed given the schizophrenic nature of the previous summer, half drought and half monsoon. It was not what they were accustomed to and they welcomed the lessening of the daylight hours with positive relief. The air was made chillier by a stiff breeze that rattled the golden leaves still clinging to the branches of the birch and aspen, and the undergrowth had turned a deep, dark, almost ominous red. Kate got out of the pickup and stood for a moment, savoring the sharp bite of autumn on her cheek.

Five feet tall, a hundred twenty pounds, a short cap of midnight black hair and almond-shaped hazel eyes with a slightly Asian fold to their lids, when she stood still she had an uncanny ability to fade into the landscape. The second and third and fourth glances came when she shifted into motion, her entire body a harmonious integration of muscle and bone, every movement smooth and confident. It wasn't grace so much as it was absolute assurance, of always knowing exactly where every limb was in relation to everything around her. Few people had ever seen her off balance because she seldom was, and Bobby Clark had been heard to say that her situational awareness was better than a Navy Seal's on his way into Abbottabad. Her gaze was steady, unflinching, and on occasion intimidating as hell.

Mutt helped, of course. No one except the about-to-be-terminally-ignorant messed with a woman whose boon companion was a half-husky, half-Arctic grey wolf who outweighed her companion by twenty pounds. Her unwavering gaze was every bit as disconcerting as Kate's, and her eyes were yellow in color and all the more daunting for that.

Although not to the woman who pulled up next to them. Ruthe Bauman had thirty years and six inches on Kate, a thin, almost stringy woman with a heavily lined face and a mop of flyaway gray hair wearing the Park uniform of jeans, Sorels, and Carhartt jacket. She waved at Kate through the windshield and donned a mask before getting out of her ancient International pickup, not quite a Model TT but in the same century.

"Ruthe, hey, long time no see."

"No kidding, Kate, I was beginning to think I was the last living person on the planet."

"Can I check your mail for you, Ruthe?" She caught the keys Ruthe tossed her by way of answering, and didn't regret the offer until she had to make three trips to carry out all of Ruthe's Amazon boxes. These had been loaded into parcel lockers with keys to them placed in the relevant post office box, an innovation forced on the post office by Covid, when all the Park rats bought everything they could online so they didn't have to go to a store and be with alleged humans who weren't wearing masks.

There was another ten minutes spent listening with outward patience to Ruthe's trenchant comments on American business practices in general and on the US Postal Service in particular. "Businesses either forgot or never figured out in the first place what business they were in. The Postal Service thought they were in the business of moving the mail, when in fact they

NOT THE ONES DEAD

were in the communications industry. Right now every single American citizen should have an email address at usps.com. Instead, we're all signed up with Gmail and Hotmail and AO fucking L."

Kate made a sympathetic noise. Ruthe's AOL account had been hacked a few months before and the entire Park had heard about it, especially the email offers to enlarge her penis. Kate waved her off when she finished her rant and went back into the post office. It was a small square room with a wall of brand-new mailboxes in three sizes and the row of parcel lockers. Cheryl's crystals and beads had been replaced with flat rate boxes, express envelopes, greeting cards, bubble wrap, and tape. Kate opened her box and was pulling out the mail when a voice said gruffly, "You're Kate Shugak."

Startled, she looked up to behold the new postmaster looming through the open half of the Dutch door that led into the sanctum sanctorum behind the mailboxes. He was tall enough that his brush cut could dust the bottom of the doorframe and his shoulders were wide enough to perform the same office for both sides at once. His hands, resting on the lower half of the Dutch door, matched the rest of him. Where on earth had he come from? WWE? Professional football? The cast of *Fast and Furious XI*?

In the month since he'd taken up the post she'd seldom heard him speak, and never before to her, so it took a moment to find a response. "You can't be open, it's Labor Day." She pulled herself together. "Yes, I'm Kate Shugak."

"Duane Jackson." He said his name with what she read as

reluctance, although she couldn't imagine why. One probably needed a name to apply for a job with the USPS.

"Nice to meet you finally, Duane." She tried a smile on for size.

It failed to have its usual effect. He frowned at her, and then at Mutt, who had accompanied Kate inside in a supervisory capacity. Kate looked down at her mail. The advertisement for an Eddie Bauer special on T-shirts was, in fact, addressed to her. "Something I can do for you?"

"There's a guy."

Kate waited.

His frown deepened into a scowl. "The guy who sold his lodge."

Enlightenment, a little. "Demetri Totemoff."

He nodded. "Him. You related?"

As of course all Alaska Native Park rats must be. "Sort of." And let's face it, in more or less the same way she was to nearly everyone else in the Park, by blood or not.

"Has he signed the deal yet?"

"He died last year. Covid. But my guess is his wife has. Alina had wanted him to retire so they could move someplace warm for a long time."

"She shouldn't have."

She kept her tone mild. "Little late to tell her so." He scowled some more and she tried to prime the pump. "Any particular reason why you would say that?"

The lines deepened in his face. "The guys who bought it. You don't want them around."

Kate didn't have the faintest idea who'd bought Demetri's lodge, as the news of the sale was only just making it to Park Air. "Oh? Why is that?"

"They're not good people. And they'll bring trouble with them."

She stared at him. "Duane, you're going to have to be a little more specific. I mean, you evidently want me to do something. What, exactly, and why?"

He shut the top half of the Dutch door in her face.

Being a people person wasn't in the job description for a Bush postmaster. Still. "What the hell?" It was a moment before she realized she'd said it out loud. There was no response from behind the mailboxes. She shook her head and let herself out the door. She let Mutt into the pickup first and then stood there for a moment, staring at the door of the post office. It was the first time anyone had ever prophesied doom at her from this location, and it was feeling a little like Scene Three of the first act of *Macbeth*. "What the hell?" she said again.

"You talking to yourself again, Kate?"

Keith Gette appeared before her. Keith was Oscar Jimenez's better half and together they partnered in a gardening business on a property off the Step Road that Keith had inherited from a deceased relative. They were gardeners who had talent and, Kate suspected, a grueling amount of work had created a business model that sold high-end herbs and greens and the only commercially grown tomatoes in the state that actually tasted like tomatoes. Covid had hit them pretty hard when half the restaurants in Anchorage and Fairbanks had closed down. "How you doing, Keith? How's business?"

He looked a little worn down. "Picking back up, I'm happy to say. We put up another high tunnel."

"You're kidding. What's that, four now?"

He smiled. "Five."

"Tell me you've got help. No way only you and Oscar can manage that much acreage."

He laughed. "Well, we're working with Jim to incorporate some agriculture classes into Herbie's curriculum, and that brings us some free labor." His face lit. "And we've put in five acres of peonies."

"Really! Nice. You actually able to make money on peonies?"

He shrugged. "We'll see. They don't weigh much and FedEx has an office in Ahtna."

"Still have to get them to Ahtna."

"You sound like Oscar. Shut up."

She laughed. "Shutting up now." She hooked a thumb over her shoulder. "You met the new guy?"

"Who, Duane?" He nodded. "Sure."

"Know anything about him?"

"No blip on the gaydar, if that's what you mean." He laughed at her expression. "Sorry, couldn't resist. Why you asking?"

"No reason. Just seemed a little off."

"Hell, Kate, everyone has an off day now and then." He left her with a wave and went inside.

A Subaru Forester whose silver paint was covered in dings

and dust slid to a halt. Van jumped out, fending off Mutt's greeting, delivered on her hind legs and involving a lot of tongue. Mutt generally went for the guys, but Van was a privileged exception. "Have you heard?"

"Heard what?"

"Midair."

Kate snapped to attention and turned to look up and down the airstrip. "Who? Where? When?"

"No idea, no idea, and I think it just happened. I was at the fire at the Roadhouse and everyone's phones went off. Didn't yours?"

Kate pulled out her phone and groaned. "I had it muted for the night and forgot to unmute."

"Sounds like a Zoom veteran to me."

"What are you doing here?"

Van shrugged. "The midair happened somewhere in the Park. Good chance any rescue or investigative efforts will stage out of Niniltna." She held up her phone. "On-the-scene reporting."

Kate nodded. "Your newspaper. Right."

"Your newspaper, Kate. You've downloaded the app, right?" Without waiting for an answer, Van jerked her head at the hangar across the strip. "I'm going to talk to George, see if he's heard anything."

"Hey?"

"What?"

Kate hooked her thumb over her shoulder. "You heard anything about the new guy?"

"The new postmaster, you mean?" Van shrugged. "He doesn't mingle much. Word is he's ex-military."

"Right," Kate said again. Her eyes narrowed. "Wait a minute. What fire at the Roadhouse?"

Food was love for Auntie Vi and this morning everything in the refrigerator and the cupboards was out on the counter. She always had a bowl of dough rising for fry bread and oil was already heating in the largest cast-iron frying pan. A Ziploc full of flour and salt and pepper sat next to a plate of caribou steaks. At the sink Auntie Vi was mashing an egg, chopped onions, minced garlic, and breadcrumbs into mooseburger, a buttered loaf pan at the ready nearby.

There were usually one or two or ten Park rats gathered around the table at Auntie Vi's, who were this morning conspicuous by their absence. Maria, Anna, and David, Auntie Vi's adopted family, were nowhere to be seen, either. The storm warnings were out. Mutt's ears went back and she tiptoed around the kitchen table and down the hall to the living room, where there was always a dog bed with a bone on it.

Kate hung her coat on a hook by the door and sidled in between Auntie Vi and the kitchen table, where Bernie was seated, looking morosely for answers in a mug of coffee and not finding any. Auntie Vi gave Kate a fiery look but there was no yelling, which gave Kate the courage to peel the plastic wrap from the bowl of dough. She began pulling balls and flattening them into rounds, which she hung over the sides of the bowl.

She got a plate out of the cupboard and covered it with paper towels. When the oil began to move she began frying the cakes.

The oven door slammed behind the meatloaf. A second frying pan crashed down on the burner next to the one with fry bread in it, splattering the oil. Kate snatched her hand back and licked it where it had been burned but it was the only outward comment she was prepared to make.

The first round of fry bread was arranged on the paper towels and sprinkled with powdered sugar, followed by another layer of paper towels. By the time all the dough had been shaped and fried, the caribou steaks had been breaded and the plate holding them had been slammed down next to Kate. Obediently she tonged them into the hot oil in the second pan. The oil began to sizzle instantly.

A quart Mason jar filled with celery stalks, sliced carrots, and green onions appeared on the table with a force that slopped the water in it over the side. Auntie Vi wasn't much for appetizers or salads and most of her greens came from cans. A dish towel slapped down and was swiped across the spill with ferocious intent.

Kate removed the mug from Bernie's hands, poured it out, and refilled it. She wasn't sure he noticed that it had been gone. Even the platter of fry bread she put in front of him failed to raise any interest. She poured herself a mug of coffee, doctored it liberally with evaporated milk and raw sugar, and sat down across from him. "Can you talk about it, Bernie?"

For several moments she wondered if he'd even heard her, and then he looked up, the picture of misery. "It's just…

everything's gone, Kate. You don't know… you can't know what that's like. I—" He looked up and saw her unsmiling face, and remembered she, too, had been burned out of her home. He dropped his head over his mug again and spoke in a mutter. "Sorry, Kate. I forgot. Of course you know."

"It's okay. Today isn't about me." She waited for a moment. "Were you able to save anything?"

"A few things. Not much."

"What happened?"

"I don't know. Something woke me up, I think it was the propane tank exploding, and I got up to look out the window and saw the bar on fire. I ran out and across the airstrip and up the back stairs. The place was filled with smoke and if I'd been thinking about it I probably wouldn't have opened the door, but I did and I think that just fed the flames because there was this big whoosh! I always empty out the register at closing every night and put the cash and slips in the safe at the house. I grabbed that and ran."

"That" was the bottle of tequila, in the bottom of which sat an extremely well pickled human finger, allegedly the price paid by one of the first people to summit Angqaq. It occupied the exact center of the table, and was, in bartender speak, the base of the Middle Finger.

Another finger, still attached to its parent hand, appeared over Kate's shoulder and shook itself forcefully in Bernie's direction. "You get that thing off table while we eat."

Bernie removed the bottle and set it down on the floor next to his chair.

"And then?" Kate said.

He sighed. "I ran for the cabins and banged on all the doors, got everyone up and out. The wind was coming straight out of the south, blowing clouds of sparks, and by that time most of roofs were on fire. When I got to the last cabin I turned around and saw the roof of the house had caught, and the eastern side, too. I had enough time to get back inside and get the safe open and shovel everything into a garbage bag. I grabbed my laptop and my go bag and threw everything into the pickup and drove it out to the road where it'd be upwind." His shoulders rose and fell. "And then all I could do was watch it burn."

He still hadn't touched the fry bread. A plateful of steaming caribou steaks appeared, brown and crisp on the outside and pink and tender on the inside, followed shortly by the meatloaf. Plates smacked down, next to a handful of silverware and a stack of paper towels. Fine dining, Park style.

The finest, Kate thought. Auntie Vi sat down between them and glared, mostly at Bernie. "Something wrong with food?"

His smile was wan. "I'm not that hungry, to tell you the truth, Auntie Vi."

Auntie Vi was outraged, or was assuming a very convincing image of it. "You!" Stab with finger. "Eat!" Another stab. "You think I go to all this trouble for it to go cold!"

It wasn't a question and she didn't wait for an answer, loading a plate with steak and bread and a slab of meatloaf as thick as a Diana Gabaldon novel and shoving Bernie's mug out of the way to make room for it in front of him.

He stared down as if he'd never seen food before. Auntie Vi huffed and loaded another plate for herself, muttering under her breath but making sure her displeasure was felt nonetheless.

"What started the fire?" Kate said.

Bernie picked at his food without enthusiasm, which was as close as it got to heresy in Auntie Vi's house. It seemed he didn't care, which struck Kate as being close to suicidal. "It started on the kitchen side, which makes sense. I guess."

"Why 'I guess'?"

"The propane tank was in the utility closet on the outside of the kitchen. If a fire was going to start anywhere..."

"Could someone have left a burner on?"

A semblance of the old Bernie emerged briefly from the Slough of Despond. "No! It's the last thing I check, every night before I lock the door. Without exception, without fail, every night, Kate." His brow furrowed. "I've been going around and around in my head. Ahtna Propane was out last week to do an annual maintenance check and fill the tank, same as every spring and fall since I've been in business."

"The furnace?"

He shook his head. "That shed's a separate building and fireproofed. It might be the only structure that didn't burn. Although I can't say for sure. I wasn't looking at it."

Kate ate some fry bread and tried not to moan with ecstasy, although it was difficult. "You said you went in the back door."

"Yes."

"Did you have to use a key?"

He blinked at her. "What?"

"You said you went in the back door. Was it locked?"

"No, I—" He frowned. "But it had to have been. I double check when I lock them. I know I did last night, too." He looked down at the plate in front of him. A knife and fork were handy so he cut off a piece of meatloaf and ate it. "Great meatloaf, Auntie."

Auntie Vi snorted at his lack of enthusiasm, but she was watching Kate.

Kate let Bernie get through his plate and reach for another piece of fry bread. "Did anything happen at the Roadhouse lately that was, I don't know, out of the ordinary?"

His brows went up. "Out of the ordinary is kind of my stock in trade, Kate."

She laughed, and he actually smiled. "I am aware," she said. "But think about it. Did you piss anyone particularly off recently? Break up a fight before it got started and made 'em both mad? Cut somebody off before they were ready to quit drinking for the night? Get in between somebody romancing one of the help?"

His eyes narrowed, the fry bread cooling in his hand. "Kate. Are you thinking someone started that fire deliberately? That it was arson?"

"Did you have insurance?"

"Sure." He gave a short, unhumorous laugh. "As much as I could get for a place that wasn't anywhere near a firehouse."

"Would it be enough to rebuild?"

His laugh this time was even more devoid of humor. "Not

remotely. I don't think anyone would have written a policy that size, and I can't really blame them. Even if Niniltna had a firehouse, by the time a truck would have got there the place would have been past saving."

"Did you try to save it?"

"I thought about getting out the garden hose but by then it would have been too little, too late. My well only runs eight, eight and a half gallons a minute."

"Were all the cabins full last night?"

He nodded.

"Got all their names?"

He shook his head. "Once a PI, always a PI."

"Bernie," she said, very patiently, "your back door was unlocked and you are sure you locked it. Your kitchen stove and propane tank had been serviced the week before. If someone did set the fire deliberately, and if one of the people occupying the cabins that night saw or heard something, we might be able to find out who did it."

He swallowed, finally, but his jaw muscles continued to flex. "You really think the fire could have been deliberately set?"

A flush was rising into his face. She greeted the signs of returning life with deep relief, although she kept it to herself.

Her phone dinged. She looked down and saw that Van had texted her a photo of the crash taken from the air. The wreckage was spread over what appeared to be a relatively small area. It was still on fire, and thankfully the photo was taken from far enough away that the details were obscure. She texted back.

Can you see the tail numbers?

Van texted back.

Can't even find the tails.

She swallowed hard. Auntie Vi would not be appreciative of her good food making a sudden reappearance. Her phone dinged again.

George says he thinks one's maybe a Beaver and the other's a Cub.

Maybe. Hard to tell.

Another moment and she texted again.

George did a low pass. I think I saw body parts.

Everything is burning.

One last text.

The smell is awful.

Even up here.

Thirteen

V AN HAD HAD JUST ENOUGH TIME TO CALL the NTSB in Anchorage after Kate left for Auntie Vi's , who promptly hung up on her when they learned she wasn't an eyewitness. Well, she was the one who had wanted the life of a journalist. An increasingly loud whine informed her of the approach of a single turbo Otter. Chugach Air Taxi, buoyed by the on-again-off-again Suulutaq Mine, now boasted two. She looked up to see one of them clad in the familiar blue and gold colors on final. When it landed she saw George looking at her through the windshield. She'd worked a summer for George, cleaning his aircraft at the end of every day, and the next day's passengers could have eaten off the floors of every one of them. He'd liked her enough to add tips onto every paycheck. The NTSB might not talk to her but George would.

She waited until the Otter taxied up to the hangar door, and then sprinted forward with the stool to place it beneath the air stairs when the door popped open. Useful almost always worked with George, as standing around sucking one's thumb never did.

"Hey, Van, what's up?" George, tall, thin, fighting fifty and the thinning hair that came with it, trotted down the stairs and turned to wave the passengers out. Park rats laden with Anchorage purchases emerged like multiple corks from the same bottle, followed by a few Suulutaq miners, or those few left after the EPA put the copper and gold mine on hold again after Biden got in. The mine owners and the mine workers and Park rats all were suffering from the whiplash of dueling ideological agendas foisted on them from Washington, DC. It made for great headlines, Van thought, but the people most nearly affected universally wished The Powers That Be would come to a decision—for or against, nobody cared which at this point—and stick to it.

"Did you hear?"

He looked grim. "About the midair? Yes."

"Did you see something when you were coming in? Smoke, maybe?"

He shook his head. "No, but from the chatter I have a pretty good idea where it went down." He grimaced. "Unfortunate choice of words, sorry."

She jerked her head at the hangar. "Is your Cub up and running?"

He looked offended. "Always."

"Wanna go see?"

He looked at his watch. "I got a couple hours before I have to turn it around to Anchorage. Why not?" Van wasn't fooled. All pilots had a macabre fascination with disasters that happened to other pilots.

She helped him roll out the Cub and waited while he checked the fuel tanks and did the walkaround. He ran the pilot's seat forward and she climbed into the back and buckled herself in. She donned the passenger headset and adjusted the microphone while he ran the seat back again and climbed in. A laminated list appeared over the back of the seat. His voice came over the headset. "Read it off for me?"

"Roger that." She took the list and read down it, waiting for his response after each item. The prop spun and caught and then they were taxiing and then the ground fell away and once again she had a front row—well, back row—seat to the best view in the world. Quilaks on the left, the rolling river valley punctuated by errant Quilaks on the right, a hint of the blinding blue expanse of the Gulf of Alaska before. In spite of the reason they were in the air she couldn't help a rush of pure joy.

She had hated every moment she had spent in Fairbanks at the University of Alaska. It wasn't UAF's fault that there were no mountains there, unless you drove all the way out to Ullrhaven and found a hill tall enough to climb and when you got to the top of it strained your eyes to the north, where if it was clear enough for long enough you might catch a glimpse of the tops of the Brooks Range. It was true what she had told Kate, that the only reason she had enrolled at UAF in the first place was Johnny. Book learning had never been her favorite thing, and she'd always known what she was good at. Lucky for her that Jim Chopin was willing to carve out enough space for an office from a corner of Herbie Topkok Polytechnic, although she didn't know for how long because the school was filling up fast with students who hailed from Ketchikan to Kaktovik. The Grosdidier brothers were taking it in turn to teach EMT classes, Dulcey Balluta, who made the best pies in the Park, was teaching home ec, and well, short version was the place was busting apart at the seams. There was a story right there all by itself. She had already written her first "Student of the Week" feature for *Kanuyaq Currents* and had banked two more.

She watched the river move past beneath them. George was keeping it low and slow, and the reflection of the Cub rippled over the surface of the water. The village of Niniltna, at three hundred plus population, give or take, was the largest town in the Park. Most of the rest of the Park's population, holding steady at two thousand from the previous census, was scattered along both sides of the riverbanks and inland in homesteads, mining claims, and the occasional high-end lodge where the rich and beautiful from all over the world went to hunt and fish and take pictures to post to Instagram so as to tell their friends, "See where I am and you aren't." Lord knew the only Alaskans who saw the inside of those lodges were the people who served those high-end guests their drinks and changed their sheets.

And when the salmon hit fresh water, every creek, stream, and river hosted its own fly fisherman, or men, most of whom couldn't tell a rod from a reel, and each and every one of whom was determined to bring back nothing less than a thirty-pound king so they could post a video of it to TikTok.

Lord. She sounded worse than Old Sam Dementieff ever had at his sourdoughiest.

"Fuck!" The Cub took a sudden swerve to the right and her head banged off the window.

"Ouch." Van put a hand to her head. The good news was she wasn't bleeding. If her heart didn't slow down she was going to hyperventilate, though. "What the hell, George!"

"A fucking drone is what the hell, Van!" He sounded furious. He pulled back on the stick and pushed forward on the throttle and the Cub grabbed air and climbed, sounding as pissed off as George was. He leveled off and stood the little plane on its right wing and brought them around in a tight circle. "Watch the sky, Van!"

She hadn't needed to be told, as she was trying to see out of all sides of the aircraft at once.

"There!" The Cub's nose dropped and her stomach floated up into the back of her throat. "Look, there! Do you see it!"

"Jesus, George, you could at least—"

He wasn't listening. "See him? Right there, on the river, that sonofabitch. He's bringing it in and not before time."

He brought the Cub down to about fifty feet off the surface of the river, not quite low enough to pull a rooster tail up behind them but close enough for Van to have to make a conscious effort to reswallow her heart. They made a tight bank around a guy in a dory painted a lime green so fluorescent it looked like a twenty-four foot Crankbait. He was standing upright, the boat rocking madly beneath his feet, wobbly legs trying to keep his balance, hands stretched out trying to catch a small black object hovering just above his head. Looking over her shoulder as they blew by Van saw the prop wash knock the drone out of his reach. He clutched for it, lost his balance, and went over the side. In what appeared to be a rescue effort the drone went in after him.

"Hey, George! The guy fell in!"

"Good! I hope the fucker drowns!" George pulled back on the stick, leveled out at a hundred feet, and folded the top half of the door down. With her face mashed up against the glass Van could see the guy hauling himself over the side of the skiff, shipping in a dangerous amount of water with him. He was shouting at them, surely something less than complimentary.

"It serves you right, motherfucker! Your goddamn drone nearly collided with my plane! You coulda killed us!" All this out the open door as they flashed by. George came around again to fly the length of the skiff and lost enough altitude on this pass that the guy dropped flat on his face to save the gear taking his head off.

"Serves him right." George slammed the window shut and pulled back on the stick. "Goddamn cheechakos bringing their fucking toys into the Park without bothering to learn the rules of the goddamn road."

Van didn't think there were very many rules yet about using drones, other than you weren't allowed to use them to hunt, but she didn't say so. There was enough steam coming out of

George's ears already, and her heart was still attempting to return to normal sinus rhythm.

Belatedly, he said, "You okay back there, Van?"

She swallowed. "I'm fine, George. That was too close."

"You're telling me." A moment went by. "Hey, Van?"

"Yeah?"

"If you could maybe not talk about this?"

"Sure."

"Especially not to Kate?"

She almost laughed and the tension began to leach out of her. "Sure."

Another moment. "Oh. And for crissake, don't write about it on that goddamn blog of yours."

"Only in the most glowing terms of your stellar abilities as a pilot, George."

"Smartass."

"What was that, George?"

"Did I say something?" She saw him sit up in his seat. "Hey, do you see that?"

She peered over his shoulder. "You mean that smoke?"

"Yeah. Right about where I thought it was, that old airstrip of Murphy's."

"Who?"

"Paddy Murphy. He had a claim out here. Came up after the Nam looking for a hole to hide in, and found one."

"Gold mine?"

"And copper. He sold out just recently. Told me he'd bought a house in The Villages on the strength of the buyout."

"What's The Villages?"

"Where old white folks go to die in Florida. He never had been able to coax a woman up here and he told me that biology indicated that a single man his age would see more action than Đăk Tô in a place like that."

It sounded like Van's idea of hell. She peered around his shoulder again, looking askance at the rolling foothills and wondering where there was a space flat enough and long enough to bulldoze an airstrip. "Isn't Demetri's lodge around here somewhere?"

He pointed. "About ten miles thataway. And it's not Demetri's anymore."

"That's right, I heard something about that. Didn't—"

"Well, hello. Looks like someone beat us to the scene."

He made a long, leisurely bank down one side of the dirt airstrip and another up the other side. There was a Cessna Caravan parked at one end. Painted white with no logos or identifying markings other than the N number—which she immediately noted—a small cluster of men in dark clothing gathered beneath one wing. One of them was peering up at them as they passed.

"Who's that?" she said.

"Never seen the plane before. Or the guys."

"Me neither. Are we close to the crash?"

He brought the Cub back to cruising altitude and put the nose back on its bearing. "Another couple of minutes."

Sitting as high up as she could get in her seat she peered again over his shoulder. On the left the Quilaks looked down their lofty, frozen noses, disdaining the presence of these puny mortals, so impractical of purpose, so ephemeral in existence. The Quilaks had been there longer than man's memory of them and would be there long after mankind had snuffed itself out, and the Quilaks lost no opportunity to speed them on their way.

It was better to sightsee, she found, than to see the wreckage scattered across a mile of brush and trees. Most of it was still burning. The two fuselages were broken and lit with a malevolent glow of flame. George brought the Cub down to a hundred feet off the ground and made a long, slow circle. Numbly, she brought up her phone and snapped pictures, one after the other. Some distant part of her mind registered his voice on the radio, calling in the coordinates of the crash. "Cub and a Beaver, I think, although it's hard to tell for sure."

Over the headset she heard someone swear and Ahtna tower told them to get the hell off the air and stay off.

There were bodies. Some of them were still burning. Others lay motionless, twisted, awkward in death, charred beyond recognition of anything but the fact that they had once been human.

Or parts of humans.

The smell of burning flesh instantly permeated the cabin. She took a long, shaky breath. "George—"

"Don't you dare throw up in my plane, Van." George's voice was tight, and she wondered if he felt sick, too. "Don't you dare!"

She closed her eyes and rested her forehead against his seat back. "I won't."

"Good." She heard him repeat the coordinates and the hell with Ahtna tower. "There are no survivors. I repeat, there are no survivors."

ATC confirmed in a tight voice and said they would inform the NTSB. George thanked them and signed off.

For something to do with her hands she texted Kate, who she could trust to be practical and matter-of-fact. Kate was, and it steadied her.

"You okay, Van?"

Her voice was a thin thread of sound. "I'm okay, George."

"Good. I'm heading for the barn."

She looked for the Caravan when they flew back over Paddy Murphy's strip but it was gone.

Fourteen

MONDAY, SEPTEMBER 5, LABOR DAY
Niniltna

WHEN BERNIE HAD FINISHED UP HIS SECOND plateful—the possibility that his situation had been caused not by malign fate but by enemy action seemed to have stimulated his appetite—Kate helped Auntie Vi clear the table and load the dishwasher, after which Auntie Vi fetched her knitting (something large made from yarn dyed a blinding fuchsia) and Kate opened the Notes app on her phone. "Okay," she said. "We're going to make two lists. First, a list of everyone who might be pissed off at you."

He folded his arms and smirked. "Kate. I'm a bartender. Pissing people off comes with the job."

"Not to the point that anyone has tried to burn you out of house and home."

The smirk died. "Fair point. You said two lists."

"The second one is the names and contact info of everyone in the cabins last night."

He raised an eyebrow.

"Look, Bernie, I know you have a well-earned reputation for keeping your customers' business their business, but in this case—"

He waved a hand, cutting her off. "Let me get my laptop."

The names of the people in the cabins were easy; they'd all paid in advance by credit card. "I didn't realize you had a dozen cabins."

"I kept filling up the ones I had so I kept adding on. Went cashless a couple of years back, got Square, got the money up-front. All someone has"—he winced—"had to do was show their ID at the bar and they got a door number and a key. Less hassle all the way around."

"How much are you charging per night these days?"

"I was charging a hundred."

Auntie Vi dropped a stitch and went hunting for it, muttering to herself.

Bernie looked defensive. "Hey, Auntie, each and every one of those cabins had a hot shower and a flush toilet. I could have Airbnb'd those suckers for two or three times that, easy. They were never empty. Tourists, fishers, hunters, Suulutaq miners on one-night stands; this summer I even had a couple of guys on a surveying trip for the National Geodetic Survey."

Auntie Vi looked suspicious. "Geodetic?"

"They measure the planet." She still looked suspicious. "Cartographers. Mapmakers."

Her brow cleared.

"Names," Kate said.

What he didn't remember QuickBooks did, although

some he was reticent about, like the borough assembly chair weekending with the commissioner of corrections, both of whom were married to other people. "They wanted the cabin furthest from the bar. They couldn't have seen or heard anything; they were too far away."

"Uh-huh," Kate said, tapping industriously. "Is there some innkeeper's oath where you swear never to reveal the names of your patrons? Because it's likely one of them burned you out."

She raised her head to watch the conflicting emotions cross her friend's face and finally settle into one she approved of. Bernie angry was a lot easier to take than Bernie miserable. His spine stiffened and his voice came out harder and stronger. "All right, Kate." He held up a hand when she would have said something else. "I get it. You're right."

He used Auntie Vi's printer to make a hard copy of a list of the most recent cabin tenants going back two weeks. Most Kate had never heard of. Some of them she knew only too well, and the thought of confronting them almost put her off proceeding any further. Almost. "All right," she said, tucking the list of names, dates, and cabin numbers to one side and taking up her phone again. "Talk to me about any upsets you saw in the Roadhouse, the same time frame. If nothing pans out we'll go back another couple of weeks."

He hesitated.

"What?"

"How much do you charge, Kate?"

"How much do you want me to find these assholes?"

In the past two weeks there had been five fights over women, one pitched battle over a man that resulted in two hundred dollars' worth of broken furniture and glassware, and eight arguments over MAGA hats. Three men and one pregnant woman had been refused service, the former because they were already drunk and the latter because it was Bernie's standing policy. Bernie had confiscated three sets of keys and put each driver to bed in a cabin, which was three nights accounted for out of a hundred sixty-eight (twelve cabins multiplied by fourteen days). There had been a minor altercation mounted by the crew of the *Sarah S* against the crew of *Kathy Q* over who had been high boat that summer. "Couple of bloody noses, nothing serious."

"This is all season-ender stuff."

He nodded, looking weary again. "Yeah. Too many young men with too much money after settling up. I'm—I was happy they were spending it at the Roadhouse, but..."

"What else?"

"Isn't that enough?"

She narrowed her eyes at him. "It's like you said, Bernie. This is all business as usual. What wasn't?"

He sighed. "There were some guys in last night. I thought they were hunters, probably from town."

"Town" was understood everywhere else in Alaska to mean Anchorage. "And?"

"I have a new server, she's kinda cute, and Mark, Luke, and Peter Grosdidier and Nathan and Boris Balluta were all trying to catch her eye. The four newbies took exception."

"What, the boys were cutting into their action?"

Bernie's voice was very dry. "It was more along the lines of they thought she should stick with her own kind."

Auntie Vi rolled her eyes. Kate sighed. "Way to read the room, guys. What happened?"

"What do you think happened? The only time the Grosdidiers and the Ballutas join forces is to repel boarders. They ganged up and the newbies were escorted from the premises."

"'Escorted?'"

"They stood not upon the order of their going, shall we say. I bought the boys a round afterward."

"Did the new guys rent a cabin?"

He shook his head. "I never saw them before. I don't know where they were staying, but it wasn't in my cabins. Good thing, too, because the Ballutas and the Grosdidiers might have started their own fire." He saw Kate's expression. "Too soon?"

"Way too soon." But Kate was secretly pleased to see a flash of the old, irreverent Bernie Koslowski surface, even if only for a moment. "Did you see their vehicle?"

"Nah."

"Do you think any of either set of brothers did?"

"Heh. They were too busy toasting the rout of the barbarians at the gate, and lying to anyone who would listen about who routed who the hardest."

"Any serious injuries?"

"Nah. No broken bones, anyway." He thought. "Maybe a busted nose. Some bruised knuckles."

Auntie Vi rolled her eyes and muttered.

"Local or from away?" Kate said patiently. "The injuries? Were any serious enough to scar someone's ego as well as their person?"

He stared at her and then his eyes widened. "Oh. Oh! Oh, I see what you mean." He hesitated. "Well. I guess they were pretty banged up, now that you mention it." He saw her look and said, "Jesus, Kate, they started it."

Kate didn't roll her eyes but she imagined it pretty good.

After a moment Bernie said, "They could have come out on four-wheelers."

She looked up.

He shrugged. "I mean, it's not like it's an unusual sound, but yeah, I heard some four-wheelers afterward. Coulda been them." He looked at her. "So you're really doing this?"

Kate closed the Notes app and set her phone to one side. "Not if you don't want me to, Bernie," she said, not entirely truthfully.

"It was probably just an accident. The propane tank…" His voice trailed away.

She waited.

He tossed off the rest of his coffee and set his mug down with a decisive snap. "No. You're right. Better to know."

"I think so, but that's just me." She waited long enough to ensure there was no further objection. Impossible to work a case for an unwilling client. "I know an arson investigator in Anchorage. He can tell us if it was an accident or deliberate."

He winced. "How much will that cost me?"

She shook her head. "He owes me one, and Jim will fly him out and back."

He sighed. "Okay. Tell Jim I'll pay for fuel."

"I'll tell him." She doubted Jim would take any of Bernie's money, especially now, but she would tell him. "Meanwhile, you'll be here?"

"Don't really have anywhere else to go, now, do I?"

"Feeling sorry for yourself doing no good." Auntie Vi slammed a clean mug down in front of him. "Have more coffee."

Fifteen

MONDAY, SEPTEMBER 12
The Park, Kate's homestead

THE DOOR OF THE CHEST FREEZER GAPED like the maw of some prehistoric beast, its interior gorged on quart Ziploc bags full of raspberries, salmonberries, nagoonberries and chopped rhubarb, along with vacuum-packed salmon filets and chunks of halibut and rockfish. She could barely get the lid closed as it was. If they got their moose this year, which they always did, where would they put it? The last thing she wanted to do was buy another freezer, because then there would always be the expectation to fill both every fall. With Johnny at UAF in Fairbanks and Van living in town, there were only the two of them, and this year of all years there was no chance of giving any of it away. It had been a great year for berries along the trail and an unusually healthy salmon run and good escapement up the Kanuyaq had ensured full freezers from Ahtna to the river's mouth, including Zoya Creek which ran in back of Kate's house. The good news was that no one was going hungry this winter. The bad news was they'd never eat all this between this fall and when the salmon hit fresh water next year.

"First-world problems," she said out loud, and closed the lid of the freezer with a firm thud. She went in the back door and into the kitchen, where a fillet of red was thawing in the sink. It was her turn to cook and she was sick of baked salmon so she was going to make salmon bouillabaisse, although if Auntie Joy walked through the door Kate would very likely be drummed out of the tribe. That year's salmon was supposed to be fried or baked, and on special occasions made into pirok. Chowder and bouillabaisse and soups and stews generally were reserved for the dog days of breakup, when last year's salmon was on the edge of freezer burn and had to be used up before the new run was up the creek.

She was tempted by the thought of pirok, but she didn't have any mushrooms, canned or fresh, and the last piece of frozen puff pastry had gone for a rhubarb tart, so she stuck to the plan. She put a pot of water on the stove. When it boiled she slid the fillet into it and turned off the heat. She drained the pot immediately, put the salmon on a cutting board, and peeled off the skin. The lazy woman's way to skin a salmon. She cut it into bite-sized squares, hoping she had removed all the bones and knowing she hadn't, and set them aside.

A deep, heavy frying pan, a splash of oil, and chopped bacon began to sizzle and perfume the air. When it was crisp she scooped it out and set it to drain on a paper towel. She got a bag of mirepoix out of the freezer, slapped it against the counter to break it up, and poured about two cups into the hot grease where it sizzled and popped. Meanwhile, she squished garlic, chopped tomatoes, and diced potatoes. There were a few slices of stale bread left so she cubed it and made croutons fried in olive oil, garlic powder, and Penzey's Italian Herb Mix, her all-purpose, super-duper go-to for croutons and everything else. In a pinch it could substitute for poultry seasoning in her justly famous two-bean stew, or so she fondly believed.

She found the homely tasks soothing. It had been a week since the double whammy of the midair and the Roadhouse burning down, and it was difficult to say which event had rocked the Park rats' world more. Bobbie had devoted days' worth of Park Air programming to people mourning the loss of the Park's only drinking establishment. Epic fistfights (including the last one the night before it burned) were rehashed and celebrated, blow by blow. Every single one of the Middle Finger shots were recounted in loving detail, with a few Big Bumpers calling in to reminisce about frostbite and altitude sickness. All the hapless tourists who had somehow found their way to the Park's only watering hole were toasted live on air. All the marriages, divorces, affairs, and one-nighters begun and ended beneath its roof were dragged out of the closet once more, although Bobby was good about bleeping out names. Well, he was when he liked the people involved.

The midair was something else again. Nine people dead, two of whom were known to the Park, and indeed to all Alaska. The other seven, a pilot and her six passengers, were Outsiders, true, but still mourned. There was an obsessive discussion fueled mostly by speculation, again on Park Air and hosted by Bobby, a pilot himself, where every scrap of detail that came to light was hashed and rehashed. It had been a partly cloudy day with the wind under five knots. One pilot was in his eighties, true, but he had the hours to prove his experience and competence. The other was younger and a woman—side eye—but she, too, had hours, if not as many as the old fart on the stick of the Cub. Every pilot worthy of the name flew the Bush with eyes wide open and one ear always on 122.75. There were more small-plane pilots per capita in Alaska than anywhere else in the world and the non-pilots flew often enough that all of them had a vital interest in aviation and aviation safety.

The NTSB was maintaining radio silence, which only meant that every new rumor was treated as fact and ran through the Park like lightning, which in this era of conspiracy theories and social media meant nothing was too weird or too ridiculous to say out loud, from the near miss of a Russian stealth jet mapping out an invasion route causing the collision, to a UFO prospecting for fresh meat doing the same.

She put everything but the salmon in the pan, added a heaping spoonful of tomato paste and chicken stock to cover along with a dried chipotle chile, salt, and pepper. When it came to a boil she covered the pan and reduced the heat. In a small bowl she put in a dollop of mayonnaise and whisked in red pepper flakes, cayenne pepper, and more squished garlic. There wasn't enough garlic in the world for Kate.

Arms slid around her from behind and someone nuzzled her neck. "Come here often, lady?"

She tilted her head back and smiled up at Jim. He was taller than her by a foot so it was easy.

He nodded at the pan. "Salmon bouillabaisse?"

"I was in the mood." She leaned into his embrace, feeling the heat and solidity of his body against her as a comfort, a delight, and an incitement to riot. "Mmm."

"Mmm, indeed." He flipped her around and she caught a glimpse of laughing blue eyes before he bent her over into a kiss that wiped every other thought from her mind. Bliss. When he allowed her to come up for air he gave her a wicked smile. "Shall we delay dinner?"

She blew out a breath. "Tempting. But no."

"Disappointing. Mostly." He let her go and got a beer from the fridge. "There's some news about the midair."

"Oh? The NTSB actually broke omertà?"

"Well, not news, exactly, but they held a press conference." His smile was half-hearted. Jim was a pilot, too. "They stressed Barr Senior's age. He was eighty-seven and still in the air."

It happened, more often than anyone cared to admit out loud. Old farts who had been flying all their lives, inimical by nature and nurture to the strictures of federal oversight, were never inclined to take the word of some fancy-ass doctor who wasn't even from around here. Most of them had been flying since their feet could reach the rudder pedals and few of them were inclined to admit the possibility of their own mortality. Kate had heard more than one of them say, "I coulda made that landing in my sleep." There were always rumors about friendly doctors who would sign off on flight physicals, too. "Well, it's not like they check your ID at Merrill."

"Maybe they should."

She shook her head. "They're working with nine hundred aircraft based there, about eight hundred of which are single-engine and privately owned. Can you imagine the shriek that would go up if every departing pilot had to go through some kind of TSA?" She reflected. "Can you imagine the shriek that would go up from TSA if anyone gave the order they had to?" She gave the bouillabaisse a stir. The aroma hit her nose and her stomach growled. So did his, loud enough to hear from across the room. "His poor family."

"Killed himself and took eight others along with him. All their poor families."

She saw him shudder. Every pilot's nightmare.

He looked at her, his expression sober. "Promise me—"

She stood on tiptoe and gave him a swift kiss. "You're a long way from eighty-seven, Jim, but I promise. Go wash your hands, it's ready."

He made an effort and it almost came out naturally. "Great, I'm starving."

She put two soup bowls on the table along with spoons and paper towels. The half a loaf of French bread smeared with butter and garlic was rescued from the oven and served up in a basket. At the last minute she stirred the salmon chunks into the chowder and let them cook on the way to the table, where she set the pot on a warming mitt.

He took his seat and filled her bowl and then his. She

topped both with the croutons and the aioli. "God, what a smell. Yum. Where's Mutt?"

"Out. Hunting her own dinner, probably."

The bouillabaisse was thick and savory and the salmon was barely cooked through and tender, and only Jim got a pin bone stuck between his teeth. "Oou 'id 'at on 'urpose."

"You served."

"Humph." He removed the pin bone with a minimum of grimace and dived back in. "You hear that the feds cancelled the offshore oil lease sale?"

"They said no one was interested in bidding."

"You think they were lying?"

She shook her head. "Bankers are the most unsentimental people on the planet. If they thought there was money to be made underwriting offshore oil exploration in Alaskan waters, there would be drilling rigs from Ketchikan to Nome tomorrow." She shrugged. "Like it or not, wind and solar are cheaper and more efficient and a hell of a lot less red meat for the tree huggers."

"So should we get solar panels, do you think? Maybe a wind turbine?"

She cast a doubtful eye toward the window, as if estimating the watts that could be harvested at this latitude. "We could look into it. I'd be happy if we weren't so dependent on fuel oil trucked in from Ahtna." She looked at him. "You should definitely think about it for the hangar. That is one big-ass roof and you might not have to chop so much wood."

He cleared the table and washed up while she built a fire in the fireplace and relaxed on the couch with the fourth and, she had been made mournfully aware, evidently the last of Becky Chambers' Wayfarer series. Jim took the other side of the couch and picked up a thick book in an orange and red cover.

"You buying books by the pound now, or what?" His last one had been a 700-page biography of Churchill.

He peered at her over the top. "Be warned, I'm going to force-march you through it after I'm done. It's like these two guys, one an anthropologist and the other an archeologist, are having a conversation about human history after they've done all the homework and now they're just talking over a beer. Or a pint, I guess, since they're both Brits. You will find chapter two especially interesting."

"You've been reading it since July."

"Late July." He turned a page. "I'm taking it slow because I want to remember as much of it as I can." He nudged her with his foot. "You?"

"An Aeluon, a Quelin, and an Akarak walk into a bar…"

He groaned. "Do I even want to know?"

"Probably not, but there may be a bedtime story later."

He brightened. "How much later?"

She hid a smile. "If you're very, very good…"

"I'm always good." This said with emphasis.

I'll say, she thought, but didn't utter the thought out loud. His ego needed no reinforcement.

They read in peaceful silence as the light outside the windows that formed the south-facing wall of the room changed gradually from day to night. It was almost dark when the door clicked open and they both looked up to see Mutt sidle inside, in what she thought was an unobtrusive manner, and nose the door closed again.

"I should never have put levers on the doors instead of knobs," Kate told her severely.

Mutt laughed at her, yellow eyes narrowed, tongue lolling out between an impressive set of what more than one bad guy had discovered were very sharp teeth. She went into the kitchen to drain her water bowl and then collapsed with a satisfied "Huff!" in front of the wood stove.

"Good hunting?" Jim said.

"Woof." She sprawled out on her side, legs askew, a position that revealed the scar on her chest left by a bullet meant for Kate the year before. The silver-gray hair was growing over it but Kate would always know exactly and precisely where that scar was.

She felt Jim looking at her and turned her head to meet his eyes. "What?"

"You're never really convinced she's coming home, are you?"

"Not any more. Not until she walks in that door." She took a long last look at Mutt, now abandoned to a food coma. "I heard the wolf pack howling last night."

"So did I." He nudged her again. "You gonna put her on a leash?"

Her head jerked up. He was laughing at her. "What I thought."

"Jerk."

"Ah, Shugak, you love me anyway and you know it."

"You being a jerk and me loving one are not co-dependent states of being."

"Ooooh, psychology. Dirty girl." He paused. "Abrupt subject change. When I left you were talking to Bernie on the phone."

"Yeah. Again."

"Did he change his mind again? Does he want to rebuild?"

A faint snore came from the sprawl of dog in front of the fire. Kate was staring out the window. He bookmarked his page and set the book on the floor. He sat up and reached for hers and did the same, and came over to her end of the couch in a gentle tackle. She settled into his arms with a feeling of coming home. They lay on their sides, her back to his front, his chin on her shoulder, watching the flames, and the slumbering behemoth stretched out in front of them.

"It doesn't sound like it. I think it's hard for him to go back out there and face it."

"End of an era."

"Yeah."

He knew her silences by now. "What?"

"There is something percolating with the aunties."

He raised his head. "Oh god, oh god. What?"

"I don't know."

"You always know."

"Not this time. I walked into Auntie Vi's last Thursday and Auntie Joy and Annie Mike were there and they shut up like someone had thrown a switch."

"Aw. Were your feelings hurt by the mean aunties?" He tickled her and she squealed. Mutt's ear twitched. "Watch it," Kate whispered. "My rabid dog will tear you a new one."

He snorted. "Fat chance. She likes me better than she does you."

Which might possibly be true.

"You were looking into the fire, you told me. Anything new there?"

"No. It was definitely arson, but we knew that from Ahtna Propane and the arson investigator, and the Ahtna fire marshal flew out and confirmed it. Both agree the valve on the tank was tampered with. They didn't find evidence of an accelerant, or anything much other than a used condom—ew—and since no one got hurt it isn't going to be a priority for the investigators."

"Any further ideas on who?"

"There was a fight in the bar the night before, but when wasn't there? Although…"

"What?"

"I can't track down the guys that started the fight. Nobody knew them. They weren't from around here."

"Hunters?"

"Maybe. Bernie said Arnie Gunnerson—you'll remember he's fresh out of the service—was there and he said they looked like wannabe military but not the real thing."

He groaned. "Great. Phony soldiers. We're lucky they didn't pull out their M4s and start blazing away. Anybody see their vehicle?"

"Nope. Although Bernie says he might have heard four-wheelers."

Jim snorted. "Like every Park rat doesn't have two or three of those already. We've got two ourselves. They weren't staying in the cabins?"

"Bernie says no."

"Huh. So they just, ah, disapparated?"

"Or something."

"Weird. What does Bernie say about the insurance? They going to pay up?"

"Not until the case clears."

He made a sound that was not complimentary of insurance companies.

A brief silence. "The reason the aunties tolerated the Roadhouse for so long is that it was fifty miles away."

"That, and he saved a corner for their quilting bee."

"True enough."

He heard the lack of enthusiasm in her voice and raised his head to look at her. "Don't you want Bernie to rebuild?"

She stirred. "I don't know."

He understood. Both her parents had died of alcohol-related causes. "He's a responsible barkeep, Kate. We could do a lot worse."

She sighed.

He nuzzled the side of her neck. "I bet I could convince you I'm right."

She shivered involuntarily as his lips traced the outline of her ear. "I doubt it, but please, do try."

Both their phones dinged with an incoming text.

"You gonna get that?" His hand was busy at the fly of her jeans.

"I would, but my phone is so far away."

"Mine, too."

"Oh, good."

The next morning Van arrived on their doorstep with the dawn, which at that time of year wasn't till seven a.m., but still. Van saw Kate's expression and held up a hand, palm out in a plea for peace. "I know, and I'm sorry. But this couldn't wait. I tried to text you last night." She saw Kate and Jim's phones, plugged in on the kitchen counter. Her eyes traveled further, to the cushions of the couch scattered across the living room floor. She looked back at Kate, who raised an eyebrow. "Uh. Ah. Well. Anyway. Something's happened, and I—"

"Coffee?"

"Sure." Van accepted a mug and the offer of a carton of half-and-half. "Thanks. The thing is—"

The brisk patter of feet on the stairs. Mutt met Jim at the bottom of them, tail wagging hard enough to create lift, jumped up to place her massive front paws on his shoulders, and ravished his face with her tongue.

"Eeyew," Jim said, although he didn't fend her off all that hard. She dropped back down to all four feet and he grabbed her head and smooched her all over. She wrinkled her nose and pulled free to unleash an enormous sneeze.

"Yeah, payback is hell," he said, and looked at Van. "Hey, kid. You're out and about early." He gave her a one-armed hug and ruffled her hair as if she was still twelve, which she wasn't and she looked as if she longed to remind him of that fact. Instead she smoothed her hair down again and stood very much upon her dignity. "Hi, Jim. I just came out because—"

"Have a seat. Kate's got a quiche in the oven." He waggled his eyebrows. "With bacon in it."

She shot Kate an apprehensive glance. "No, coffee's fine, but there's something I—"

"Nonsense," Kate said, "you're here and there's plenty." Shortly thereafter they were seated around the table and Jim for one was stuffing his face for all he was worth. Bacon and eggs in a butter crust were just the restorative for an energetic night. He winked at Kate, who had no trouble interpreting its meaning and hid a grin behind her mug.

Van, belatedly recognizing the error of her ways, ate and drank without comment. Jim cleared the table and refilled everyone's coffee. Kate took a sip. "Now, then. What brings you all the way out here so early?" She smiled. "Not that you aren't always welcome, Van."

She meant it sincerely and Van knew it, but she had just been ever so slightly spanked and she knew that, too. They could have answered their phones last night and this whole scene would never have happened, but she resisted saying so in case she was then made to wait through lunch to impart her news.

And news it was. "I got a tip."

Kate looked at Jim. "What kind of a tip?"

"An anonymous tip."

When she said nothing more Kate said, so obviously manifesting an outward patience that Van knew she had just about run out, "Concerning?"

Van shoved her mug to one side. "There's an extra body."

Before the silence got too long, Jim said, "An extra body."

"In the wreckage of the midair. There were two people in the Cub, right? And seven people in the Beaver. So nine dead. But they've found a tenth body in the wreckage."

Mutt put her head on the table next to Jim and gazed up at him with adoring eyes. He scratched her ears and her tail thumped the floor. "No ID?"

"Didn't say."

"Male or female?"

"Male. The email I got said a tenth man was killed in the midair and they'd just found his body."

"Email? Show me."

"That's the thing, Kate. Right after I got the email? It disappeared out of my inbox."

"Did you delete it?"

"No."

"Did you check your spam filter? Your trash?"

She nodded. "It isn't there."

"Did you confirm there was an actual tenth body?"

"I called the Alaska regional office of the National Transportation Safety Board in Anchorage. I identified myself as press and I said I had information about the midair. They connected me to someone who said he was with the major investigation team. I told him about the email."

Kate exchanged a glance with Jim. "Well? What did he say?"

Van swallowed. "He said he wanted to see the email and could I forward it to him. I said I would, and that was when I found it was gone. When I told him he hung up on me."

"But he didn't deny it," Kate said thoughtfully.

"No."

"It took them a week to realize they had an extra body in the wreck?" Jim looked at Kate. "That's some sloppy investigating right there."

She met his eyes. "Or…"

He sat back. "Or someone is trying to keep it quiet. But why?"

Van drank more coffee, although it had to be cold by then. "There's something else."

"What?"

She took a deep breath. "When we were flying back from the wreck."

"You and George?"

She nodded. "We flew over an airstrip. George said it belonged to some old miner, Paddy Murphy?"

"Old Pat Murphy." Kate nodded. "I remember him. Didn't I hear he'd sold out and drug up?"

"That's what George said." Van swallowed. "There was a plane parked on the strip. White, unmarked except for the tail number."

"Which of course you noted." Jim's voice was dry.

Van held up her phone. "When we got back I looked it up on the FAA registry."

"And?"

"And it's registered to the federal government."

"Any particular department?"

"The Department of Justice."

Mutt, who was lying on the floor between Kate and Jim, heard something in the quality of the silence that followed that made her raise her head.

"Interesting," Jim said at last.

After a moment he added, "That wasn't in the story you posted about the crash site."

"I didn't see them doing anything other than being there. And they weren't at the crash site, per se. The strip is well short of it."

Kate crossed her arms and frowned at the table. "What's this have to do with the tenth body, if it exists?"

Van gave an uncomfortable shrug. "Maybe nothing. It's just another weird thing, you know? Three in a row. Feels, I dunno, itchy."

"Three?" Jim said.

"The Roadhouse burned down, it looks like deliberately. The midair, same day. And the DOJ on the scene, also same day."

Jim looked at Kate. "Wanna go for a ride?"

Sixteen

TUESDAY, SEPTEMBER 13
The Park, Paddy Murphy's claim

"WHEN WE FLEW OUT HERE GEORGE SAID we were on a straight line for Demetri's lodge."

"Not Demetri's anymore." Jim's voice sounded noncommittal over the headset but Kate looked at him from the right seat. They were at five hundred feet, flying as slow as Jim's 206 could without falling out of the air. Kate rode shotgun, Van was in the back with Mutt next to her.

"Who did buy it?"

"Nobody seems to know," Van said. "So I got curious and went up to the Step."

"And yet your car still runs."

"I heard that," Van said with feeling. "Anyway, Dan wasn't there but you know that map he's got on the wall in his office? The property is still colored green and the owner is listed as 'Private.'"

Kate remembered the one-way conversation she'd had with

the new postmaster. *The guys who bought it. You don't want them around.*

"I remember, last May sometime, I think? George said he saw a Herc headed in that direction when he was on his way back from an Ahtna run."

"I remember Demetri lengthened his airstrip a while back," Kate said. "So his high rollers could fly straight in from town in their private jets."

"Yeah, I remember," Jim said. "George was a little torqued about that. Said he was going to sue Demetri for restraint of trade."

"There's the strip," Van said suddenly.

Jim put the Cessna into a shallow bank, circling the strip once. It was laid out almost exactly north to south, carved from the side of a foothill with enough rocky crags interrupting its descent to make him wary. The surface of the strip looked deceptively pothole-free from five hundred feet but he'd been fooled before and he was pranging no planes that day. A rudimentary trail on the upside of the strip led up the slope, at the top of which was a small moss-covered roof surrounded by a threatening ring of encroaching spruce and birch and alders.

"Is it long enough for you to land on?"

"The question is, is it long enough for me to take off again?"

"Whoever it was got that Caravan in and out again on last Monday."

"True that." He leveled off, put the nose on the strip, and dropped down to fifty feet off the deck, rocking back and forth so he could check the surface from both sides. They came to the end of the strip and climbed again. "Yeah, it's long enough. Surface looks okay. Little narrow."

"You saw the black crosses."

"One at each end," he said cheerfully, "but nobody here to wave us off, so…"

"You better hope nobody's putting down on our strip while we're out here."

"They'll see the cameras and take off again."

He'd put Ring cameras on both corners of the hangar facing their airstrip. "Right. Forgot."

Black crosses on the end of a remote strip meant that except in emergencies landing on them without prior permission was prohibited by their owners. The whole point of remote strips, however, was that they were remote and usually unattended, which thwarted oversight. Years as a state trooper had taught Jim that just the sight of a security camera hanging from the eave of a house or over the door of a cabin inspired an immediate one-eighty in the most curious and/or larcenous of passers-by.

He put the Cessna down at the northernmost inch of the strip and used the entire length of gravel to roll out, stopping, Van told him, almost exactly where the Caravan had been parked. "Nice work if you can get it," he said, switching off and hanging his headset from the crossbar. He opened the door. "Coming?"

They bailed out after him, Mutt jumping neatly over Van and making a perfect four-point landing on the gravel of the strip. A black bear poked her head out of the brush of some alders, followed by the three smaller heads of her cubs. Mutt gave one bark from deep in her throat and all four decided they had urgent appointments somewhere else. A cow moose with two calves, born this year by the size of them and most likely the reason for the bears to be lurking around, melted out of the brush, crossed the strip, and melted back into the brush on the other side. Even after a lifetime spent watching them it always amazed Kate how effortlessly something that big could simply vanish from sight from one second to the next.

"What are we looking for?" Jim said.

"The federal government didn't come out here for no reason," Kate said.

"Is it any of our business?"

She looked at him, one eyebrow raised. "We are still in the Park, right?"

He rolled his eyes.

In the meantime Van was trotting back and forth, examining the strip's surface. Kate shook her head and moved off the strip, bushwhacking through the thick undergrowth, which proved to be mostly blueberries, a lot of them. "You got any Ziplocs in the plane, Jim?"

"Sure." He fetched a couple of gallon bags and picked with her. The berries were as big as her thumbnail and when she popped one in her mouth it burst with flavor and sweetness. "We really need more berries?"

"Pick."

"Picking."

They did so in amiable silence for a while, moving steadily down the edge of the strip. When it ended, Kate straightened up to stretch her back. "Hey. Look there."

As he'd noticed before in Kate World, when she lasered in on something, other and more interesting things brought themselves to her attention. Jim followed her pointing finger and saw a tiny clearing in a circle of scrub spruce, all of them brown and dying from the depredations of the spruce bark beetle. She sealed her bag and set it down on the edge of the strip and set off. He followed.

The clearing was obviously manmade, and... "Look. Someone had a tent pitched here. See where the stakes were? The holes?"

The undergrowth was dank and rotting in place but push it aside and the indentations were easily spotted. "Yeah, and look here, where the lines for the rain fly scored the bark on the tree trunks."

"I'll bet—yeah, look, he pulled some rocks out of the edge of the strip for a fireplace."

"And then scattered them."

Mutt went crashing through the brush next to them and flushed a flock of ptarmigan into the air, accompanied by a cacophony of indignant squawks.

"Guy wasn't going to starve, that's for sure. Not if he knew what he was doing." Jim looked around. "Cleaned it up pretty good. Could be a hunter spotted his moose from the air, sat down, pegged out a campsite so he could shoot it the next day. Following the rules."

Mutt reappeared. Her tail was wagging so hard it was almost a blur. She was carrying something in her mouth.

"What have you got there, girlfriend?"

Mutt pranced forward and laid her kill proudly at Kate's feet. She backed off and plumped down on her butt. Kate knew her duty and pulled out the Ziploc she always carried and produced a piece of salmon jerky. Gulp. After which Mutt cocked an eye at Jim, who obliged forthwith with praise and caresses, to Mutt's immense gratification. Recharged by all this adoration she wheeled and charged back into the brush again.

What Mutt had found was covered with dirt and leaves and Mutt slobber. Holding it gingerly by one edge, Kate gave it a shake, provoking a shower of leaves and needles and dirt. The object resolved itself into a ball cap.

"A hat?" Jim said.

Kate tried to keep the disappointment from her voice. "Yes."

"What's the logo?"

She turned it so that the crown was facing her. "I can't—it's really dirty. Wait." She beat it against her calf, and more of the dirt fell free. The logo was on an oval-shaped badge centered on the crown. The body of the hat was blue, the brim was red, and the badge itself had perhaps once been white. "It's not that old after all," she said, "it's just really dirty. And something's been chewing on it."

"Something large or something small?"

"Something small." She handed it to him.

"Good to know. Standard ball cap. Patriotic colors, red, white, and blue. What are those letters?"

"We might have to take it home and wash it before we can read them." She beat the hat against her leg once more. "Or no, wait, there you go." She held it up so that it caught an errant ray of sunshine. "J—6—4—9."

"J649." Jim shrugged. "Doesn't ring any bells for me. Probably a designation for a new Winchester load."

Kate sighed. "Any random hunter from Anchorage could have lost a ball cap here. For that matter, it could have belonged to Paddy Murphy."

Jim reached into a pocket for one of the plastic bags that was always on call there. "Force of habit," he said when he saw Kate's look. He stowed the cap in the back of the Stationair.

Van came up to them. "Look what I found."

It was a bright shiny new cartridge. Jim took it from her. "Winchester .30-06 Springfield." He handed it to Kate.

"Not fired," she said. "And hasn't been out here long otherwise it would show some weathering." She handed it back. "Pretty sure it won't fit the mag of a Glock 19M."

He smiled. "No." He saw Van's look. "Feeb's chosen sidearm. Your friends probably didn't drop it." He jerked his chin. "Spotted a trail from the air, starts off halfway up the strip."

"I saw that. Probably goes to Murphy's cabin."

"Yeah, saw the roof. We should mosey on up, take a look."

"Better hope the new owner doesn't show up."

"I heard that." He didn't try to hide a shudder. "Gold miners. Scary fuckers."

"I heard that."

The trail was narrow and rocky but not too steep and not all that long. They made a lot of noise to let the bears know they were there. In fifteen minutes they had arrived. The clearing looked larger than it had from the air, surrounded by the ubiquitous outhouse and shed. The cabin looked like it had been there since the stampede, made of logs gone dark with age, its roof covered with moss and the last holdouts of forget-me-nots and seed heads of columbine, pink pussytoes, cranesbill, Siberian wild iris, and chocolate lilies. They had migrated to the ground around the cabin with gay abandon, too. Would have been pretty in June.

"Guy liked flowers," Van said, puffing up from the rear. "Can't be all bad."

"Mmm." Depended on if he'd planted them on purpose. Kate looked down at Mutt and held out her hands, palms out. "Search."

"Wuff." Mutt put her nose down to the ground and began quartering the clearing.

A croak above them caused Kate's head to tilt back and find the large, blue-black raven perched high in the limbs of a black spruce, surveying them with critical attention. He expressed his opinion of their intrusion into his domain with a series of pithy clicks and clacks and croaks, before launching himself from his perch, dropping a big glop of poop that just missed Jim, and flapping off in high dudgeon. "I keep seeing where people say only the rat and the cockroach will survive the end of days. I think they're wrong. I think the raven will inherit the earth, because it's smarter than either of them and can eat them both."

"What's with the search command?"

"I hold my hands up to show her I don't have anything specific for her to find. She knows I'm interested in anything that doesn't look or smell right to her."

"How the hell did you train her to do that?"

She shrugged one shoulder. "Repetition and reward. When she did what I wanted I gave her a treat. It helps that she's really smart."

"The wolf in her."

"Yes."

"She ever turn on you?"

Kate was silent for so long after he asked this question that he stopped watching Mutt troll for unusual scents and turned to look at Mutt's other roommate. "Kate?"

He was generally pretty good at deciphering Kate's expression but not this one. She looked closed off, remote, unreachable. Alarming. She stirred finally to give him a wintry smile. "It was after I moved home from Anchorage."

He'd acquired a great deal of information about the incident that had moved her home, in bits and pieces let fall in passing by others. The thin, white scar that bisected her throat literally from ear to ear was by now almost invisible to someone who didn't know where to look, although the rasp it had left would very likely always be present in her voice. He did his best to make his question sound indifferent. He didn't care if she answered or not. Sure he didn't. "You never told me how Mutt came to you."

"I wasn't…" She paused. "Doing well. I wasn't sleeping, eating, hell, bathing. People would come to the door. I wouldn't let them in, not even the aunties.

"Then one morning, early, I heard this whine outside. Kind of low key but constant. Something about the sound of it pushed me to open the door." She shook her head. "And there was this pup, four, five months old, obviously part wolf, mistreated, nearly unconscious. Really only half alive.

"Well. She was bleeding all over my doorstep. Couldn't have that, so I picked her up. She snapped at me. She didn't connect, but even then her teeth looked big and sharp. And then—"

"What?"

"I don't know. It's hard to explain. We stared at each other for the longest time. Or at least it felt like it. All I know is, she made no further objection. I brought her inside and cleaned her wounds, sewed up a couple of gashes. I remember being grateful she didn't have any broken bones. She didn't so much as whimper. I gave her some eggs beaten in milk and she slurped that down. Got a moose roast down from the cache and started giving her that a few bits at a time.

"A month later she was good as new, and truth to tell, I expected her to leave. I wouldn't have stopped her. When she wanted out I opened the door and closed it behind her. If I heard a scratch at the door I'd let her in." She shrugged. "There was always a scratch."

"And the training?"

They both watched Mutt follow her nose around the little circle of open space in the stand of spruce trees. Her tail was a tight curl, her ruff ever so slightly raised. "She's on to something."

If so, she wasn't yet ready to share. "It's funny. I look back now and I see that it was her that initiated the training. She was never going to be a dog who played fetch and spend the rest of her time snoozing in front of the stove. She brought me a hare."

"I beg your pardon?"

"It was February. She brought me an Arctic hare, its neck broken very neatly. At first I thought she was trying to feed me, and then I thought she was asking my permission to eat it, but that didn't make sense because if she had after she'd caught it I never would have known."

"Always better to ask forgiveness than permission."

"Heh. Yeah. So I started going with her on her excursions and over time she basically showed me how to train her to find something or someone. One thing led to another and I ended up with this genius-level roommate." She jerked her chin. "And there she goes."

Mutt shoved through the undergrowth on a somewhat

easterly heading. Jim started to follow and Kate held up a hand. "Wait. She'll tell us if she wants us to come."

Kate went to the door of the cabin. It was unlocked. She pushed it open. The windows, one small square per wall, had been boarded up and the only light came from the doorway she stood in. It was smaller than her cabin had been, with no loft, one stove, a table, a chair, and a small bed in one corner. She squinted into the dark and then thought to get out her phone and activate the flashlight.

The bed was still made. A built-in counter with a tin washpan served as the kitchen. She saw the package of plastic razors, ripped open on the shelf above. And the bathroom, too, apparently.

She turned around, the beam from her phone illuminating the interior of the cabin in brief snapshots. There was a cardboard box full of old paperbacks. A small tower of Blazo boxes, one each for underwear, shirts, and pants. A hook next to the door with a Carhartt's jacket hanging from it, stained from many years of use, the hood ripped and sewn together again with what looked like dental floss.

She came out the door and saw Jim coming out of the shed. "What did you find?"

There was a frown in his eyes. "ATV and a sled."

She saw the outlines of a four-wheeler and a snow machine behind him. "He must have sold as is?"

He heard the question in her voice. "I guess he flew out."

She jerked her head at the cabin. "His bed's still made and he left his clothes behind. Razor, too."

"Where'd he go?"

"I think Dan said Florida."

He relaxed slightly. "Wouldn't need Alaskan clothes in Florida, I guess. Or a snow machine, either, come to that."

They looked at each other. It sounded perfectly reasonable, and felt absolutely wrong.

Behind them Mutt barked once, high and sharp.

"Uh, guys?" Van. She sounded a little shaky.

The mound of dirt was the standard three by six. An attempt had been made to conceal it with leaves and branches, foiled by Mutt's nose.

Jim looked indescribably weary. "Kate, did anyone actually see Paddy Murphy leave the Park?"

"I don't know."

Jim fetched a shovel he'd seen in the shed. It was a shallow hole. The thin layer of dirt over the hard rock that formed the backbone of the Quilaks would make every grave in this area so.

They uncovered it enough to see the body. It was lying face down. They could tell by the red hair showing through the dirt.

"They didn't even wrap him in a blanket or something." Van's voice was high and thin.

"Van." Van didn't move. "Van," she said with more emphasis. The girl looked at her with haunted eyes. "One of us needs to keep an eye on the plane otherwise we might be walking out of here. Would you, please? Don't forget to make noise on the way down."

Van turned and went without a word.

Kate waited until Van was around the cabin. "Mutt. Follow."

When Mutt was gone Kate looked at Jim across the grave. "I suppose he could have died of natural causes."

"Then who buried him? And why wasn't the Park invited?"

She sighed and jumped down into the grave.

Seventeen

TUESDAY, SEPTEMBER 13
The Park, Paddy Murphy's claim

VAN WASN'T TOO PROUD TO RECOGNIZE the relief she felt when Kate dismissed her from a scene that was already ugly and was going to get more so fast. She told herself she'd seen enough and she'd already got all the photos she needed anyway.

Yeah. That was why she left.

She went slowly, taking care over tree roots and rocky outcroppings. There was a rustle in the bushes to her left and she remembered Kate's admonition and started to sing, loudly. After a moment she realized her subconscious had chosen the MonaLisa Twins' cover of an old Beatles' tune. "Maxwell's Silver Hammer" might not be the best choice under present circumstances, and then Mutt shoved her way out of the brush and loped off down the trail in front of her. She relaxed. Nothing bad could happen to her with Mutt along.

They got to the bottom of the trail and walked across the strip to the Cessna. She opened the door and climbed into the left seat. Unless and until she learned to fly herself it was the only chance she'd ever get to put her hands on the yoke.

She'd just stretched her legs to put her feet on the pedals when Mutt started to growl. Van looked out the door, which she had left open. "Girlfriend? What's going on?"

The growl increased in volume.

Her heart began to beat faster. "Mutt? What's wrong?" She slid out of the aircraft and looked over Mutt's head.

Two men were coming out of the trees at the end of the airstrip. There were wearing desert camo fatigues and both of them had rifles over their shoulders. What she found frightening was the pistols strapped to their sides.

Mutt stepped in front of her. The growl increased to a snarl, rising and falling in volume and menace with her breath.

Both men stopped short. The younger one put his hand on his pistol. "Well, hey there, pretty lady. Is this your dog? We're harmless, you can call her off."

He might have sounded more convincing if he hadn't been smirking and his eyes hadn't been giving her a long, slow once-over. Her skin crawled inside her clothes.

His companion was older, and expressionless by comparison. He said nothing, which frightened her more than the younger man's leering, although she couldn't have said why.

"You don't hurt me, she won't hurt you." Van was proud her voice was steady. "Excuse me a moment." She got out her phone and activated the video. "What do you want?"

"Hey now, is that nice, is that friendly? Tate?" But the younger man's voice was wary now.

"Shut up, Al. Put that away, miss." The older man's voice was flat and hard and told Van its owner was used to being obeyed.

But then so was Mutt. She snapped loudly. The younger man jumped and then looked embarrassed and finally angry. "Why don't we just shoot her, Tate?"

Van had heard enough. She filled her lungs with air and shouted at the top of her voice. "Kate! Jim!"

The younger man laughed. "Oh sure, you—"

"Kate! Jim! At the airstrip!"

Mutt put back her head, pointed her nose to the sky, and let loose with a long, moaning howl, rising and falling in pitch, loud enough to be heard fifty miles away.

The younger man paled. "Is that a wolf? Jesus, Tate, is that a fucking wolf?"

In the distance, a faint howl answered him.

Jim found a tarp in the cabin and they lifted the body out and rolled it up, wrapping it securely at both ends with duct tape.

"The trooper will be pissed that we moved it."

"Almost certainly," Jim said, "but we couldn't leave him here."

There was a moss-covered wheelbarrow in back of the cabin. It had a flat tire but it was downhill to the airstrip and it was manageable and better than trying to carry the body downhill between them. No way was Jim going to try a fireman's carry.

The body had been in the grave long enough for rigor to pass off and he didn't know how well it would hold together under rough usage.

They'd almost made it to the bottom when they heard Van yell their names. And then they heard Mutt howl.

Kate was in front and she moved from a careful pace to an accelerated running stride from one step to the next and was gone from sight a moment later.

"Kate! Goddammit!"

Jim abandoned the wheelbarrow and ran after her. A confused impression of tree limbs and needles and leaves grabbing and lashing and a feeling of increased speed as the trail swooped downward. He banged into the stump of an evergreen and careened off that into its vengeful sibling who caught at his hair and ripped at his clothes. He pulled free and kept going and he didn't try to be stealthy about it because he wanted whoever had set Mutt off to hear him coming.

After what felt like entirely too long he crashed out of the brush and momentum kept him going four or five steps onto the surface of the strip. He had to jump so he didn't trip over the edge and fall flat on his face. Quite the entrance for the hero riding to the rescue.

A tableau of four people and a dog stood frozen in position next to the Stationair. He walked toward them, trying to get his breathing under control. He had mostly achieved that by the time he reached them. "Gentlemen," he said pleasantly. "I'm Jim Chopin and this is my aircraft. How may I help you?"

"You can call off that fucking dog, for one thing." The younger, skinnier man's voice broke on the last word.

His companion was older and made of sterner stuff, but he had his hand on his sidearm.

They both had sidearms, as well as rifles slung over their shoulders. They wore matching camo fatigues over tactical boots and caps pulled low and tight.

"Hunters?" Jim said, still pleasantly, although he wouldn't have believed them if they'd said yes.

"No, residents."

"Really? Where?"

"We got a place back aways." The older man gestured vaguely behind them. "Just out for a ride."

Given the continuous rolling thunder of Mutt's bladder-evacuating growl, Jim had to admire his sangfroid. "You came across the creek? From the air it looks a pretty steep climb."

The older man shrugged. "We crossed upstream."

Mutt's lips peeled further back from her teeth and the snarl increased in volume.

"Tate, I'm going to shoot that fucking wolf if it comes one step closer!" The kid started to pull his gun.

"Al, don't—"

Afterward Jim never could remember seeing Mutt move. One moment she was standing stiff-legged between Kate and Van and the two men, and the next Al was on the ground. He'd managed to pull his weapon, a nine mil auto, but Mutt had her teeth clamped around his wrist. At some point he must have divined telepathically what she was going to do because in the same moment Jim discovered he had gone for his ankle holster. He had it out and pointed at Tate before Tate had his sidearm all the way out of the holster.

"Nobody move until I say so." He took several quick steps to the left, clearing his line of fire. Tate swiveled so as to keep facing him. "Kate, call off Mutt."

"Mutt. Release."

Mutt opened her jaw and stepped back. There wasn't more than saliva on the kid's arm but he squalled like he'd been bitten to the bone. "Fucken wolf coulda took my arm off! Shoot the goddamn monster, Tate!"

"Little busy, Al." Tate kept his eyes unwaveringly fixed on Jim, as well he might.

"Kate, disarm them."

Kate hauled the kid back to his feet and stripped him of rifle and sidearm in the same motion. She pushed him to one side and he was still shaky enough to stumble further away. By the time he'd caught his balance she was standing directly behind his partner, the muzzle of her requisitioned pistol lodged firmly in his spine. "Please don't move. I am unfamiliar with this weapon and I have no idea what the trigger pull is."

She wouldn't have wasted her breath on the kid but this man was older and smarter and stood motionless. He let her push his hand away from his holster and straightened his arm so his rifle strap would slip free.

She took the weapons to the edge of the airstrip, unloaded both rifles and one handgun and threw them into the alders.

She walked to the other side of the strip and threw the rounds and the magazines into a tangle of devil's club.

She did so love Alaska. It was always on her side.

She held the remaining pistol muzzle down as she came back to stand near Jim, but not so close as to get in his way or get hit by ejecting shell casings, hot from being fired. She'd learned that lesson in a hard school.

The fact that two men would be down and probably dead immediately afterward she regarded with complete indifference.

"You can retrieve your weapons after we leave," Jim said. "What are you doing here, again? I know you're in the middle of a national park but this bit of it is private property."

"We don't have to tell you shit," the kid said. His cap had fallen off when Mutt knocked him down and his head had been shaved painfully close, and recently, too, if the scabs were any indication.

"Mutt," Kate said.

Mutt took a step forward. The kid took a step back, closer to Tate.

"Where is your property, exactly? I don't remember Paddy Murphy having any close neighbors."

"None of your fucking business, you filthy squaw—"

Tate hit him with the back of his hand, almost casually, without taking his eyes from Jim. The kid went down flat on his back again, this time with blood gushing from his nose. "Mind telling me why you are here?"

"We know Paddy. We flew out to check up on him."

Tate went very still. "Did you find him?"

"Yes." Jim jerked his chin. "He's back up the trail a ways."

The man's eyes narrowed. "I'd like to say hi to him, make sure he's okay. Since we're neighbors and all."

"Not today. Today I suggest you start walking back toward the creek." Jim twitched his Glock toward the end of the runway. "The trail starts off the end of the strip there."

For a long moment Kate thought the situation could break either way, but then Tate reached down to pick Al up off the ground and stood him on his feet. "See you around."

"Anytime," Kate said.

Tate looked at Kate. He almost laughed, and then he looked more closely at her expression and decided against it.

They watched, unmoving, until the two men had disappeared into the trees.

"Van?"

Van hadn't moved once during the entire encounter.

"Van!"

She turned to look at him, her eyes the size of salad plates.

"Here." He held out his hand.

She stared at his automatic as if she'd never seen a gun before. "I know you know how to use one of these. Back up Kate while I go get Paddy. If one of those assholes so much as pops his head out of the bushes, shoot."

Awareness returned. She took the sidearm. Once he saw her forefinger against the outside of the trigger guard, he turned and headed up the trail.

"Mutt, go!"

A moment later he heard Mutt panting at his heels.

When he got back with the body in the barrow the women were standing with their backs to each other, both of them pale and watching the brush in either direction. They'd already opened the back doors, and now helped him place the body inside. Kate unloaded the second handgun belonging to the two wannabe soldiers and disposed of it and the ammunition while Jim dumped the wheelbarrow off the side of the strip.

He returned to the aircraft to do a very thorough walkaround. He climbed in and closed the door. Kate was buckled into the right seat. Mutt was half on Van's lap in the back. He handed Kate the laminated checklist.

"Auxiliary fuel pump."

"Off."

"Flight controls."

He worked the yoke and rudders. "Free and correct."

She ran through the entire checklist top to bottom. He had enough hours in the Cessna now that he didn't always use it but today the routine had a calming effect on all three of them. The engine caught on the first try and his hands were steady as they lifted into the air. He put the nose on Niniltna and he might have put on a little more speed than he normally did. "Van. What happened?"

He heard the shake in her voice even over the headset. "I was waiting at the plane like you said. They walked out of the brush. They wanted to know who I was and what I was doing here. The young one made some of comments. You know."

He and Kate exchanged a glance. They did know.

"I was really glad to see Kate come charging out of the trees." A ghost of a laugh. "Like the cavalry. But then I was afraid they were going to shoot Mutt. Who were those guys?"

"I don't know," Kate said. "But they sure seem ubiquitous lately." She looked at Jim. "They knew Paddy was dead."

"They were surprised to hear he was just up the trail, weren't they?"

"They'll go looking for him."

"First thing. And they won't find him." Jim jerked his head at the back of the plane.

Behind them Van hugged Mutt and stared unseeing out the window. "Why did the older man hit the kid? Was it because he called Kate a bad name?"

"No. He was making sure the kid didn't get them both killed." Kate turned to Jim. "When did you start wearing your backup piece again?"

There was no hint of apology in his voice. "Right after Bobby had his run-in with those assholes in June."

The rest of the journey was accomplished in silence.

Eighteen

THEY STOPPED BRIEFLY IN NINILTNA TO leave Paddy's body in the chest freezer at the trooper post. "Should we plug it in?"

Jim had emptied the freezer when he resigned and closed down the post. "I don't know. I guess so. Rigor mortis is about as far as I went in forensic expertise. I don't know if freezing it will screw with the autopsy."

"It'll deteriorate more if we don't."

He bent over and picked up the plug to stick it in the outlet.

They went outside and Jim called it in to the trooper post in Tok. It was clear from his side of the conversation that they didn't quite believe him because he had to repeat everything two and three times. "Look," he said finally, "I've had a long morning. I'm tired, and I'm going home. What's next is up to you."

He ended the call and grinned at Kate. "I should have quit this job years ago."

"Liberating?"

"Fucking emancipating. Let's go home."

"Fine by me."

Jim set the Cessna down in a runway paint job of a landing and taxied to the hangar. They sat for a moment without moving, until Kate said, "Do you want to put her back inside?"

He looked over the fuselage in the direction of Prince William Sound, which was where all Park weather came from. It was a calm, clear, crisp autumn afternoon with no haze gathering on the horizon, yet. "Let's leave her out. Might want to go somewhere else today."

They chocked the wheels and adjourned to the house, and the second pot of coffee for the day was barely perking before the sound of an aircraft on approach at alarmingly low altitude caused the mugs to vibrate where they sat on the counter. Jim's head came up. "Sounds like Ranger Dan's 172."

Kate groaned. "We left the plane out. He knows we're here."

Twenty minutes later the man himself tramped up the steps and banged on the door. Stocky, red-haired, blue-eyed, and freckled over every inch of exposed skin, he wore a brand-new vest from Copper River Fleece that featured a salmon-and-bear-paw trim. He accepted a mug of coffee and a piece of cold breakfast quiche he ate with his fingers, grunting his appreciation.

"To what do we owe this unexpected honor?"

Dan gave his mug an expansive wave. "Yeah, yeah, I know

I'm supposed to call before I land. But I saw your SUV with wings and I knew you were home, and hell, I'm practically family, aren't I?"

Kate, hiding her amusement, put the cushions back on the couch and took a seat. "Sure. You're our bratty cousin who keeps borrowing money on the promise of paying back the last loan."

Entering into the spirit of this Jim said, "No, he's that cranky uncle who only watches Fox News and only listens to Ted Nugent." He considered, and then added fairly, "Or Eric Clapton."

"Don't let Kurt hear you say that."

"Noted." Jim seated himself beside Kate. Van sat at the table, iPhone out, Notes app at the ready. Dan surveyed her with disfavor. "All of this is off the record."

She closed the app and set the phone to one side.

Dan snorted. "Like that really works."

"It better," Van said mildly, "if I ever want a source to trust me again."

He clearly didn't believe her. "Whatever."

"What's up, Dan?" Kate said.

Dan leaned forward, resting his hands on his knees, and fixed her with a beady eye. "Howie and Willard."

Kate groaned, Jim rolled his eyes, and Van got up to go to the bathroom.

"I don't think I even want to know," Kate said. "Besides, what do you think I can do? They're grown men, both of them, and even Bobbie Singh has never managed to keep either one of them in jail long enough for them to be scared straight."

"Well, to be clear, Willard's never been in jail," Jim said.

"Yeah, yeah, incompetent, undue influence, we've all heard it a hundred times, and it's true anyway, Willard can't be held responsible for every illegal thing Howie sets him up for." She glared at Dan. "What have they done now?"

"Tiffany—one of the rangerettes—caught them using a drone to hunt a moose."

"Rangerettes?"

Dan gave an impatient shrug. "What I call the interns. They were all girls this year."

Jim laughed. Kate, getting back to the point, said, "Tiffany caught Howie and Willard hunting moose with a drone in the Park?"

"Where else? She had her phone with her, Kate. She's got it on video."

Kate put her head back and closed her eyes. "Oh, great."

"I mean, come on, we all know what a tinkerer Willard is. Howie ordered the drone and left Willard alone with it for five minutes and next thing you know they had to take it outside to give it the old test drive and then why wouldn't they take it on their hunting trip just to see what they could see?"

"Howie knows it's illegal to hunt with drones."

"He swears Willard didn't and that Willard was running the drone."

She sighed. "What do you want me to do? Go take the drone away from them?"

Dan fidgeted. "Well—"

Jim leaned forward. "Dan, where were they hunting?"

Kate glanced at him, surprised. Dan said, "North of the mine. And yes, before you ask, the season was open. Not that I don't think they'd just gotten there. The glimpses I caught of their camp on Tiffany's video looked like it had been there for a while."

"And they only got one moose?"

"Howie couldn't hit a 747 if he was standing under the wing, as you well know, and in his own words Willard 'don't mess with no guns.' It was probably divine intervention they got this one."

"North of the mine." Jim rubbed his chin, thinking. "Howie still using that old .30-06 of Louis Deem's?"

Van and Kate both gave him sharp looks.

Dan shrugged. "No Deem relative has yet to show up to run the boys off his homestead and claim the contents, so I guess so."

"Tiffany didn't arrest them?"

"She's new to the Park. She doesn't know them and I think Willard's size scared her. She took the video, hopped on her ATV, and hauled ass."

Everyone's phones dinged. Van got to hers first. She clicked and scrolled and swore beneath her breath. "Jo Dunaway, of course, who else. Whoever sent that email wasn't lying. Everyone has the story about the extra body." Van looked indignant. "I wonder if they emailed all the reporters in the state, waiting for one of us to bite?"

"Male but no ID," Jim said, reading from his phone.

"And no speculation if the body had already been there or…" Kate looked up.

"Or what?" Van said.

"Or been planted there in hopes nobody'd notice one more body among so many," Dan said, with relish.

This sally did not go over as well as he had thought it might and for the first time the chief ranger woke up to the invisible pall that seemed to hang over the room. "What's going on?"

Jim looked at Kate. She said, "Did you actually see Paddy Murphy leave the Park, Dan?"

He frowned. "No. He told me he was going when I ran into him at the Riverside. Well." He shrugged. "He was telling everyone, at the top of his voice."

"When was that?"

"June, I think? Mid-June, maybe? I didn't see him after that. I figured…" His voice trailed away as he realized what their questions meant.

"Yeah." Jim took over. "We found him buried in back of his cabin this morning."

"Oh shit."

"We think it's him, anyway. It looks like his hair."

"How did he die?"

"That'll be for the trooper to find out." Kate looked at Jim. His voice was as impassive as his expression. Once a cop. The fact was that they had uncovered enough of the remains to determine that the back of Paddy's head had been hit hard enough to break his skull, and that he had been shot once in the chest.

Mutt barked outside, and Kate went to the window to see an unfamiliar pickup emerge from the alders that edged the lane between the house and the road and come to a stop next to Van's Forester. Mutt had planted herself in front of the stairs leading up to the front door. She didn't bark again, but then she didn't have to. The occupants of the pickup remained inside with the doors firmly shut.

Kate strolled over to the door, slipped on her tennis shoes, checked their fit (she didn't want to raise a blister between the front door and the deck), grabbed her hoodie and had an oddly difficult time feeding the teeth into the zipper.

Behind her she heard Jim not even try to hide a chuckle.

She sauntered out onto the deck, ignoring the stairs, and paused in front of the railing that faced the yard. One hand shading her eyes, she peered at the pickup. "You folks lost?" She didn't bother raising her voice.

The driver's side window cranked down an inch and a half. "Are you Kate Shugak?"

"And if I am?"

"Is that your dog?"

"She does live with me, yes."

"Is she going to bite us?"

"Not unless I ask her to."

A pause while the two people in the cab conferred, both of

them taking it in turn to peer through the windshield at her, at Mutt, and then back at her.

She let them look, because she knew what they saw. A five-foot nothing Alaska Native woman, maybe a hundred twenty pounds with her shoes on. Dressed in jeans and a white tee under a navy blue hoodie with a UAF Nanook logo and a pair of scuffed Asics, hers was not the most formidable presence. Or she hoped it wasn't, because she worked at it hard enough.

Mutt was far more intimidating, all the more so because she so obviously enjoyed scaring the pants off anyone who crossed her path, furred, feathered, or Homo sapiens—as the two wannabe soldiers this morning had been schooled. If there was a more impressive sight than a one hundred forty pound half-husky, half-gray wolf, ruff extended, lip up to display a magnificent set of canines, yellow eyes narrowed and intent, Kate didn't know what it was.

The window cranked down again. "I'm Frank Barr Junior. My sister Elsa is with me. We want to talk to you about our dad."

Well, hell.

Nineteen

TUESDAY, SEPTEMBER 13
The Park, Kate's homestead

THEY SAT AT THE DINING TABLE, LOOKING uncomfortable. Kate sent a bright smile over their heads. "Dan, Van, great to see you both. Let's get together again soon, okay?"

Dan grumbled and Van sulked but they both left.

"Coffee?" Jim said, ready with mugs and carafe.

"Thank you," Frank Barr Jr. said. "It was a long drive from Anchorage."

"You drove straight through?"

He shook his head. "Overnighted in Ahtna."

"Still a long drive."

"It is," Barr Jr. said with feeling. Elsa, who had yet to say a word, nodded agreement.

"Why didn't you fly?"

"Because the closest we could get would have been Ahtna and I didn't feel like hitching fifty miles."

Dan chose this moment to take off from the airstrip out

back and buzz the house close enough to rattle the glassware in the cupboard. Barr Jr. raised his eyebrows. "You got a strip?"

"Who doesn't?"

Brother and sister were of medium height and spare of weight with pale, freckled skin, blue eyes, and light brown hair, although she had a lot more of it left than he had. They wore Pendleton shirts, jeans, and Sorels under Carhartt jackets, none of which were on their first outing. Their hands were large-knuckled and scarred and looked like they worked for a living.

In spite of herself Kate liked what she saw. "You folks hungry?"

Barr Jr. looked at his sister. "Long drive from Ahtna. We could eat."

Kate pulled the leftover salmon bouillabaisse out of the refrigerator and put it on the stove. There were three pieces of fry bread left; she nuked them and set them on the table with butter and honey. Steaming bowls appeared shortly thereafter and Barr Jr. grunted involuntarily when the first spoonful went in.

Kate went into the kitchen, followed hotfoot by Jim. "Do you want me to stay?"

"Yes."

He filled his mug and opened the cupboard, fishing around in back until he found the bag of Dare Maple Leaf cookies she had hidden there. He smiled serenely into her scowl, dumped the cookies into a bowl, and carried it to the table.

She joined him, pinning an expression of polite interest to her face while behind it, oh behind it, she was planning a terrible revenge.

Barr Jr. sat back from the table and hid a burp behind his hand. "Excuse me. That was great, Ms. Shugak. I didn't think we were going to get anything to eat until we got back to Ahtna tonight."

"Where are you staying?" Still being polite.

"The new Aspen."

"Oh, of course." Tony and Stan's Ahtna Lodge not being good enough for them. Which was not a kind thought, of which Kate was briefly ashamed, but only briefly. Now, more or less post-Covid, when the remnants of their twenty-first-century plague showed only occasionally in masks still worn by elders like Ruthe Bauman, Kate was determined to spend her money as much as possible in local and in locally owned businesses. Of course, she thought, remembering Ruthe's half dozen Amazon boxes, it wasn't always possible.

On the other hand, obviously the Barrs weren't running for office. Definitely a point in their favor. "How can I help you, Mr. Barr?"

"Frank, please."

"And Kate." She looked at the sister.

"Elsa. Glad to meet you, Kate. We hear good things." Elsa's voice was lower than her brother's but they sounded as much alike as they looked.

"Who from?"

"Morris Maxwell."

"How do you know him?"

"He was referred to us by Victoria Muravieff."

"How is she?"

"So far as anyone can tell, fine. Still in recovery, so far as I know. She's not the most social person."

Which could have had something to do with the fact that Victoria had been imprisoned for thirty years for a murder she did not commit, and no one in Alaska other than her daughter had thought she was innocent. "How is Max?"

"He said you'd ask, and I was to tell you that he was a couple of martinis behind and that he expected you to make good on that sooner because he wasn't going to be around for it much later."

"He's been dying since I met him five years ago. He'll outlive us all."

"We only wish. All the old lions are leaving us. Clem, Ed, Arliss, Joe."

Auntie Balasha, Kate thought. Demetri.

"Dad." This from Elsa, who swallowed the last bite of her fry bread, wiped the butter from her fingers, and gave Kate a steady look. "I assume you've heard."

"That the NTSB, in their infinite wisdom, have decided the cause of the crash was pilot error? Yes."

Elsa waved a hand. "Oh, they're not saying so yet, but they will. We have sources." She glanced at her brother.

"And you want me to—"

"We want you to prove that it was not in fact pilot error. That someone was trying to kill my father, and succeeded. The

Beaver that also came down was just in the wrong place at the wrong time."

"Bad luck on them."

Jim's comment was free of irony but he got a long look from Elsa anyway. "And you are Jim Chopin, am I correct?"

"You are."

"AST, retired. Max spoke well of you, too."

"Thank him for me."

"Do I understand that in hiring Kate we also hire you?"

"I'm just the pilot. I drive the plane where she tells me to."

Her gaze flicked back and forth between the two of them.

Barr Jr. leaned forward. "Kate, you have something of a reputation for—" He hesitated.

"Pursuing lost causes?" Jim said.

Kate damned him with a glare. He raised an eyebrow in return. Deny it if you dare.

Barr Jr. smiled, which was something of a revelation. Until that moment sour had looked like his factory setting. Which reminded her of Abel. She knew it, and knew it inclined her to listen to Barr Jr.'s case when she also knew she should show both Barrs to the door with her apologies. "How much do you know about my father?"

She sat back. "What everyone knows."

Franklin "Frank" Barr, Sr., born in Oklahoma, had joined the Marines out of high school and stayed in long enough to serve in Korea. "First in at Inchon, he used to say, although he did not approve of any part of the Korean conflict and left the service after the armistice in 1953. His troop plane stopped in

Anchorage on the way home and there wasn't anyone waiting for him in Oklahoma so he took his discharge here. He grew up on a farm so he wasn't frightened of heavy equipment and the US Coast and Geodetic Survey took him on." He smiled again. "One gathers there were some wild times. He took a survey crew out to the Alaska Peninsula by barge and another one overland to the Rampart Dam site. He decided there had to be an easier way to travel than by Cat train, so he learned to fly and got a license and started his first business flying freight out of Fairbanks."

"Beaufort Air," Jim said.

Barr Jr. nodded. "Made his fortune flying freight and crew for RPetCo. Sold out in 1993, and you know how that ended up."

"Oh yeah," Kate said. The buyer of Beaufort Air had been an asset stripper from Outside. Flights were cancelled without notice, tickets weren't honored and never refunded, and a lot of Alaskans flyers had been very annoyed. Barr Sr.'s reputation had taken a beating and for a while he had simply disappeared from the scene. Many thought he had moved out of state.

"So he bought a Cub and went beachcombing."

"That's when he found the dinosaur graveyard."

Barr Jr. nodded. "Crumbling out of a bank between Shishmaref and Kivalina. He was smart, he called the Associated Press reporter for Alaska first, and as soon as the photographs hit the wire *National Geographic* got involved, and after them the Smithsonian, and then the American Association for the Advancement of Science, and next thing you knew, Frank Barr

Senior was a salty but lovable old fart who had significantly advanced scientific understanding of the Jurassic in Alaska."

"The University of Alaska Fairbanks gave him an honorary degree," Elsa said, her mouth twisting up in a reluctant smile. "He loved that."

"And of course it helped that he bankrolled the dig, all expenses, transportation, food, lodging," Barr Jr. said. "He even hired a couple of locals to make sure the cheechakos didn't stumble into a grizzly."

Elsa nodded. "Which made the locals happy, not to mention the scientists."

"Redemption," Kate said, which produced an uncomfortable silence but she didn't walk it back because it was true.

Barr Jr. cleared his throat. "And then they started drilling offshore in the Arctic again, only all the people who'd been there in the seventies and eighties were dead or gone, and—" He shrugged.

Elsa took up the tale. "And Dad was the only one around who remembered that you don't put lettuce in the freezer when it comes off the plane in Deadhorse. So he started Ikiak Air, and that was his second fortune."

"What was he doing in the Park?"

Elsa looked at Barr Jr., who said, "Looking at properties for sale."

"For what purpose?"

Barr Jr. shook his head. "The old man played his cards pretty close to his chest. I figure the high-end tourism business. Lot of people out there with more money than they know what to do with, just looking for someone to help them spend it. Ikiak Air is already doing a substantial luxury charter business in state. Dad was looking into acquiring a small private jet so he could bring clients in from Outside. I heard him say more than once that he couldn't believe what the lodges were charging at that level. I think he wanted a piece of it."

Kate looked at Elsa, who shrugged. "He talked about the film industry, too. He might have been looking for locations for potential productions."

"What film industry? I thought the state did away with the film subsidy."

Elsa shrugged again. "I expect he thought he'd bring it back."

Kate expected so, too. "Did he ever talk to an old miner by the name of Paddy Murphy?"

Barr Jr. shook his head but Elsa nodded. "He told me he'd bought Murphy out, that Murphy was packing up and would be out by October first."

"And remind me who was with him the day of the crash?"

"Art Gorst Junior. Son of Roy Gorst Senior, COO of Beaufort." Barr Jr. exchanged a glance with his sister, its meaning indecipherable. "Art Senior was Dad's partner in Ikiak Air."

"Okay," Kate said. "Look, Frank, Elsa, I'm very sorry for your loss. I can't begin to imagine the shitstorm that must be blowing up around you right now, and I understand the natural feelings children have for a parent. However. Your father was eighty-seven years old and still flying?" She shook her head. "I don't want to take your money under false pretenses. I can't promise you any result from my investigation that would differ from the official one."

Another sibling glance. "There is something we haven't told you."

"Oh?" She looked from one to the other. "Which would be..."

"As I said, we have a source," Elsa said.

"And?"

"You've heard they found a tenth body in the wreckage, one that was on neither aircraft?"

"So far as they know," Jim said. "I admit a third person in a Super Cub would be a squeeze, but there were empty seats in the Beaver."

Elsa shook her head, very certain. "There are witnesses on the ground at the Ahtna airport who swear the people who boarded were every one of them on the manifest. We talked to them this morning. Art and Dad were in the Cub, and the pilot and six passengers were in the Beaver. The tenth body is someone else altogether, not involved with either flight."

"Okay," Kate said. "But the body in question—Look, you guys are Alaskans. You know how often people disappear in the Bush. Many of them are never found. What makes you think this person isn't one of them?"

"It's a man," Barr Jr. said. "And he didn't die in the crash. He was shot."

"Twice in the chest, once in the head," Elsa said.

Jim's lips pursed in a soundless whistle. "Mozambique drill."

At Elsa's questioning look, Kate said briefly, "It's a method of execution favored by organized crime. Do they know the weapon yet?"

"An automatic, they think a Glock."

Kate frowned at them. "You are very well informed."

"So are you," Elsa said. "So is anyone with as much time served in the state as we have."

Kate thought about it, conscious of their eyes on her face. "The extra body is, I admit, an anomaly. As is, certainly, the means of his death in these circumstances. But I don't see how your certainty that Frank Senior didn't cause the accident factors in."

"I was recently widowed and I moved back in with my father to keep house for him," Elsa said. "I can attest to the fact that he was very much all there. He'd forget things now and then but who doesn't? Flying was second nature to him. He had more hours than any ten pilots you can name, including you, in spite of all your OJT time in the air." She nodded at Jim. "No offense."

"None taken, but I'm only forty-four. Give me time."

Elsa gave a brief smile. "Understood. However, allow me to reiterate. There is no way my father accidentally or otherwise veered into the flight path of another aircraft."

Her brother was firm in agreement. "I worked with him every day. He just bought all three of us new MacBook Airs and he had his up and running before I did, without the aid of a twelve-year-old, I might add. This wasn't a man afraid of either old or new technology. And he'd been flying that Cub for over twenty years. He didn't climb into it, he put it on. He had eyes in the back of his head when it came to Bush flying because he knew—none better!—how many amateurs we've got in the air up here."

Kate sighed. "If I take this job, I will have to ask questions. A lot of them, many of which will feel intrusive and unnecessary and possibly even offensive." Kate looked from one to the other. "You understand that in an investigation like this one, there will be no such thing as privacy. Nine people were killed, and now there is a tenth victim in the mix. I'll be asking a lot of uncomfortable questions of a lot of people. Further, the NTSB will have their teeth well and truly set into this investigation by now and they won't take kindly to someone private nosing into what they consider to be their business. I will do my best to stay off their radar, but…" She paused. "What do you want me to say when they ask me who I'm working for?"

Barr Jr. smiled. This one was devoid of humor. "Tell them the truth."

Elsa leaned forward as if to intensify the intensity of her response. "Yes. Please. Tell them it was us."

"What do you think?"

They were standing in front of the windows overlooking the yard, watching the pickup—a bright blue brand-new Dodge Ram Charger—do a three-point turn and nose back into the alders.

"Are you asking me if you should have taken the job? Because I like my liver right where it is."

The corners of her mouth quirked. She examined the check in her hand. "He had the bookkeeper print it out before he left Anchorage." She showed it to him.

He whistled. "Nice."

"They wanted me motivated." She sighed. "Now I have to earn it."

"Where will you start?"

A flock of Canada geese overflew the house. Further south, where the Kanuyaq was edged on either side by marshes, a column of many more geese spiraled up into the air. "I always hate their honking in the fall."

He agreed. "Much better to hear it in the spring when they're coming back."

The vee folded itself into the column. Some signal must have been given that only the geese could hear because the top of the column began to peel off, eventually forming an immense dark mass heading south.

"California, here I come."

Kate smiled. "Better them than me." She looked up at him. "I'd like to know who was on that Beaver."

He raised an eyebrow. "You think—"

She shook her head. "As a means of ruling them out. If you were still on the job, you would do the same."

"Truth. Where do we start?"

An hour later they had both run down the batteries on their cells, but they had a picture of the Beaver's manifest and fell to comparing notes. "Kenny Hazen said it was a flightseeing trip, no stops, there and back again. And he sounded more than a little miffed at the way the NTSB shut out the local police force."

"That's the feds for you. The Ahtna air dispatcher, Lucy Purnell, gave me the manifest." Kate raised a brow at the affectionate tone in his voice and he grinned. "I might have kept company with her for a while back in the day."

She rolled her eyes. "Who didn't you keep company with?"

For some reason the fact that she was so secure in their relationship that the mention of one of his exes provoked no further response made him feel warm all over, but he wasn't going to say so. She nodded at the list.

"Let's have it."

"Passengers first. Ron and Carolyn Wollard, 67 and 65, Las Vegas, Nevada, both retired. He was Coast Guard, she was a nurse. Their daughter, Jennifer, 39, also Coast Guard, stationed in Kodiak. Nathaniel Belisle, 38, Jennifer's fiancé, also Coast Guard, also stationed in Kodiak."

"Ouch."

"I know. A helluva hit for one family to take."

"Not to mention the Coast Guard. The other two?"

"Jacob Nakata, 33, Seattle, Microsoft exec, tech side, not admin. Courtney Melendy, 19, also Seattle, a model and his girlfriend."

"Pilot?"

He grimaced. The loss of a good pilot was always painful to another. "Amber Macintosh, 36, relocated to Ahtna for the summer because that was where the job was. Permanent residence in Anchorage. The Beaver was hers. Lucy said Macintosh treated it like it was an only child and that there was no way anything was ever going to go wrong with that plane in the air. After she got that off her chest, she said it was Amber's last flight of the season and that it was a blankety-blank shame that the redacted FAA couldn't see its way clear to make sure expletive deleted old geezers who were probably blind and deaf and senile to boot weren't flying who shouldn't be."

"I could probably handle the profanity," she said mildly.

"I didn't edit. It's the way she talks."

"What, she's a Sunday School teacher in her off time?"

"No, she just wasn't as careful on the air a time or two as she should have been and the FCC came down on Ahtna Air for it."

"Ah. Did Macintosh have an A&P license?"

He shook his head. "No, but Lucy said she annualed the Beaver herself and got a mechanic she knew in Anchorage to sign off on it. She gave me his name and I called him. He was the guy at Spernak who checked out the Stationair before I signed the check. He says she knew what she was doing and, same as Lucy, said that she loved that aircraft like it was her own child."

Kate scrolled down and back through the list of names and details she had tapped into the Notes app on her phone. "Nothing on the surface rings any bells."

"For me, either."

"On to the Cub, then. Bought by Barr Senior in 1994. Allegedly he's the only one who has flown it since. Let's check with the kids to be sure."

Jim made a note. "Mechanic?"

"I can't imagine Barr Senior ever skimping on the maintenance of any plane he got into, but, yeah, we need to ask the kids who his mechanic was and check to be sure."

Jim added to his note.

"I called Kurt. He ran a quick check on Barr Senior and Art Gorst. On the surface it looks like Ikiak Air is debt-free, makes its payroll, and pays its bills on time. The FAA gives them a clean bill, too, no violations or complaints." She sat back, frowning. "I want Kurt to do a deeper dive into all of them. We'll need to talk to the NTSB, or try to. We're going to have to go to Anchorage."

Jim, who had realized this the moment Kate accepted the check, said, "We're good to go. But—"

"What?"

"Speaking of staking out their air route, I'd like to look at the wreckage first."

"Isn't the NTSB still waving people off?"

"We can always finesse a flyby on the way to town."

"Little out of our way. We should have done that this morning."

"I meant to, but—" They both thought of the confrontation at the airstrip. "Besides, you heard Dan." He grinned at her. "We've got an SUV with wings. It was built for going out of our way."

Twenty

I N THE END, IT WAS A WASTE OF AV GAS. THERE was no one at the crash site and nothing large enough to be seen from the air remained of the two aircraft. Jim reduced speed as much as he dared and made a long, low circle of the area. The death scene of nine people and the dump site of a tenth had been reduced to charred areas of vegetation. A clump of black spruce had burned down to the branch.

"They worked fast."

Jim's voice was grim over the headset. "By now everything is laid out in a warehouse in Anchorage."

"Or in the morgue." Kate looked up to scan the horizon in all directions visible to her. That was so not the way she wanted to go.

Anchorage

It was partly cloudy with a stiff breeze coming out of the northeast but the view from the Quilak Range to the Chugiak

Mountains was always superb and this afternoon was no different. Flying, it was a little over two hundred miles, compared to driving, which was over three hundred. It might be possible to fit more into the back of a pickup than into the Stationair but Kate would take the flight over the drive anytime.

"Where you going?" she said when he turned south down Knik Arm.

"A permanent tiedown at Lake Hood came open and I grabbed it. Hood's closer to Ted than Merrill, if you have to catch the red-eye to Seattle."

They landed on the dirt strip without fuss in spite of the 737s breathing down their necks next door at Ted Stevens International Airport, the aforementioned Ted. Jim taxied to the tiedown, located between a cherry-red Stearman biplane and an elderly Cessna 172. They HAD to wait for an Uber with a cargo hatch big enough to include Mutt. When they got to the townhouse the driver—a morose, incurious older gentleman dressed in a suit and an impeccably tied tie—deposited them on their doorstep, popped the hatch for Mutt to jump down, and was off without even asking them for a five-star rating. "He'll get one anyway," Jim said. "I do love mute in my Uber drivers."

Kate had changed the keyed deadbolt to a wireless keypad and opened the door with the app on her phone. Inside, Mutt remained by the door, yellow eyes fixed sternly on Kate.

"I think Mutt would like to stretch her legs," she said. "Come with?"

He shook his head. "I'll call Kurt, let him know what's up."

"Tomorrow morning, soon as he can see us."

"He's going to think we're nuts."

"Won't be the first time."

"True that."

Mutt terrorized every small animal with wings and without from Westchester to Earthquake Park and back again, and not limiting herself to small animals, either. Given the fact that Anchorageites were regularly kicked to death by moose in their own backyards and so had up close and personal experience with nature red in tooth and claw, they could be remarkably twitchy when Mutt in all her lupine glory appeared around the corner on the bike trail. Especially when they had a dog on a leash. It was rank prejudice for which Kate saw no reason. It wasn't like Mutt did more than lift her lip at them, after all.

The two of them arrived back at the townhouse reinforced by the notion of their own omnipotence and bounced back inside to discover Jim in the kitchen putting together a scratch dinner after a quick run to City Market. He had not forgotten Mutt, who retired to the backyard with what looked like the left femur of a wooly mammoth. "I went up to 10th and M, too," he said when Kate's eyebrows went up.

Through the back door Kate watched Mutt take up residence on a square of scrap carpet Kate had laid out for her the previous year. "She looks happy."

"A run and food and she's good. You're much harder to

please." She came up behind to peer around his shoulder. "Speaking of which…"

"Pork stew with black beans and corn."

"Did you stick in a chipotle chili?"

"I did."

"Did you get cilantro and sour cream for garnish?"

"I did."

"And for bread?"

"I got a baguette from Fire Island." He grinned down at her. "You and Mutt. Always thinking with your stomachs."

"Well, yeah."

He laughed and tapped the wooden spoon against the edge of the pot and put the lid on. "We'll let it come to a boil and then dump in the beans and she'll be good to go. Want something to drink?" He reached into the refrigerator and pulled out a Sprite Zero.

"You really are the perfect man."

He waggled his eyebrows. "I try."

She'd tried a phone call to the local NTSB office when they landed. No luck. She tried again now. No luck again and this time they were less polite about it. She tossed the phone on the counter and reached for a knife, a cutting board, and the cilantro. She chopped it and dished up it and the sour cream, then sliced the baguette and set it on the table. An Alaskan Amber for him, the soda for her in a glass full of ice, and they sat down to steaming bowls of thick stew exuding an aroma that titillated the salivary glands and the alimentary canal in equal measure. Kate moaned over the first bite. "You are so hired."

Afterward she cleared the table and put the dishes in the dishwasher as Jim let Mutt in and started the fire in the gas fireplace in the living room. When Kate joined him on the couch facing the picture window, the last of the light from the day was beginning to fade from the sky. The wind had calmed and the surface of the lagoon was like a mirror. A lone cyclist pedaled by, the white noodles of his Airpods the only distinguishable thing about him in the dusk.

"You know," Kate said, "the last time I was sitting on this couch, someone shot through that window just to make a point."

"Ah, yes. Mr. Smith." Jim got up to close the drapes. "Love to meet him one day."

"I bet."

He sat down again and draped an arm around her shoulders to pull her close. In front of the fire Mutt put her head on her paws and lapsed into somnolence.

It was like an episode of *Leave it to Beaver*, Kate thought. Not that she'd ever seen the show. There were great gaps of American so-called culture in her life experience. Came from growing up without television.

"What?"

"What what?" she said.

"I can hear you thinking. Can't you be still for a few minutes, even between your ears?"

Her voice was muffled against his shirt. "That was scary this morning."

"We were definitely outgunned."

"I didn't know you were that quick on the draw." She raised her head. "I didn't know you had anything to draw."

"Yeah. Well."

"You weren't a Boy Scout, were you? There isn't a Billy the Kid merit badge?"

"Shut up, Shugak."

She chuckled and leaned into his shoulder again. "Van was terrified at first but she seemed to recover pretty quickly."

His chest rose and fell in a sigh. She raised her head again. "What?"

He looked a little shamefaced. "I texted to make sure she got home okay, and made her promise she would stay there at least for tonight."

She laughed.

He pulled back to give her a quizzical look. Whatever he saw there must have reassured him because he drew her back under his arm and rested his cheek on her head.

They sat there for a long time, not talking, not reading, just being, until it was time for bed.

Kurt Pletnikof's office was on the seventh floor of an office building downtown. Kate, Jim, and Mutt walked up from Westchester, paused for refreshment at Snow City Cafe where the staff were wise to Mutt and welcomed her with bacon crisp, just as she liked it. The three of them were in the elevator of the office building at nine fifty-nine a.m. and at Kurt's office door on the stroke of ten. The sign on the wall next to the door was in plain brass letters, *Pletnikof Investigations*. The door opened into a reception area furnished with seating. Copies of *PI Magazine* were arranged in a meticulous row on the coffee table. In spite of timing their arrival to opening hours to the second, a man was already sitting on the couch leafing through one of the magazines. He was in his forties, dressed in a blue suit his belly had outgrown, a blue button-down, and an electric-blue tie with tiny gavels printed on it. Jowls were threatening his face and he looked cross, as if he was aware of the jowls and knew there was nothing he could do about them. He looked up when they entered. His eyes widened when he saw Mutt and he paused in the act of flipping a page. Well, more like he froze solid, but Kate always tried to be kind.

Mutt looked up at her with a smug expression that said, *I've still got it.*

Beyond the seating area was a desk and at that desk sat one Agrifina Fancyboy, a young woman who looked like Awkwafina and who dressed like the post-Stanley Tucci Anne Hathaway in *The Devil Wears Prada*. Ms. Fancyboy (her preferred title, as she never hesitated to instruct those who erred toward informality, like Kate) had been born on the Y-K Delta but she was living the Fashion Week on Fifth Avenue dream, or as close as she could get to it in Anchorage, Alaska. Her steel-gray two-piece wool suit, four-inch stilettos, and meticulously mascaraed eyelashes were proof.

Whenever Kate tried to put on mascara she poked herself in the eye with the brush, so she'd given up on it early on. Ms. Fancyboy frankly terrified her, although she did her best not to let it show. "Ms. Fancyboy."

"Ms. Shugak." Ms. Fancyboy nodded at Jim. "Mr. Chopin."

"Ma'am."

"Mr. Pletnikof asked you be shown in as soon as you arrived." Ms. Fancyboy rose to her feet. "This way, please."

"Wait a minute," the guy on the couch said. "My appointment was—"

"Mr. Pletnikof will be with you shortly, Mr. Morrison." Ms. Fancyboy opened one of only two doors behind her desk and said, "Ms. Shugak and Mr. Chopin, sir."

She stepped back, they stepped inside, and the door was closed firmly behind them. One had the feeling that until Ms. Fancyboy willed it, they would remain there.

At his desk Kurt stared after her with stars in his eyes. "I love that woman more than life itself."

"Good thing, since you're engaged to her," Jim said.

"Mutt! Hey, girl, come here and give Uncle Kurt some love."

Mutt pranced over and proffered her ears for scratching, after which she accepted a beef stick from a jar Kurt kept in a drawer just for her as only her due.

"I don't know why you don't weigh three hundred pounds," Kate told her.

Mutt jumped up on the couch in the corner, turned around three times, and sat down to enjoy her beef stick in proper form.

Kate and Jim sat across from Kurt. "Jim filled you in yesterday?"

"Yeah..." Kurt hesitated. "I don't get why we're doing this, Kate. It's a waste of our time and their money."

"I told them that, Kurt, in almost those exact words. What can I say? We've had clients with more money than sense before this."

Kurt rolled his eyes. "Well, then, of course, we must investigate the cause of this crash. Which cause could not possibly be as obvious as an octogenarian in the left seat." He shook his head and opened his laptop. "I've got addresses and histories on the pilot and passengers in the Beaver. Two Coasties, an ex-Coastie and a retired nurse from Vegas, a tech lord from Seattle, and his trophy girlfriend Lily Chee. Not the real Lily Chee, I don't mean, but some teenage runway queen. Guy was fourteen years older than she was. Pervert."

Kate had no idea who Lily Chee was and didn't care unless she figured into the case as something other than a victim. Or unless she'd met the tech lord on Jeffrey Epstein's plane, which sounded plausible, except that Epstein, yay, was dead.

"The Coasties were only stationed here, the ex-Coastie and the retired nurse were one of the Coasties' parents and they never lived here and have no local contacts in state other than professional. I did a quick skim of public records in Kodiak and their names don't pop. I can go deeper if you want, get in touch with their COs, but..." He shrugged.

"The tech lord and his arm candy never set foot in the state before that day. They literally got off Alaska Airlines 573, got on a charter for Ahtna, where they got on the Beaver to go flightseeing. The charter was still on the ground in Ahtna waiting to take them back to Anchorage when the pilot heard about the midair. He's based out of Anchorage and I talked to him last night. Said he'd never met either of them before, got the trip by a referral through the Microsoft travel department." He waved a hand. "Some kind of executive perk, I dunno."

He swiveled back to face them, linking his hands over his belly. He looked good, fitter than Kate had ever seen him, and he was dressed a lot better, suit with the jacket off, silk tie pulled a little loose at the throat, hair in a stylish cut. She was pretty sure his shoes were new and polished to a mirror shine. Especially if Agrifina Fancyboy had anything to say about it. He'd come a long way from the guy in the broken-down cabin in the Park, poaching bears for their bladders to sell on the black market.

"Honestly," he said now, "I don't think we need to bother with the passengers in the Beaver. At least not at the moment, not unless we stumble across some new piece of evidence."

Jim looked at Kate. She nodded. "What about the Beaver pilot?"

He sighed again. "You sure their money's good?"

She nodded at his laptop. "We use the same bank. Should have cleared by now if it's going to."

He actually did verify that the money was in their account. Of course, he'd been shot on the first job Kate had hired him for. Even if you were only halfway bright, almost dying made you focus on the important things in ways almost nothing else could. And Kurt, it turned out, was even smarter than Kate had figured when she bankrolled Pletnikof Investigations.

"Okay then," he said, marginally more cheerful. "Amber Macintosh, thirty-six, pilot, owner/operator of a 1966 de Havilland Beaver. The pilot I talked to this morning knew her. Says her rep was good, she never forgot where in the Bush and when she left anybody, she always picked them up when she said she would, and she kept her aircraft maintained. They both flew for the Iditarod Air Force one year and fell into conversation at one of the checkpoints. Said she was over the moon because she'd just paid off the plane, it was hers now, free and clear. Said she was volunteering for the race to celebrate and because she hadn't flown much of Alaska west or north before. Said he called her after the race to ask her out but she turned him down. No reason, just no. Seen her to wave to off and on since then." He looked at them. "You want more, we'll have to sic Tyler onto it. God knows we got the money."

"How is Tyler?"

"Fine, so far as I know. I haven't seen the guy since he first came to town."

"Still hiding out?"

"I think he thinks so but no one's come knocking at our door looking for him. And he did exfiltrate himself from Fairbanks pretty efficiently." Kurt grinned. "We talk on the phone—he uses burners, changes them out every single blessed day, I have to wait for a text before I can contact him. His email address changes every day, too."

"How do you know what address?"

"He texts me when he gets up. Which is usually around eight o'clock at night. I swear to god the kid has never seen the sun."

Jim raised his eyebrows. "That takes talent, living in Alaska, at least in the summer."

"How about Barr and Gorst?" Kate said.

"Ah, well, now. Barr was an Alaskan old fart of the first water, and what you know I know and so does every other person who was born here. Made his first fortune flying freight and passengers for Royal Petroleum Company, aka RPetCo. Sold off Beaufort Airlines without looking too closely at the person who signed the check, who promptly stripped the once-proud Beaufort Air and sold it for parts. People were pissed. There were death threats and his wife left him. So he climbs into his Super Cub—the same one he was flying in the midair, FYI—and found that dinosaur graveyard. Big hullabaloo by all the usual suspects and they all came trailing network TV crews. The guy was basically a reality TV star before there was such a thing. Somebody quoted in his obituary said 'The camera loved him.' I dunno." He indicated his laptop. "There are clips on YouTube and he looked and sounded like a cranky old fart to me. Coulda been Old Sam Dementieff if Barr Senior was taller and, you know, Eyak." He ran a hand through his hair, mussing his stylish do in a way that would surely wring Ms. Fancyboy's heart. "Then the oil companies started drilling offshore again and Barr Senior was about the only one left in state who knew how. He started another airline and he made another fortune."

"Some people do have the knack. What about Gorst?"

Kurt leaned back in his chair and laced his hands behind his head. "Well, now, there's where things get at least a little interesting. Finally. Art Gorst Junior, forty-five, was the son of Art Gorst Senior, who was Barr Senior's chief of operations at Beaufort. Gorst Senior died before Barr Senior started his second airline, so Barr Senior took on Gorst Junior as partner. Gorst Junior did the grunt work along with Barr Junior while Barr Senior ran operations." He paused. "I get the vibe that Gorst Junior was something of an underachiever. Good-looking, fun to be around, but it was the opinion of the guy who knew both him and his dad that Gorst Junior had been handed too much too young and never learned how to make it himself."

"Old story. What's interesting about that?"

"There are rumors that Gorst Junior has been fudging the Ikiak Air books, and that Barr Senior didn't know it."

"And Barr Junior didn't know, either?"

"My guy says not."

They all thought about that for a while. "Doesn't help us, though, does it," Kate said.

"Uh, yeah, if Gorst Junior was going to take out Barr Senior he wouldn't have been in the same plane with him."

Kate ignored the sarcasm. "Was Gorst Junior a pilot?"

"No."

"Barr's kids said we could have free rein of the Ikiak Air office, look at anything we want."

Kurt brightened. "Give Tyler a way in and he'll make them sit up and beg."

"Gorst Junior have any family?"

Kurt snorted. "Guy I talked to last night called Gorst a world-class bed-hopper. He married three, four times, the guy couldn't keep count. The last one stuck. A couple kids."

"Which may be why he was—"

"Or was not..."

"Or was not," Jim said obediently, "hurting for money. Three kids. That's a lot of child support."

"Did Macintosh have relatives?"

"There's a brother Outside, Illinois. He's hired someone to pack up her stuff." He tapped his keyboard and Kate's phone chimed with an incoming text. "That's her address. The movers will be there today—" he checked the time "—right about now. They'll let you in on my say-so but make it quick."

"Kurt, you are amazing."

His chest puffed out. Praise from Kate Shugak did not come often. They got up to go and he snapped his fingers. "Hey?"

She turned. "What?"

"Is it true? Auntie Balasha died of Covid?"

"It's true."

"Damn." He was silent for a moment. "Of all of them, she was the only one who really listened, you know?"

"I know."

Twenty-one

WEDNESDAY, SEPTEMBER 14
Anchorage

AMBER MACINTOSH'S APARTMENT WAS A modest rental in a nine-plex in Spenard. Hers was upstairs on the end furthest from the street. The movers were waiting and impatient at having to. Jim slipped them both a twenty but their expressions told him it wouldn't hold them for long. Although Mutt, plunking herself down in the open doorway, would provide anyone added incentive.

One bedroom, one bathroom, with a corner desk in the living room out of which she ran her business. "No logbook," Jim said, rifling through a drawer, "but she probably had it with her."

"You always carry yours?" Kate was looking through a pile of mail the landlord had left on the coffee table.

"Always. Never miss recording an hour of flight time."

Hours at PIC—or pilot in command in the air—were a measuring stick for every pilot, small plane or large. The more hours, the bigger the stick, where said stick was almost certainly a euphemism for something else, even for women pilots. Only the oldest of Alaskan old farts understood the meaning of a low number on their driver's license; this was similar in the world of aviation and not just in Alaska. "How many hours have you got?"

"Seven thousand nine hundred and forty-two." He looked up. "Plus an hour and a half for yesterday's flight. Remind me to update my log this evening."

"That count your hours in the helo?"

"Oh, hell no. A couple hundred, maybe, and that's probably generous."

"Almost eight thousand." Her eyes got a faraway look. "Eight thousand hours, twenty-four hours a day... that's almost a full year in the air."

He shrugged. "When I was posted to Nome I flew nearly every day, weather permitting. Tok, too, and same thing after we built the post at Niniltna. Not to mention all the flying to whichever courthouse had jurisdiction to testify in whatever trial. The job builds hours fast."

"And Macintosh?"

"How old did Kurt say she was?"

"Thirty-six."

He thought. "Assume she graduated high school at eighteen and Embry-Riddle at twenty-two, and that she's spent less time on the ground than in the air since. Fifty-five hours to private pilot certification. Another ninety for instrument rating. I think it's around four hundred more for a commercial pilot's certificate. Then there's multi-engine and I forget what all."

He shrugged at her look. "Everyone wants to fly for Alaska Airlines. The glamour is all in the big jets."

"She didn't."

"No," he said thoughtfully. "She didn't, did she." He sat down in the desk chair and opened the laptop. He tapped the touchpad and sighed when the desktop opened obediently. "No password."

"Honestly." Kate's voice came distantly from the bathroom. He heard the door open on the medicine cabinet. "People have no respect whatsoever for hackers. Think of what Tyler would say."

Macintosh's internet provider had yet to discontinue her account. He clicked around and found the laptop's IP address and texted it to Kurt. He didn't have to wait five minutes; he didn't even have to wait two before things began happening on the desktop that had nothing to do with him. Taking care not to touch the keyboard he pushed back from the desk and stood up.

"Tyler in?"

"I hope so." He followed the sound of her voice into the bedroom, where she was going through the closet. "What have we got?"

"Jeans and button-downs. She must have been wearing the bomber jacket."

"Typecasting."

She turned her head to give him and his black leather bomber jacket the beady eye. "Uh-huh." She turned back to the closet. "One little black dress, one pair of dress shoes, good quality but not exactly Givenchy." She pointed. "Want to check the shelves?"

One shoebox filled with old paperwork, another with aviation certificates, including her diploma from Embry-Riddle. "Impressive," Jim said.

"What in?"

"Aeronautics. Jesus."

"What?"

"She took an associates' degree in maintenance while she was at it."

"Why didn't she sign off on her own annuals, then?" Her voice sounded muffled.

"Twice as careful on the ground, twice as safe in the air."

"See how well that worked out for her." Her voice changed. "Jim."

He turned and saw that she had raised the mattress so she could look under it. He stepped forward and took the weight and she reached for a nine by twelve manila envelope lying in the exact center of the box springs.

He let the mattress down gently. "Surprise."

She was disgusted. "It's such a cliché. Hiding stuff under the mattress. Geeze."

"No password."

"Yeah, okay, but still."

"I hear you."

"Unaddressed," she said, turning the envelope over. "And unsealed, just the metal clasp." She hefted it. "Pretty bulky."

"And the suspense builds."

"Yeah, yeah." She opened the clasp and emptied the envelope on the bedspread. They stood looking at the contents for a long moment without speaking.

"Well."

"Yeah." Jim drew out the word.

"We should probably count it."

In fact, they counted it twice because they both thought their first count must be off.

"Sweet Jesus," Kate said. "Twenty-two thousand four hundred dollars. That's a lot of cash to be hiding under your mattress."

"And it's not like this is a gated community or anything. I mean, it's Spenard, for crissake."

"Could be worse. Could be Muldoon."

He laughed, which eased the tension a little. "What the hell was Macintosh up to?"

"She was doing something she was getting paid for in cash. Either it was work that no one wanted a paper trail for, or income she didn't want to pay taxes on, or both." She frowned.

"What?"

"It's an odd amount. Twenty-two thousand four hundred."

"Twenty-five would be a rounder number? Maybe it was twenty-five originally. Maybe she blew a couple thousand in riotous living when she got paid."

Kate looked around at the bedroom and snorted. He got her point. The dishes, the flatware, and the pots and pans were your basic four-person sets from Walmart. The coffee maker was a one-cup pour through, the coffee ready-ground from Safeway. The freezer was filled with Stouffer's frozen dinners. Her work clothes were by Eddie Bauer, her underwear by Hanes. The only art on the walls was a framed print of a red Beaver on floats, taking off from Lake Hood. They'd check the tail number to be sure but he was certain it was Macintosh's. If she'd paid a professional photographer to take it, it was probably the most expensive item in the apartment.

He looked back at the money. Good old American greenbacks in packs of used twenties. "Easy to spend." He looked at her. "What do we do now?"

She stared at him.

He hooked a thumb over his shoulder. "I don't think we want to leave it behind for them. At the same time, if we call the cops, they will surely point out that I no longer have any standing in law and what the hell am I doing here?"

Entering into the spirit of this, she nodded. "And we bribed our way into this apartment to begin with. They could by rights arrest us for B&E." She thought. "Well, entering, at least."

"So, no cops. But what do we do with the money?"

"Got a pen?" He did. She got out her phone and took several photos of the money and the envelope spread out across the bedspread, which was a fluffy comforter with big colorful flowers printed all over it and the only sign of either femininity or style in the entire apartment. She put the money back in the envelope and this time sealed the flap as well as fastened the clasp. She wrote something, crossing the flap, and handed it to him to read. "Witnessed to contain $22,400 in $20 bills by Kate Shugak and Jim Chopin." She'd signed and dated it and handed him the pen.

Dutifully he signed and dated where indicated. "Speaking of evidence. Somebody could make a case that we actually found the whole $25,000 inside."

"I'll take my chances. Pick up the mattress again."

He did so and she replaced the envelope. "Hold it for a minute." She replaced the envelope where she'd found it and took a photo of that, too. "Okay."

He set the mattress down. "That it?"

"The best we can do. This way it has at least a chance of getting to the brother."

"And we know now that Macintosh was some bent."

"Which might have nothing to do with the midair."

He sighed. "True."

"And it is possible she simply hated banks."

"Who doesn't?"

Ikiak Air was housed in a large hangar on the east side of 7R/25L at Ted. Kate checked out their website en route. "Didn't I read something about how they've stopped drilling offshore again?"

"Yes. Because they're able to—what do they call it —"

"Directionally drill?"

He'd forgotten that she'd put in time in Prudhoe Bay. "Yeah, but it's different now. They drill straight down on land and then dogleg to—that's it, horizontally directionally drill. Say that three times fast without stuttering."

"So no need for ice roads out to the islands anymore."

"It's trending that way, according to the story I read. Why?"

She looked up from her phone. "Because Ikiak Air's website looks a lot more like a fixed base of operations than it does a carrier. Lounge, catering, conference rooms, Wi-Fi. For the aircraft they got fuel, ground crew, rented hangar space."

"Huh." He was silent for a moment. "Don't remember the kids mentioning that."

"Suppose they could have forgotten."

He quirked an eyebrow at her.

They followed Spenard to where it crossed International and became Jewel Lake, turned right on Raspberry and turned right just before it became Kincaid Park, where they found themselves on the edge of a large aviation industrial park. There were air freight shippers, small airlines, aviation service companies, a helicopter outfit with helicopters taking off and landing sequentially and continuously from a pad in front of the door, a business park with a dozen individual offices, and a LifeMed building with the distinctive orange-and-white caduceus on the wall. It was a logo known to every Bering Sea deckhand who ever got a fish hook in his eye and had to be flown out from St. Paul on an airplane with that logo on the tail to Providence in Anchorage or Virginia Mason in Seattle.

They pulled into a parking space next to a hangar four times the size of Jim's with office space over and beside. The scream of an engine signaled the approach of an aging 727 with an RPetCo logo on the tail. They got out and watched as it stopped in front of the hangar. It was what they called the combi, two freight igloos forward and seventy-two passengers aft.

No passengers got off, only crew, and that crew was two pilots total. Ground crew boarded, popped the top of the freight section and a forklift came forward to remove the two igloos.

"They must be shipping gold ingots to make book on that flight," Jim said.

They went inside—Mutt trotting between them, tail up, ears interested—where they were greeted by a subdued woman who introduced herself as Susan Whitcomb and said she was the office manager. "Yes, Barr Junior called to say you would be coming. Frank's office is right there." She examined their driver's licenses carefully and pointed. "Art's office is down the hall. His name's on the door."

"Could we have a tour of the facility first?"

She eyed Mutt. Mutt, very much on her dignity, raised her chin and curled her tail a little tighter. She cherished the notion that it made her look more husky than wolf and thus less threatening. Nothing could be further from the truth but far be it from Kate to tell her otherwise.

Over her head Jim smiled at the office manager and she caved at once, because of course she did. The lounge had a full self-serve bar and, as advertised, Wi-Fi access. The conference rooms were all black walnut and brown leather and wall screens for Zoom calls and Ted Talks and remote board meetings. Upstairs there were half a dozen small rooms each equipped with a desk and a chair, "Private office space," the office manager said.

"Do you have a rate sheet?"

She led them back downstairs to her office, also nicely furnished and within shouting distance of the president and CEO's office as that was right next door.

Jim took the sheet of paper Whitcomb handed him and read down it. "Wow." He handed it back.

She gave a faint smile.

"Can you tell us a little bit about your bosses?"

Whitcomb was as tall as Kate was short and as fair as Kate was dark and she looked surprised that Kate could speak. "My... bosses? Oh." Her voice flattened. She indicated the chairs in front of her desk and sat down behind it. Mutt took up station equidistant between Kate and Jim, ears up, all attention, as if she could understand every word being said. Maybe she could.

"You mean Art as well as Frank and Barr Junior."

Whitcomb was the only one who called Frank Barr Sr. "Frank" instead of "Barr Senior." Kate wondered about their relationship. Barr Sr. had been eighty-seven; Whitcomb was maybe forty, but May–December romances at the office were nothing new under the sun. "Can you talk to us a little about both of them, please?" She had meant it as a request but Whitcomb heard it as an order and flushed.

Jim, the old smoothie, inserted himself into the conversation, pulling Whitcomb's attention his way. "Anything you can tell us will be such a big help, Sue."

Whitcomb looked dazzled and who could blame her. "Art is— was useless for anything but glad-handing. Frank gave him the job because he and Art's dad came up together in the old days and Frank figured he owed it to him after Art's dad died." She stopped, clearly struggling with what came next.

Jim didn't say anything. So, Kate thought, good cop, bad cop. Not trying to be nice about it this time she said, "We are informed that Gorst Junior might have been cooking the books and that Barr Senior might have found out about it."

Whitcomb flushed again, more deeply this time. She looked at Jim, who gave her a placating smile. Between the deep blue eyes, the wide, white smile, and the skin bronzed from a summer spent outdoors, it was enough. "Maybe tell us about the business first," he said, and that slow, deep voice was the last straw. A tear slid down Whitcomb's face and Jim, radiating sympathy in the way only very tall, utterly confident men can, leaned forward to push the box of Kleenex sitting on top of her desk to within her reach.

"Art had no interest in aviation other than how much he could pull out of it to fund his various amusements." She pulled a tissue from the box and dabbed her eyes. "Oh yes, he was a notorious player. His most recent wife, Courtney, finally had enough and threw him out. Two kids, both still in grade school. He had others. Frank never said but I think the grandkids were why he gave Art the job."

Jim wasn't going to say it so Kate had to. "You and Gorst Junior—"

Whitcomb carried on as if she hadn't heard, speaking

directly to Jim. "Frank was— Frank was the real deal. Smart, honest, and god was the man capable. He could fly anything, he could spot a commodity before anyone else knew there was someone to sell it to, and he was just the best boss. He was willing to pay top dollar for top tier people. He was demanding but he never blindsided you, told you up front what to expect so you always knew where you were with him." She waved her hand. "That's not just me talking. Ask anyone who works here. Frank Junior would say the same."

Someone stuck his head in the door. "That G-2 from Houston just landed, Sue."

"Take care of them for me, Adam, would you?"

"Sure thing."

She turned back to them. "This place ran like clockwork, money in the bank, bills paid on time, deadlines met. The drilling companies were very happy with us, signed on the dotted line every time." She lost her composure for a moment. "And boy do they pay well, and they never question the charges. They're the easiest customers to deal with I've ever met and I've been in business since I graduated from high school." She paused. "Or they were."

"What happened?"

"They moved operations onshore and when you fly into Deadhorse instead of an ice strip on the Arctic Ocean things get a lot more competitive."

Jim gave her another smile to prime the pump. "That would be when the FBO came into being."

She brightened. If she'd had a tail it would have been wagging hard enough to compete with Mutt. "It was Frank's idea, and like all Frank's ideas, it turned to gold practically overnight. There were already others in business here but Frank's idea was to cater to the high-enders, the guys rich enough to have their own jets and willing to pay for privacy. They can get good booze and nice conference rooms anywhere, but privacy is really what they want and that's what we offer. Frank came up with an NDA and made all the employees sign it and spelled out exactly what it meant. One leak and the leaker was fired. Like I said, he paid well and he treated us like human beings. It wasn't a job anyone wanted to lose just so they could brag to the *National Enquirer* about that time Leonardo de Caprio came through with Timothy Treadwell."

Too bad the bears didn't get both of them, Kate thought. "Gorst Junior," she said.

Whitcomb sighed and looked at Jim. "As I said, Junior is— was good at glad-handing and not much else. Frank hired him to drum up business. Not that we needed it."

"He wasn't cooking the books?"

"Junior wouldn't know a double entry from a double header," Whitcomb said flatly. "He drew a salary to go to Chamber of Commerce meetings. First he stayed in state, and then he started attending meetings Outside." She bit her lip. "I hate to admit it but he did bring in business."

"What kind of business?"

"People with money, which meant money in the bank for us. Wasn't our business how they made it. Frank started hoping out loud that Junior had made the turn, that he was going to be a useful member of society from now on, maybe Courtney would take him back, he could start being a real father to his kids." She sighed. "Frank always did dream big.

"The new people started using the conference rooms to meet local businessmen, and again, money in the bank, yay us. But one day, Frank came into my office really upset. He said Erland Bannister was in Conference Room B talking with some guy from Chicago."

She didn't notice Kate stiffening at the mention of the name. Jim certainly did and so did Mutt. "Erland Bannister?" Jim said very carefully indeed. "The Alaska businessman?"

Whitcomb shrugged. "I'm not baked Alaska. Frank recruited me out of an FBO in Scottsdale ten years ago, and I never have paid much attention to the news, so I'd never heard of him." She blew out a sharp breath. "Frank was not a fan. He said Bannister was a liar, a cheat, a thief, an embezzler, and a murderer. And he said that was only on Bannister's good days. On his worst days, Frank said, he was… worse."

Kate was liking Barr Sr. more and more.

"He waited until the meeting was over and on their way out pulled Bannister aside and told him he wasn't welcome at Ikiak Air and not to come back." The color washed out of her face and she looked fixedly at the hands clasped on the desk in front of her.

"What happened?"

"Bannister laughed in his face." Whitcomb spoke in a voice barely above a whisper. "He told him to talk to his partner."

"Art Junior."

"Yes. Junior wasn't here, of course, so Frank had to wait for him to come back from schmoozing with the Las Vegas Rotary Club or whoever. They went into Frank's office and closed the door. I didn't hear the words but we all heard the shouting. Junior stormed out and from then on he was hardly ever in the office."

"When was that?"

Whitcomb thought. "Year, year and a half ago?"

Bannister had died the previous November, so probably more like a year and a half. "But Gorst Junior was in the Cub with him."

"I know." She raised her hands in a shrug.

"What was the purpose of the trip?"

"Frank was spending a lot of air time flying around the more scenic areas of the state looking for properties to buy. I don't know why. I was pretty sure he had another big idea but he wasn't ready to share."

"Why take Junior with him?"

A short laugh entirely lacking in humor. "He didn't say but best guess is Junior was in the process of reconstituting himself as a realtor. The last refuge of incompetents and scoundrels."

Kate stirred. "Do you have a list of the properties Frank Senior had bought recently?"

"Of course."

Jim smiled at her. "Could you print out a list?"

She positively fluttered. "Certainly." She turned to her desktop, tapped a few keys. An unseen printer clicked and whirred. The piece of paper was still warm when she handed it to Jim. Jim looked at it and showed it to Kate, pointing to a name.

"I see he bought an old mining claim from a Patrick Murphy," Kate said. "Was Art Junior the listing agent for the property?"

"Yes." Whitcomb rolled her eyes. "Frank said that Art Senior had known Murphy back in the day. That he probably just went with a name he knew."

Which is precisely what an Alaskan old fart would do.

Jim stirred. "Barr Junior said we could have access to your records."

Whitcomb led them to Barr Sr.'s office and left them to it. Jim pulled out the IP address and texted it to Kurt, who passed it on to Tyler. As at Macintosh's, a few moments later icons began opening and closing on the screen. He averted his eyes.

His phone rang. "Hey, Kurt. I just sent—"

"Yeah, yeah, I got it, Tyler's on it." Jim eyed the screen, which now resembled the tiles in the roller cage of a bingo game. "You still at Ikiak?"

"Yes."

"About done?"

"Yes."

Kurt heaved a sigh. "Drop by here on your way back?"

Jim didn't like the sound of Kurt's voice. "What up?"

"Not on the phone."

Worse and worse. "On our way."

Twenty-two

WEDNESDAY, SEPTEMBER 14
Anchorage

K URT WAS LOOKING AT KATE WITH apprehension.

Correction: Kurt was looking at Kate as if he was afraid she might explode with the fury of a Javelin missile launched at a Russian tank in Donbas. Only in his office.

Jim was sitting right next to her and he could relate. Mutt moved ostentatiously to Jim's other side.

"Macintosh flew for Erland Bannister?" Kate's voice was level, even pleasant, which only ratcheted up the tension in the room.

"She kept a log of all her manifests on her computer, and Tyler says she was religious about entering expenses on QuickBooks." He caught Kate's eye and hurried on. "But yes, she flew for Erland. In fact, she flew him in and out of the Park on multiple occasions for two years, dating back to the discovery of the Suulutaq."

"Why don't I remember seeing her aircraft on the strip?"

"She flew him direct to the mine, bypassing Niniltna. I called George Perry. He remembered because it pissed him off that she was doing him out of the business. George says they stopped in Niniltna now and then to meet up with Outside investors that started flying in on their corporate jets after they paved the airstrip."

"Two years," Jim said. "Up until he died?"

Kurt nodded.

Jim looked at Kate. "How she paid off her plane."

From beyond the fucking grave. Kate felt a little light-headed, what with all the repressed wrath. She looked at Kurt. "But that's not all, is it?"

Kurt looked miserable. "No."

She attempted a smile and ceased when he flinched. "Don't keep us in suspense. Spit it out."

"Remember those two goons who kidnapped Martin?"

There was a momentary silence. "I remember," Jim said. "Bernie called them Ace and Deuce. He gave me the glass with the fingerprints on it. I passed it on the FBI." He turned to Kate. "What were their names?"

Kate drew in a deep breath and let it out again, very slowly. The lightheadedness was not improving. "Carmine DiFronzo and Milton Spilotro."

Kurt nodded. "Those are the two. They were listed as the only passengers on a flight in the list of Macintosh's ledger, I'm guessing days before Martin went missing."

Jim distinctly remembered the day Howie Katelnikof, that little weasel, had materialized at the homestead with a plea to find his cousin. "What was the date, exactly?" Kurt told him. "Yeah. That fits."

Kate looked out of Kurt's window. It was one of those crisp, clear September days, after the leaves had begun to turn but before they had fallen. Fresh snow covered Susitna, and a hundred miles further north, the ever-white peaks of Denali and Foraker graced the horizon, albeit less awe-inspiring at this distance. Hull-down, she had heard a sailor call the effect of distance on massive objects. From Kurt's office, Denali looked like the caricature of a woman's breast and Foraker like a loaf of Wonder bread. She'd seen them up close, both from the air and from the ground. She knew the difference. "What else?" she said to the mountains.

"I hate it when you do that."

"What else, Kurt?"

"I had Tyler run a check on all the debtors that were listed in her QuickBooks account. She had a lot of work from Outsiders. One of them was a law firm in Chicago."

Kate looked at him. Jim said, "Oh hell no."

Kurt nodded, still with that wary eye on Kate. "Cullen and Associates."

She heard Susan Whitcomb's voice in her head. *He said Erland Bannister was in Conference Room B talking with some guy from Chicago.*

"Kate?"

Jim leaned forward so he could look her full in the face. "Kate?"

Kate blinked, as if coming out of a trance. "Where does her brother live, again?"

"Macintosh's?" Kurt tapped a few keys. "Illinois."

She looked at him. "As in Chicago, Illinois?"

He gaped at her.

"You think she was planted here," Jim said. "But Jesus, Kate." He looked at Kurt. "How long has she been in the state?"

Kurt had anticipated the question. "She got her driver's license here four years ago."

"So, again, the same year of the Suulutaq discovery."

"Which Erland was hip-deep in."

"Yes." Kate withdrew her gaze from the long view. "Kurt, do you have any friends in the local NTSB office?"

He shook his head.

She tapped her knee. "I've had no luck getting through to them. Ask Tyler if he can access the records of the investigation into the midair?"

Kurt looked infinitely relieved at the change of subject. "No problem." So long as Tyler could do it without blowback, but that wasn't information he felt it necessary to volunteer in this moment.

"The cause of the crash, and the identity of the extra body Jo Dunaway told everyone they found." She looked at Jim. "We've talked to Barr Senior's kids. Seems like we ought to check in with Gorst Junior's ex before we head home."

Jim rose and Mutt, overjoyed, leaped to her feet.

"Kurt?"

"Kate?"

"I think a list of what locations in Alaska Cullen and Associates were paying Macintosh to fly to would be useful."

He looked relieved all over again. He knew very well that what she really wanted him to do was locate Erland Bannister's grave so she could desecrate it. "We'll get on that. Hey, Kate?"

She turned at the door. "What?"

"Remember who we're working for, okay?"

She gave him a faint smile. "So far it looks like Barr Senior is the good guy. I don't think his kids can complain."

"So far."

She nodded. "So far."

Courtney Gorst was the whole package—gorgeous, smart, and seriously pissed off. "Sure, I'll talk to you about him," she said, stepping back to open the door wider. "I sure wouldn't want you to get the wrong idea about good old Junior. Oh." This as Mutt followed Kate inside. Courtney shrugged. "Welcome one, welcome all."

They followed her through to the living room and waited for her to bring coffee. The smell of fresh baked chocolate chip cookies was in the air and Jim hoped some would make an appearance. His wish came true as Courtney, a woman with more—and more impressive—curves than the Daytona Speedway returned with a laden tray. Her eyes were large and dark and bottomless, her mouth large and lavish, her hair a thick brown disciplined into a sleek, modern cut, her skin a pale cream. She wore a lavender shirt open-necked with the sleeves rolled up to the elbow over a pair of black slacks fresh from the cleaners. There were jeweled flip-flops on her feet that matched the color of her shirt, polish on her toenails that matched the polish on her fingernails, and a silver ring in the shape of a breaking wave on her right-side fourth toe. Above all, she had that indefinable aura some women had as a birthright—that she knew her own worth down to the last pheromone and she wasn't going to just give it away to the first guy who asked.

She set the tray down and sat opposite them, crossing her legs and smiling at Jim, wholly ignoring Kate. Kate nudged him and he realized a cookie had stopped halfway to his mouth. It made the rest of the journey and he chewed mechanically, washing down the tasteless crumbs with a swallow of coffee that might have been Valvoline for all he knew.

"What wrong idea about Art?" Kate said, when it became clear Jim wasn't going to.

Courtney Gorst transferred her gaze, reluctantly, and Kate got that. Good thing or she might have been irremediably pissed off. It was the second time today, for crissake. She hoped her annoyance didn't show and was further annoyed when she saw the smile in Courtney's eyes. A woman like Courtney always knew.

She answered Kate. "I wouldn't want you to get the wrong idea about Junior." Amazing how thin those lips could get when she pressed them together like that. Now she looked less like Angelina Jolie and more like the Wicked Witch of the

West. Kate hoped Jim noticed, or at least that it would break the spell. It didn't. "What would be the wrong idea?"

"That he was any kind of a good guy."

"Specifically?"

Courtney shrugged. "Unfaithful husband, absent father, lousy provider." She drank coffee. She hadn't taken a cookie, and given that figure, Kate doubted she ever would. "The fact of the matter is that I was seduced by a pretty face."

Kate was less interested in Gorst Jr. at home than she was in Gorst Jr. at work. "Did he talk about work?"

"Yes, of course, that would be why you're here." Courtney's disdain would have been paralyzing if Kate had let it be. She set her cup down precisely centered in its saucer. "He was neither a good nor an honest man at home, Ms....?"

"Shugak."

"Ms. Shugak. It would be foolish to expect he would be at work." She sighed and for a moment—for a moment only—she looked older than her years. "He let drop a few bits and pieces now and then. He thought Frank Barr was a fool. Well, so did I, when he hired Junior." She shook her head. "He always talked big, Junior did. There was always some story about some bigwig he'd met on his last trip Outside, how the money was going to come pouring in and Frank would have to step aside and let him take over the business."

Jim appeared still to be frozen in the space-time continuum. "Come pouring in from where?"

Courtney shrugged. "All over. This last trip? Chicago."

"Any particular name?"

"Some law firm he'd brought in as a customer a couple of years ago."

"What were their interests in Alaska?"

Another shrug. "What are anyone's interests in Alaska? Oil. Gas. Minerals. Fish. What else is there? Junior said he thought Barr Senior was looking for property to buy up that he could later sell to the Suulutaq at a profit."

The Suulutaq Mine had been doing exploratory drills for two plus years and they kept extending the underground reach of their copper and gold deposit. Kate could see them buying up nearby existing mines no matter how small on the theory that the deposit went even further. "Do you know where he and Barr Senior were going that day?"

"A couple of properties that looked ripe for the plucking." Courtney was bored with the subject and smiled again at Jim, turning up the wattage.

The front door banged open. "Mom! We're home! Mom? What's that car doing in the driveway?" There was a cascade of thuds as coats, shoes, and book bags hit the floor, followed by a stampede of feet. Two children, eight and ten or thereabouts, clustered in the doorway and cast disapproving looks. "How come they're eating our cookies?"

Courtney laughed and stood up. She was still a femme fatale and no mistake, but her reaction to the children manifested in tolerance and love. "There are more in the kitchen. Go, go, I'll be right there."

They thundered off to the back of the house. She looked at Kate and Jim. "Any more questions?"

The spell had been broken, Kate was relieved to see, and Jim rose to his feet. "Could we call you if we do?"

"Certainly." She fluttered her eyelashes at him. "I'll be here all week. See yourselves out, won't you?"

She grinned at Kate as she passed her, and this time it was more an invitation to share the joke. Kate found she didn't dislike Courtney Gorst as much as she thought she had.

Mutt, however, lifted her lip at the widow.

Kate gave her an extra scratch in the place she loved best, just behind her right ear.

They took the Forester back to the townhouse, stripped the bed and left the dirty sheets and towels in a pile for the housekeeper, and called for an Uber to take them to Lake Hood. The Stationair was where they'd left it and looked as if no one had given it so much as a second glance. Jim did the walkaround while Kate freed the tiedowns. They got in and strapped down. "Over the top or around?"

The high over Southcentral was hanging in there, making the afternoon too beautiful to waste. "Around."

They were in the air ten minutes later and out of Anchorage air space shortly afterward. They went north and east through Tahneta Pass, the Talkeetna Mountains to the left and the Chugach Mountains to the right, all the peaks covered with a healthy layer of early snow. "Gonna be a cold one," Jim said over the headset, and Kate nodded. Denali and Foraker loomed larger than life to the northwest until Jim put the nose on home and relaxed into that state of observant vigilance practiced by all experienced pilots.

"Hey."

He looked at her. "What?"

"Mind if we go home by way of the Step?"

"You want to talk to Dan?"

"I want to look at his map."

"Uh-huh. Should I ask why?"

"One of those itches I can't scratch."

He leered at her. "Happy to scratch your itch any day, baby."

She laughed, and, content, he altered course by a degree or two to the north. He also switched to the Park HQ channel and called ahead to make sure Dan was there. They set down on the gravel strip a little under eighty minutes later and found the chief ranger waiting for them, beaming. "Been a while."

"Been a whole day," Kate said.

"Since you visited me at home," he said severely. "To what do I owe the honor?"

"I want to look at your map."

He shrugged. "Be my guest." He led the way inside and to his office. "What's up?"

Sixty percent of the state was still in federal hands, that amount whittled down over the years by transfers to the state and the Alaska Native corporations. The fact was more than half the time you spent in the air in the Park you were flying over federal lands. It bred a low-level but endemic resentment in the people who lived there and Chief Ranger Dan O'Brian spent a significant amount of his time in ensuring those federal lands he oversaw provided its residents no cause to shoot up boats, planes, and ATVs bearing the NPS logo.

"Everything in private hands is still red, right?"

"Yes." Dan came to stand next to Kate. "What's going on?"

She pointed at a red splotch in the lower right-hand corner. "That's Demetri's lodge?"

"Yeah. Well, it was."

"Do you know who bought it?"

Dan shrugged. He looked tired, but then he always looked tired toward the end of the season. Summer meant fishing and tourism and, let's not forget, construction, and right after summer came fall, when the hunters apparated in Harry Potter-style from Anchorage and Outside, trophy hunters competing with subsistence hunters. Too many of the former couldn't find the game management unit listed on their permits and too many of the latter were too impatient with so-called hunters who cared less about the meat than how the rack would display on the walls of their offices. "It's a corporation, I forget the name. I haven't had time to run them down." He sighed. "Or get out there, for that matter."

"No idea why this corporation bought the property?"

He shrugged again. "Demetri's concern was commercial. I'm guessing theirs will be private. Best guess is they're going to turn it into some kind of corporate retreat for board meetings and executive weekends, like that." He sighed. "I'm down with that. For one thing it'll mean a lot less traffic in and out. We can hardly keep up as it is. Probably mostly be summer traffic, too. I don't see board members choosing Alaska in February for a retreat when they could pick Maui instead."

The building felt quiet. "Summer help gone for the year?"

"All the interns are. I'll hang on to the part-time rangers through moose season, and bring them back in January when caribou season starts."

Momentarily diverted Kate said, "There will be one this year?"

"Yeah, their population has come back up a lot over the last couple of years. I hear they might even be issuing cow tags. Anyway, yeah, my part-timers are all out in the field at the moment. Howie Katelnikof isn't the only asshole out there with a drone." He brooded over that for a moment. "Why are you so curious about who bought Demetri's lodge?"

"Paddy Murphy sold his claim to Frank Barr Senior."

Dan's eyebrows went up. "Did he, now."

"He did, and I'm wondering if he pissed off someone else who wanted to buy it. And who."

"Particularly who," Jim said. "She's got an itch she can't scratch."

Dan grinned and Kate gave him a ferocious glare. "Don't you dare."

Speech withered on his tongue but the grin stayed firmly in place. He looked like a leprechaun when he grinned, only taller.

"We're hearing Barr Senior was buying up a lot of private properties in these parts."

"They say why?"

"Various theories but no one knows for sure. Barr Senior didn't share well. One of the rumors is he was looking for property to buy up that he could later sell to the Suulutaq at a profit."

"Thinking lightning might strike twice, eh?" Dan scratched his chin. "Stranger things have happened, but the EPA is going to shut the Suulutaq down for good, or so this administration says."

Kate snorted. "So it says. They haven't done it yet."

Dan's eyebrows ascended into his hairline. "Why, Kate Shugak, I'm shocked, shocked to hear you express such doubt in the pure motives of my boss."

The three of them looked at the picture of the President of the United States on the wall, and looked away again.

"Barr Senior's office manager says Gorst Junior was Paddy Murphy's realtor, and that he brought the deal to Barr Senior. No mention of the claim. Could be he didn't mention it to her."

"Huh." Dan looked at Kate. "What has any of this to do with the price of tea in China?"

"I don't know yet, but someone has been camping out there."

He frowned. "I didn't know Paddy Murphy well but he was okay. There was never any heavy lifting to do with him. He mined his gold and he stayed mostly sober and he didn't try to pet the bears. Who the hell would want to kill him?"

No answer, because there wasn't one.

"Any idea how long the body had been there?"

"A week, maybe," Jim said. "But that's just a guess."

"Wait a minute." Dan leaned forward. "That cap you found. You thinking it might have belonged to his killer?"

Jim pulled the cap out of his pocket, where it seemed to have taken up permanent residence. "Maybe. Again, just a guess. All we've got is a lot of disconnected evidence and uninformed speculation."

Dan picked up the cap and smoothed out the plastic so he could look at the logo again. "I've never seen this logo, but—"

"But what?"

"Shut up and let me think." He frowned at the logo for what felt like a long time. Kate shifted in her seat. He trained the frown on her. Jim marveled at his courage.

The frown finally cleared from his brow. "Harry and Marge Bachman."

"Harry and who who?"

Dan pawed through the flotsam and jetsam left by the federal paper tsunami on his desk. "It was right here, damn it." File folders and loose papers slipped down all four sides of his desk. "Here!" He opened the folder and summarized the list of complaints. At the end Jim said, "That was a really dick move on the guy with cancer."

"Dick moves all around. Who the hell are these people who think they can tell my people where they can and can't go in the Park? That's my privilege!" Dan recollected in whose presence he was speaking and his ears went red.

Kate was not taking offense on behalf of the Indigenous of Alaska or the Niniltna Native Association today, however.

She ran her forefinger across the map until she found the lake where the Bachmans' charter had dropped them off.

"Kate?" Dan came around his desk and looked over her shoulder.

The lake was almost equidistant between Paddy Murphy's claim and Demetri's lodge.

Jim had come to stand behind her, too, and she heard the intake of his breath. "Dan, can you find out who bought Demetri's lodge? I asked Kurt but he hasn't gotten back to me."

"Maybe." He stared at her finger on the map.

"You heard about Bobby getting run off the road in June?"

"Who hasn't?"

She told him about their experience at Paddy Murphy's the previous morning. Jim added the encounter in front of Bingley's on July first, about which she had completely forgotten.

"You think it's the same people? My complaints, and Bobby's near miss, and your thing at Paddy's?"

She turned her head to meet his eyes. "Once is happenstance, twice is coincidence—"

In unison they finished Goldfinger's immortal line. "—the third time is enemy action."

Dan took a deep breath and let it out slowly. "I might maybe have a few bells I can ring."

Twenty-three

WEDNESDAY, SEPTEMBER 14
The Park, Kate's homestead

THEY FLEW DIRECTLY HOME FROM THE STEP to the homestead strip, overflying Niniltna. If they'd been driving, there would have been no avoiding being spotted by someone and the word going forth that they were back. There was much to be said for having your own aircraft and your own strip. Mutt agreed. She waited just long enough for the door to open wide enough before going airborne. In a bound she had disappeared into the brush without so much as a backward glance.

"I feel so used."

"Relax. She'll be back and all over you before you know it." Kate helped push the 206 into the hangar. They closed the doors and for a moment they stood watching the sky darken and the stars wink into life one by one.

"Going to be a cold one tonight." He zipped up his jacket. "Might actually freeze."

"About time." A last quarter of moon appeared above the

horizon. "I remember Emaa telling me once how she was in Anchorage in 1969 when they landed on the moon for the first time. She was at a friend's house, watching it on TV."

"Yeah?"

"She said she thought by now we'd be able to see the lights of lunar settlements from Earth."

The last of the light drained from the sky as if someone had pulled the plug. The glow of the moon increased, but not from human outposts on its surface. "If she'd been running NASA, we would be."

They walked to the house and stopped short at the sight of Van's car parked out front and lights shining through the windows.

"Well, hell," Jim said.

"Not that we don't love the kids." Kate's response was automatic and without enthusiasm. She was tired and she wanted some quiet time to think about everything they had learned over the past three days. At the moment her brain felt constructed of rabbit holes, too many of them, none of which led anywhere revelatory or even useful.

They went inside to find Van frying Spam, hampered by the fact that Johnny had his arms around her waist and his chin on her shoulder. "Hey. We were hoping you'd get back tonight." She nodded at the counter. "I've got rice cooking and I brought eggs. Do you guys know how empty your refrigerator is?"

Jim opened the refrigerator door. "But there is beer."

"I brought that," Johnny said.

"You are welcome here anytime."

Van laughed, and Johnny gave Kate a hearty hug.

"How'd you get here?"

"George had a freight run to Fairbanks. He always calls when he has a deadheader to see if I want a ride home."

Jim took a long swallow from the bottle. "And just how did you think you were going to get back again?"

Johnny grinned at him.

Johnny Morgan was Kate's son, adopted by her after his father died and a few other events that everyone tried and failed to forget. His father had been tall and so was he, with broad shoulders, long wiry limbs and large hands and feet. He was putting on muscle and at the same time growing into a craggy set of facial features that were individually forceful and collectively rugged, brow, nose, and chin, and a wide mouth made for an infectious grin. He looked more a man and less a boy every time she saw him. She wasn't too proud to admit—privately—that the realization hurt her heart a little.

She set the table for four as Van set the browned Spam on a paper-towel-lined plate. She cracked ten eggs into the frying pan and turned the heat all the way down.

"Please tell me we've got some soy sauce." Kate checked the refrigerator and found half a bottle in the door.

"Thank god for that," Johnny said. "Otherwise we would have had to fly to Ahtna to buy some."

"'We.' Heh." Jim set down his beer and ripped off paper towels for napkins.

"You've spent enough time with your feet under the

Aguilars' table. Don't tell me you wouldn't have been first in the plane."

Van chuckled. She looked far more cheerful than frying Spam and eggs called for. Kate put the soy sauce and the rice cooker with a spoon stuck in it on the table. They sat down and fell to. For a while there was silence around the table.

"Where were you?" Johnny said when he came up for air.

"Anchorage."

"Why?"

Kate eyed his empty plate, which he had literally swiped clean with his fingers. "Don't they feed you up there?"

He made a face. "If you can call it that."

She relented. "I remember."

"I'll clean up." Jim rose to his feet. "Kate, why don't you start a fire?"

Mutt nosed her way into the house as Jim was about to join them, looking very cocky and extremely well fed. Jim plucked a feather out of the corner of her mouth as she pranced by. He held it up. "Hmm. Brown fading to white. Have you been terrorizing the local ptarmigan population, Mutt? And did you leave any for us?"

Mutt, meantime, saw Johnny and let out something perilously close to a shriek before launching herself from the center of the living room to make a four-point landing in his lap and assaulting his face with her tongue. "Augh! Get off me! Mutt! Geez!" She laughed at him, her tongue lolling out of her mouth, before consenting to being shoved to the floor.

She thought about sitting on his feet but the fire and her quilt beckoned. Exhausted from hunting down her dinner and by her duties as the welcoming committee she flopped down as close to the flame as she could without setting herself on fire and stretched out, in her elongated state taking up most of the length of that wall.

"Whew." Johnny wiped his face off on his sleeve and settled back next to Van on the couch. "So, what did you go to Anchorage for?"

Jim looked at Kate, who shrugged, and gave them a brief précis of their activities.

"Seems kind of Don Quixote. I mean the guy was in his late eighties, had some kind of episode in the air, and ran into the only other aircraft around. It's awful but it happens."

"Windmills we got plenty." Kate scrubbed her hands through her hair and Van watched enviously as it settled back into a perfect black cap. A skinny sleeveless dress, a long string of beads, and a pair of patent leather Mary Janes, and Kate Shugak wouldn't have looked out of place in a 1920s speakeasy. Except with more muscles. Whereas Van herself always looked like a bed where the corners of the sheets were always coming unstuck.

She looked at Johnny, who was looking at her with a smile in his eyes. He dropped a kiss on her nose and she settled back against him, oddly comforted. "Windmills?"

"Tell them the rest," Jim said. "They might see something we didn't."

So she did. There followed a thoughtful silence. "Maybe we

should have driven a stake through Erland Bannister's heart before we buried him," Johnny said.

Kate looked drained. "By his works shall ye know him."

"What happened to Jane?"

"Out on bail, waiting for trial."

"You could ask her—"

"No." Jane Wardwell was Johnny's egg donor and not a friend.

Jim was made of sterner stuff. "She was closest to him before he died. She knows where at least some of the bodies are buried."

Kate's phone rang from where it was plugged in on the counter. She didn't move. Johnny, whose phone had not left his person since she'd bought him his first one, gave a long-suffering sigh and got up and brought it to her.

"What'd you have to go and do that for? Now I'll have to answer it." She looked at the phone and Jim saw her expression change and the kids saw his and Mutt's head came up and she stared at Kate through narrowed eyes that were a lot less friendly than they had been when she'd walked in.

"No Caller ID," Kate said, holding it up so they could see.

The kids looked bewildered, until they saw Jim's expression, and then they looked frightened.

He tried to get his expression back into some kind of order. "Don't answer it."

"He'll keep calling."

"Block him."

"I can't. No number to block. And he might accidentally

say something useful." She closed her eyes for a brief moment and then opened them again. "Hello."

"Kate Shugak?" A young man, very polite, and sounding entirely too familiar.

"Speaking."

"Please hold for Mr. Smith."

A click, followed by the sound of that elderly voice with the distinctive whispery quality and Shakespearean cadence that set Kate's teeth on edge. "Thank you, Seth. Ms. Shugak, hello again."

"What happened to Jared?"

"His services were made available to the industry."

"What industry was that again, precisely?"

A chuckle. "How delightful to be speaking to you again, Ms. Shugak."

She said nothing.

"Hello?"

"You called me, Mr. Smith. I presume you have a message and you won't hang up until it's delivered."

"Well, I was hoping we could chat for a bit, as friends do. However, I remember your tendency to stick to business." He gave a delicate cough. "Very well, shall we come to it, then? You will remember our last conversation."

This call is merely to advise you that it would be best for your health, and the health of your loved ones, if you, shall we say, averted your eyes going forward. That is a very handsome dog you have, by the way.

Kate's eyes went to Mutt, who was on her feet, teeth bared,

a low, rumbling growl issuing menacingly from somewhere between her fourth and fifth ribs. "And must I remind you, Mr. Smith, of what I said?"

"I believe it was something on the order of banning my organization from your state. Quite amusing." His voice hardened. "I did tell you my organization has broad interests. Your current line of inquiry is… concerning. As are the questions generating from your colleagues."

Kate got up and went to the counter, fishing through the detritus there until she found a pad and pencil. She wrote quickly and held it up so Jim could read it. He looked at her. NOW, she mouthed. He took his phone and went out on the deck. "I'm afraid I'm at something of a loss, Mr. Smith. To which investigation are you referring? It wouldn't do me any good to cease my work altogether."

"Oh, my dear Ms. Shugak. I am disappointed in you."

"Did anyone ever tell you, Mr. Smith, that you sound exactly like President Snow at his most poisonous?" And Kate hung up and ran outside. "Do you have him?' He handed the phone to her. "Dan? Dan?"

A mumble. "'Sec, m'eating." A noisy swallow. "What?"

"Did you make any of those calls you said you would?"

Dan sounded bewildered. "Yeah, a couple, while I was making dinner. "What—"

"I need you to pack an overnight bag and get in your plane and come here."

Now he sounded befuddled. "To your house?"

"Yes, now, right now."

"Tonight?"

"Yes, dammit, tonight!"

"But your strip doesn't have any lights."

"There will be lights." She looked at Jim.

"Yeah, but—"

"Dan, just come. I don't think it's safe for you on the Step right now."

His voice changed then. "Oh Kate, come on. I'm out here at the ass end of nowhere and it's dark. Who could find me even if they wanted to?"

"Just come, okay? Safety in numbers."

A long pause while he thought it over. "I think you're nuts, but okay. I'm on my way. Will I at least get some of your bacon waffles for breakfast out of it?"

"If you're alive to eat them, sure. Here's Jim again." She handed him the phone. "Tell him about the beacon."

She went back inside and looked at Van and Johnny. "I need a favor."

They assembled at the strip. Jim flicked on the floods on the hangar, which illuminated the central portion of the runway. Van took her Subaru to one end, Johnny took Jim's pickup to the other, while Kate took hers to the corner opposite Jim's pickup. She ran back to the shop and got out the ATV, which started blessedly at a touch. Too bad she couldn't bring out the sled but the lack of snow would wreck the belt. She turned on the headlights and followed Mutt's tail back to the strip. She parked the ATV and killed the lights and the engine. She ran across the strip to the hangar, Mutt romping around first her and then Jim like this was the most fun she'd ever had in her life. "Have you heard him?"

"Relax." Jim was looking at an electronic gadget, the green glow of the screen reflecting up into his intent expression. "He conned the Park Service out of that new 172, remember? Newish, anyway. And it's only seventy-eighty miles." He looked up and smiled. "We got ourselves arranged pretty smartly. Give him a few more minutes."

As the words left his mouth they both heard it, the buzz of a small plane's engine. Definitely a Cessna. "Van! Johnny! Now!"

She ran back across the airstrip and started the ATV and hit the lights. She ran down to the end of the strip to her pickup, climbed in and started it and turned on the headlights. Across from her she saw the lights of Jim's pickup come on, and at the other end the lights of Van's Subaru came on. She got out and stood outside to look up. The aircraft was closer now and she could hear it over the sound of her truck. Then she saw his lights, the landing light on the leading edge of his left wing, the flashing beacon up top, the navigation light, and the strobes on the wingtips. He brought the aircraft around in a tight bank, pilot-side down. Checking out the accommodations. She took a quick look at the airstrip. The vehicle lights formed a patchwork line. He made one full circle, straightened up, waggled his wings, flew out a ways and turned back, lining up his approach. She could hear the blare of the stall signal briefly before he touched down light as a feather just past the black X Jim had put at both ends. The plane rolled to a halt right next to the hangar. Nice.

Kate turned off the pickup and ran to the ATV, which she drove across the strip. As she hopped off she heard Dan say, "Didn't use it. Didn't need to," and realized he was talking about the beacon. "I know the heading and I could see where to put 'er down fine. You guys definitely have a future in airport design." He heard her approaching and looked around. "Kate."

"Dan." There was a wealth of relief in her voice. "Good to see you."

"Yeah, again because it's been so long. Now what the hell, Shugak?"

"Let's put your ride in the hangar. The explanations will keep until we're back at the house."

"Can't wait to hear this one." But he didn't sound too cranky. Probably the promise of bacon waffles.

The 172 tucked in neatly beside the 206 and they closed the hangar doors and Jim killed the floods. Kate took the ATV and Jim and Dan the pickup. Van and Johnny were already at the house. "Dan can have the couch. Sheet, blankets, pillow?" These were produced.

Kate, whom overwhelming relief had made suddenly weary, looked around at the circle of expectant faces and quailed at the thought of a full explanation. She met Dan's eyes. "Short version. Someone called tonight and warned me to stop asking questions."

His ginger eyebrows went up. "Warned? Or threatened?" His tone indicated that his version of Kate Shugak did not succumb to mere warnings.

"I believe these threats to be credible. Hence the sending up of the storm flag."

Johnny bristled. "Questions about what? Who was that guy?"

Jim stepped forward. "Been a long day for everyone. Let's leave the night watchman on duty"—he nodded at Mutt, who gazed at him adoringly—"and get some sleep. Time enough to hash this over in the morning."

Dan looked meaningfully at Kate. "When there will be bacon waffles."

She was too tired to laugh. "When there will be bacon waffles."

Twenty-four

THURSDAY, SEPTEMBER 15
The Park, Kate's homestead

AND THERE WERE. ALONG WITH FRESH-brewed coffee—the good stuff special ordered online from Waimea Coffee Company—crisp bacon crumbled into the waffle batter, and maple syrup hot off the stove. Dan's eyes rolled up into his head at the first bite. "Omg. I might just have had an orgasm."

"Ew," Van said. Johnny and Jim were too busy stuffing their faces to say anything.

By dawn's early light the boogieman and his threats were reduced to manageable proportions. The table cleared, they sat around over mugs of coffee as Kate told the tale with interpolations and emendations from Jim and, surprisingly, Van.

"I didn't get the chance to tell you last night. I took a photo of that ball cap Mutt found and I showed it around the village, asking people if they'd seen it before and where and who was wearing it. Like that. I went up to the post office first, because everyone goes there." She shook her head. "Every question I asked, his answer was, 'Did you have a question about your mail?' I gave it up and went down the hill. Finally hit gold at the Riverside, where Nathan Balluta told me that the guys at the Roadhouse who started the fight that last night? He said all four of them were wearing the same cap."

Kate stood up and started to pace. "Who might be guys from the same group of people who have been threatening visitors to the Park, according to reports received by Dan. They come into the Roadhouse and get pounded by the Grosdidiers and the Ballutas. Bernie has the combined brotherhood throw them out of the bar. Must be Tuesday, right?"

"Sunday, actually."

"You know what I mean. Then, very early that next morning, someone mickied with the valve on the Roadhouse's propane tank and burns it down.

"Later that morning two planes collide in midair in the Park just north of Demetri's lodge. Yeah, yeah, I know." She waved off Dan, who had dared to open his mouth to speak. "He sold it; it's not his lodge anymore." She stopped in the middle of the floor, hands on her waist, frowning at the white socks on her feet.

"A week later Van here gets an anonymous tip that a tenth body had been discovered in the wreckage of the crash. Turns out a lot of reporters got that same tip, so someone with knowledge of the investigation was obviously trying to stir things up. No ID on the body, male." She shot a look at Jim.

"And somehow the Barr siblings discover and share with

us the information that this victim had been shot twice in the chest and once in the head."

Dan jumped. "What?"

"They still haven't broken that last bit in the regular press," Kate said. "There is enough weird shit going on here that some of it must be related. How, I can't even begin to imagine, not yet, but we fly out there, taking with us Mutt"—Mutt yipped—"aka the Nose. She does what she does and finds us"—Kate nodded at the table where the ball cap lay, still filthy inside its Ziploc—"that, and, not coincidentally, Paddy Murphy's body, also shot."

She turned and paced back to the window and here she stopped, staring unseeingly out at the glorious panorama spread out before her. "Van, in your new job you've got your nose stuck in everyone's business. Dan, in your job you're everywhere all the time. Jim, you spend half your time at the school and kids are notorious for being wired in through their belly buttons to all the gossip. What have you seen? What have you heard? What off thing has someone said to you?"

She spun around. "Okay, I'll start. The day of the Roadhouse fire and the midair I drove in to Niniltna to check the mail. Our new postmaster, who has not said one word to me since he arrived, asks me if I know who Demetri sold his lodge to. No, I say. And then he tells me they're…" She searched her memory for the exact wording. "He said the guys who bought Demetri's lodge, we didn't want them around. He said they weren't good people and that they'd bring trouble with them."

"A tad vague," Jim said.

"That was it?" Dan was skeptical.

"That was it. He issued his proclamation and then closed the door in my face."

"Doing his best impression of the Oracle at Delphi," Van said. "Only, you know, a guy."

"And nobody could figure out what the hell she was saying, either. At the time I shrugged it off. Maybe Jackson knows the new owner from a previous life, and he's got a beef with him. It happens."

"I checked on the Department of Lands website after you left yesterday," Dan said, "and guess what? The ownership of the lodge is now listed as private."

"You can do that?"

Jim nodded. "You can take your home address off your driver's license now, too."

"It's because of doxxing." They looked at Van. "On social media. Somebody opens an account on TikTok or Twitter, and they list their phone number and…" She waved a hand. "I don't know, the exact shade of their Nice'n Easy hair dye."

Kate thought of all the times Kurt had found the home address of a person of interest right there on their own Facebook page.

Van shrugged. "It's the first place people look when they're mad at you—"

"Or are just plain nuts." This from Johnny.

"—and next thing you know they're outside your house, and some of them bring guns." Van shrugged again, a little apologetically this time. "Doxxing."

"I'm so glad I live in the Park," Kate said with feeling.

"Where everyone's address is a post office box."

"Not to mention which, everyone in the Park is armed to the teeth," Dan said.

Jim snorted. "Make that everyone in Alaska. On the job whenever I had to fly Ravn to a crime scene I knew at least half the other passengers were packing."

"Much as your life is worth to knock on the wrong door hereabouts."

"Why cops hate responding to DVs."

They brooded collectively about that for a moment.

"However. To answer your question." Dan breathed on his fingernails and buffed them against his shirt. "I called in a favor from a friend in the Lands Department in Juneau last night." He fished out a piece of paper torn from a lined yellow tablet. "She says 'private' in this instance stands for BB LLC."

"Dan, you star!"

"Yeah, well. Read it and weep." He tossed the piece of paper on the table. "The company doesn't have a website and then you called, so I didn't get any further than that."

Jim squinted at Dan's awful scrawl. "A PO box number?"

"Unfortunately, this one's in Midland, Texas."

Van and Johnny were already busy on their phones. "No mention in the state's Chamber of Commerce in Texas or Alaska."

"Or the Better Business Bureau. And nothing on LinkedIn." Van looked up. "Who are these guys?"

"Bilbo Baggins LLC?"

"Béla Bartók LLC?"

"Big Brother LLC?"

"Big Boobs LLC?" Dan quailed beneath the glare from both women. "Sorry."

"What else?"

"Well." Dan hesitated. "There's Howie and Willard and their goddam drone."

"What's weird about that? It's Howie, the little weasel, business as usual."

"Okay, yeah, but hunting with a drone is a first for them."

"Did—who did you say it was—catch them at it? Like, an on the record catch? Drone in the air, rifle fire, moose on the ground?"

"Tiffany. And she got video on her phone of Howie shooting the moose and Willard bringing the drone back down."

Kate thought about it. "Maybe not weird, but different. Where were they?"

"That's what makes it weird. They had four-wheeled out to a small lake."

Kate looked impatient. "You told us that already. What's weird about that?"

"It's in the same general area as Paddy Murphy's claim."

Kate looked at Jim. "Did you keep that cartridge that Van found?"

He fished it out of his pocket and handed it to Dan.

Dan looked at it. "Winchester .30-06 Springfield. Who else in the Park has one of these, I wonder."

"Who doesn't?" Kate nodded at the kitchen. "There's a box of them in the junk drawer."

Dan looked disgusted. "And Howie, that little weasel, is just the kind of careless little fucker to drop something and not be bothered to pick it back up again."

Kate got out the *Alaska Atlas & Gazetteer*. "Where's that lake again?"

Dan found the page and pointed.

"That's practically in Canada."

Dan nodded. "I flew out there and didn't see anyone."

"In the 172?" Jim said. "With the NPS decal on the side?"

Dan rolled his eyes. "Yeah, yeah, I get it, the Sign of the Fed, everybody run for it."

Kate's forefinger traced a circle connecting the marks. Demetri's lodge. The lake was to the north and east, where Busted Flat Peak was almost on the Canadian border. Paddy Murphy's property was to the north of Busted Flat Peak and slightly west. She found a pencil and circled all the marks and then put her thumb against the scale and held it first between the lodge and the lake and then between the lodge and the claim. Way too close to ignore.

Dan shook his head. "What the hell is going on down there?"

"Whatever it is, they've been getting away with it because nobody noticed."

"A bunch of people noticed," Dan said, holding up the folder he'd brought with him that held the complaints he'd received.

They thought about that for a while. "Okay, Van. You and George and the DOJ."

"What?" Johnny.

"What?" Dan.

Van gave Johnny an apologetic look. "I was at the Roadhouse. I heard about the midair and I went back into town and hitched a ride with George to take a look at the crash site. So off we go and first we fly over Murphy's airstrip and there's an unmarked Caravan with a bunch of guys standing around dressed like Will Smith and Tommy Lee Jones. We keep going and we find the crash site." She swallowed hard and Johnny put his arm around her shoulders. "It's just as horrible as you can imagine. And then we come back. The Caravan was gone by then, but I got the tail number on the first pass and I looked it up when we got back. It's registered to the Department of Justice."

There was a moment of startled silence. "Okay, this will end well," Johnny said.

Kate looked at Jim.

He sighed. "The carpentry class got a temp job this summer. The pay was sweet. Came with bunks and burgers and a big screen TV with *Call of Duty* and *Grand Theft Auto* and joysticks for everybody to play during their off hours. Of which there were not many, as I understand it, because this was a rush job, with the promise of a bonus if they finished early and passed the inspection."

"What were they building?"

"A church."

"Where?"

"That's what's weird. They couldn't say. They had to sign a

non-disclosure agreement. They couldn't say who hired them and they couldn't say where they built the church."

"What denomination?"

"They weren't told."

"That makes no sense," Johnny said. "The whole idea of a church is to seduce as many people into the cult as possible. Gotta tell the world what you're doing so they'll beat a path to your door."

Kate glanced at him. Johnny's grandparents had been evangelical Christians. It was one of the reasons he'd hitchhiked from Arizona to Alaska to move in with her. He might be just a tad prejudiced against organized religion on that account.

"They did let a couple of things slip in conversation," Jim said. "They had to fly there and back. No road in. A Navajo. Pretty slick, Pavel said. Felt like their own private plane. And then the rest of them shut him up before he gave anything else away."

"What else?"

"Their last day a pastor flew in on the plane they were leaving on, the Navajo again. The church had an inaugural service and the boys were invited to attend."

Johnny made a face. "Trying to convert 'em."

"Maybe. They weren't successful."

"Why not?"

Jim looked a little conscious. "I was eavesdropping. They were in the shop and I was in the hall, so I didn't get all of it. What I did hear sounded a little nutty."

"Like?"

"Like abortion is murder and homosexuality is a crime."

Johnny snorted. "That's what passes for mainstream evangelical Christianity today."

"Yeah, but there was more. Pedophilia and bestiality are about to become legal in the US, and global warming is God's judgement on a sinful world, and the end times are coming and we all have to ready ourselves for Armageddon and the Rapture."

"And only the people in that church are getting into heaven," Johnny said.

"I guess."

Dan shook his head. "I only wish I could say I'd never heard anything crazier than that."

Kate was watching Jim. "Why the NDAs?"

Dan raised his eyebrows. "Someone's pretty determined to maintain their privacy, be my guess."

"There is something going on that they don't want to be generally known," Van said.

"Whoever they are," Johnny said.

Foreigner's "Urgent" began playing somewhere and Kate found her phone. "Kurt, I was just going to—" She stood up straight. "What?" She sounded very quiet and preternaturally calm, but Mutt materialized at her side, never a good sign. "Is anyone hurt? You? Agrifina?" She closed her eyes and exhaled. "Good. What's the damage?"

She listened, her face slowly creasing into a frown. "All right. Don't go home, Kurt. I'm not joking. Get Agrifina and go somewhere safe. Is there somewhere safe you can go? Good. No," she said sharply. "Don't tell me and especially don't tell me over the phone. Do you need money? All right. Find somewhere to hole up and don't tell anyone where you are."

Jim could hear Kurt's voice. "Not even you?"

"Especially not me. In fact, buy a couple of burner phones and text—no, email me the new numbers as you use them. We still have the enhanced encryption on our Gmail accounts, right? Good. What's Tyler's phone number du jour?" She scrabbled for pen and paper and scribbled the number down. "He knows who I am, right? He'll take my call? Good. All right, go, now. Don't screw around, Kurt. Remember Mr. Smith? He called." She winced and held the phone away from her ear. "Never mind that, get moving. Now."

She hung up and looked at them. "Someone started a fire at Pletnikof Investigations."

"How?"

"A small explosive device placed on or near Kurt's laptop."

"He left it at the office? Doesn't sound like him."

"He and Ms. Fancyboy were out to dinner. He planned on going back afterward to catch up on this and that. Probably why the whole building didn't burn down."

Her phone dinged. She called back. "Tyler? Kate Shugak here. Kurt put you in the know? Good. First, anything you can on an organization with the name 'J649.' Next, anything at all on BB LLC." She paused. "Tyler, no-way no-how can that be traced back to him, or Pletnikof Investigations, or me." Again she had to hold the phone away from her ear for a moment.

"Yes, I know, you are the best. Remember Mr. Smith? He's involved. I don't know. I don't know. I don't know. No, I don't know much, that's why I need you." She hung up and stood for a moment, unmoving.

Jim watched her. He'd seen that vacant look before. "Kate?"

Something snapped into place behind her blank expression and she looked up. "Cisco Barre."

He gaped at her.

"The guy with the mom and all the towhead kids."

"Uh. Yeah."

Dan snorted, Van rolled her eyes, and Johnny snickered.

Kate looked impatient. "In the two fancy RVs? In Niniltna, the first of July?"

Realization dawned. "Oh. I remember now."

"You remember what he said?"

Jim couldn't remember much beyond Barre behaving as if Kate Shugak's existence was unworthy of acknowledgement. He felt a return of the slow burn he had felt that day. Yeah, he remembered that pretty well. "What, specifically?"

"He said they'd just bought a property in the area and were having it renovated, and in the meantime they were getting to know the neighborhood."

He made an effort. "Okay?"

"But he was familiar enough already with the neighborhood to know about the Alaskan Barrs."

Something clicked, finally. "Barre with an e."

"Exactly."

"BB LLC," he said. "Barre Something LLC."

She spread her hands. "Maybe Cisco has a brother. Barre Brothers LLC."

Dan still thought Big Boobs LLC was a better name, but he thought so silently.

"Kate?" Van looked hesitant. "You said anything weird."

"I did. What you got?"

"I forgot until this minute. What Dan said about Howie and Willard's drone reminded me."

"And?"

"When we went to look at the crash site? George followed the river down to, I don't know, about Ruthe's, I guess, before we cut east. On the way we overflew a boat, a big wooden skiff with a big-ass kicker, one guy in it. He was flying a drone and we nearly ran into it."

Johnny sat up. "You never said."

"Kinda overshadowed by subsequent events. Anyway, George was about as pissed off as I've ever seen him. He brought the Cub right down on the deck and buzzed the guy. The guy was trying to catch hold of the drone but he fell overboard and George's prop wash knocked the drone in after him."

"And then?"

Van shrugged. "We headed east. George was pretty steamed. Don't think he cared much if the guy drowned or not."

"Didn't call it in?"

Van shook her head.

"Okay by me," Johnny said, color retuning to his face.

Van smiled at him and squeezed his hand.

"Who was the guy in the boat?"

Van fidgeted. "Well…"

"Spit it out."

"He'd spent the day before in Niniltna. He's a *National Geographic* photographer and he's doing a Kanuyaq River trip from source to mouth. I interviewed him for the paper." She nodded at Kate's phone. "Go to the app."

Kate looked guilty.

Van looked exasperated. "Haven't you downloaded it yet? Give me that!" She snatched the phone out of Kate's hand and tapped on the screen. "There," she said, shoving it back, and looked at the rest of them meaningfully. Dan and Jim were already following the path of least resistance and were looking as industrious as possible over their screens. Johnny was watching them with a smirk.

Van pointed at the screen. "Right there, that little square."

Kate opened Google instead, entering something into the search box. She tapped again and stared at the result for a long moment before looking up. "The range, even on the highest end commercial drone, is only two to four miles."

Jim met her eyes and saw the same relief there he knew she saw in his own. "Good to know."

Dan was irritated. "Why? Why is that good to know?"

Jim leaned forward again and tapped the atlas. "Because the lake, where Willard flew his drone, is eight to ten miles north of the crash site."

Realization dawned. "So not near enough to have caused the midair."

"Exactly."

Kate was staring into space, phone forgotten in her hands. "Kate."

Jim's deep voice penetrated the fog and she looked around to meet his eyes. "I've been looking at two aircraft in the air and trying to figure out how they ran into each other over such a very large air space. Especially in September, after the season's over."

"And?"

"And I should have been trying to find out who else might have been in the air with them." She paused. "Or what." She took a deep breath. "Okay, this is what we are going to do." She pointed at Jim. "You are going to take them"—she pointed at Johnny and Van—"to Fairbanks."

"What!"

"Like hell!"

Kate raised her voice. "I have just had a credible threat against me and mine. You're mine. You have to—"

"Who is this Mr. Smith?" Van looked from Kate to Jim. "And why are you so scared of him?"

The question stopped Kate in her tracks. Her mouth opened and closed and nothing came out. She looked at Jim, who shrugged and spread his hands. She looked at the ceiling and closed her eyes. "Okay."

She opened her eyes and looked at Johnny and Van. "I don't know who the guy is. You remember when those two yahoos kidnapped Martin last year? Because it turns out he's heir to the Kanuyaq Mine and their boss wanted it? Mr. Smith worked for their boss, Erland Bannister was involved, and the upshot is that they sent someone to Anchorage to shoot up the townhouse while I was there."

"What!"

"What the hell, Kate! You never told us about that!"

"He called and we had quite the nice chat. He threatened me, I told him to get the hell out of Alaska and stay out, he threatened Mutt, and we hung up. I didn't hear from him again until last night."

"He threatened you?" Johnny was horrified.

"He threatened Mutt?" Dan was horrified.

Mutt barked, which brought the meeting back to order.

Into the silence Kate said, "He's connected, through a law firm in Chicago. And Erland Bannister was involved there, too."

"Of course he was. Because Erland Bannister."

"These people play for keeps, Johnny. Which is why I want you somewhere safe. You're my hostages to fortune. I can't do what I need to do while I'm worried about you."

"Now just hold on there." Johnny rose to his feet, standing as tall as his father had. He looked... formidable. When had that happened?

His face was flushed. "I understand that it's hard for parents to accept that their children have grown up." He spaced the words out deliberately, as if making sure she understood each of them. "But I am no longer a child, I can look after myself, and I make my own decisions."

Van stepped to his side and slipped her hand into his.

The expression on her face was identical to Johnny's, and as implacable. "As do I."

Kate felt unaccustomed tears prick her eyes and willed them back with a fierce effort. When Johnny referred to her as his parent it always felt as if he had handed her a Nobel Prize. Jim was wearing his best "I have no opinion in these matters" face but Dan was nodding his head in agreement.

"This is our home, we're staying, and we're helping however we can. You of all people should know we can because you taught us how."

"Besides," Van said, "I'm a reporter and a publisher and this is a breaking story. I'm not going anywhere."

The mutual declaration of independence momentarily silenced the room.

"Okay," Jim said when he thought the friendly fire had died down enough for him to emerge from cover. "Next plan."

"You're right." Kate closed her eyes and gave a small laugh that broke in the middle. "I'm sorry. Past time for me to be making decisions for you."

Johnny and Van, still stiff with the outraged dignity of youth, were by no means ready to forgive and forget.

"Woof!"

Everyone jumped, and it broke the spell. "Another country heard from," Jim said. There was nervous laughter. "What's next, Kate?"

"You think we could find one or two of your carpentry students in the dorm?"

He shrugged. "Most of them, probably. This semester's just getting started. And after that?"

Kate opened the contacts on her phone and scrolled down until she found what she was looking for. She tapped the number and held the phone to her ear. Someone answered on the first ring. "Special Agent James G. Mason, please." She listened. "I see. No, no message." She hung up and looked at Van. "If Special Agent Mason is Airbnbing it somewhere in the Park, do you think you can find him?"

Van stuttered a little. "I—ah—I guess so. Probably."

"And after that?" Jim said, watching Kate.

"After that…" Kate hesitated. "After that, we'll see."

Twenty-five

THURSDAY, SEPTEMBER 15
Niniltna

JIM, KATE, VAN, AND JOHNNY FLEW INTO Niniltna in the Stationair. Dan's blood was up and he was unwilling to give up the hunt so he followed in the 172.

The Herbie Topkok Polytechnic Academy occupied a large, two-story building on the edge of the Kanuyaq. Van disappeared into her office, followed by Johnny, while Jim led the way to the carpentry shop, where it was freezing because all the windows were open to disperse the sawdust hanging in the air. Everyone sneezed multiple times anyway. When the tears cleared from Kate's eyes she saw that the room had been recently studded and Sheetrocked. No paint had been wasted on it. The ceiling was a solid phalanx of LED shop lights, rendering the room into the place where shadows go to die. The walls were lined with tool kits, the center of the floor was taken up with work tables interspersed with saws and sanders and drills and grinders, and every six feet the floor had been plumbed with brass electrical outlets.

Jim saw Kate looking at the outlets. "Can't never have enough power, nope."

Kate, who had lived half her life without electricity, knew better than a California boy like him how true that was. "Pretty orderly for a shop."

He tried to hide his pleasure at her approval and she repressed a smile. He'd been a trooper for more than twenty years. He was more used to drunks vomiting the pint of R&R they'd just flatfooted down the front of his uniform than he was at receiving compliments and he was still learning how to accept one.

One burly young man wearing goggles was running a two-by-four through a sander. A slight young woman was measuring and marking a slab of three-quarter-inch pine board for cutting. Both looked up at their entrance. The man switched off the sander and pushed his goggles up. The woman said, "Hey, Jim."

"Hey, Sharon. What are you working on?"

"Shelving for the new dorm rooms."

"Good job. Pavel, got a sec?"

The man nodded and doffed his goggles.

"Pavel, Dan O'Brian, chief ranger of the Park, Kate Shugak."

Pavel nodded at Dan, took a longer look at Kate. He was thick through the shoulders and chest, with long arms, a physique perfected by generations of pulling nets from the Kuskokwim River. His eyes were a smoky topaz and set on high, flat cheekbones clothed in skin like brown velvet. His thick black hair stood up all over his head as if he'd cut it himself without looking in the mirror. Maybe it grew that way naturally, but she doubted it.

He looked familiar. "Where are you from?"

He took his time answering, which all by itself told her he was Alaska Bush born and raised. "Bering for high school. Napaskiak before."

She avoided looking him in the eye. "Your last name Chevak?"

"Yeah."

She risked a brief glance at his face. "Any relation to Stephanie?"

His expression didn't change, exactly, but somehow, something inside himself got the signal to become infinitesimally less aloof. "My cousin."

Kate allowed the corners of her mouth to indent in the merest hint of a smile. "She's a friend."

"She said."

Jim, who had kept quiet in the face of this delicate exploration of Alaska Native connections, cleared his throat in a suggestive manner. "Pavel, you were one of the guys who built the church, right?"

And Pavel's face promptly closed right back up again. After a moment, he gave a wary nod.

"I wonder…" Jim produced the Ziploc and flipped it so that Pavel could see the logo on the ball cap inside. "Was anyone wearing a cap like this where you were building that church?"

Pavel held out a hand and Jim gave him the bag. The young man's hands were large-knuckled and covered with scars and looked ready-made for swinging a hammer, and yet there was a grace and surety to the way he turned the bag in his hands and then held it up to the light. He studied the logo for several moments, his expression giving nothing away.

He handed it back to Jim. "Not caps."

Jim looked disappointed. "Well, it was worth a try. Thanks—"

"Not caps," Kate said, addressing the third button of Pavel's shirt. "Maybe a sweatshirt with the same logo?"

Jim held his breath.

"Not a sweatshirt," Pavel said. "The guy who supervised us wore a jacket. Dark green. Like the old Alaska tuxedos. With that logo. And..." From the corner of her eye Kate saw him make a gesture over his left breast. "Like in the service."

"Insignia?" Kate said.

"With rank?" At Pavel's look Jim said, "Private? Sergeant?"

"Captain."

"Did you get paychecks?"

"Cash."

"How did you get all your tools and supplies out there?"

"Everything was out there already, the two-by-fours, the T1-11, the Sheetrock, the PVC, the cable, nails, screws, everything. Including the tools. And they were all new. Stanley."

Whoever hired Herbie's apprentice carpenters wasn't broke. "How did they get all that stuff out there?"

"They had a Herc that brought in supplies every week." He turned back to his task.

Dan gave a low, admiring whistle.

"Pavel?"

He didn't answer and he didn't turn around, all his attention focused on the wood and the sander.

"That's enough." Sharon frowned at them. "I don't think Pavel should say anymore. They had us sign some paper that said we wouldn't and they gave us a shit ton of money to make sure we wouldn't."

The clinic was on the other end of the village, a ten-minute walk. Fishing season was over and hunting season hadn't been open long enough for friendly fire casualties to start coming in, so they didn't have to wait on patients being treated. Three of the four Grosdidiers were there, Mark, Luke, and Peter. Fortuitous, because those were the three who had been at the Roadhouse the night before it burned down. Mutt bounced forward to exchange greetings and, as usual, tribute in the form of beef jerky was paid. "You are a shameless panhandler," Kate said.

Mutt stayed where she was. Peter had found just the right spot between her ears.

Jim pulled out the ball cap. "Any of you ever seen this logo before?"

They passed it around. Mark shrugged, Peter spread his hands, but Luke frowned.

"What?" Kate said.

"I don't—oh yeah. The assholes at the Roadhouse were wearing these. Van was showing this around, wasn't she?"

"Tell us about the fight."

Peter shrugged. "There were these four assholes the size of André the Giant, drinking at the bar, playing grab ass with Allie and Chloe or trying to because Allie and Chloe weren't having any. The Balluta boys were in, blowing their settlement—"

"All three of them? Not Albert, surely."

"No, Dulcey has Albert tied to her tail for good and all. He doesn't get out much anymore." He sighed. "Lucky bastard. No, this was just Boris and Nathan, and you know how the two of them are always on the lookout for new talent. Well." He looked a little conscious, and so did Mark and Luke. Matt might be taken but it wasn't as if the younger Grosdidier brothers didn't spend most of their off hours chasing women themselves. The ratio of men to women in the Park was ten to one the last time Kate checked, and Allie and Chloe were undoubtedly part of the reason why the three younger Grosdidiers were at the Roadhouse themselves that evening.

"Yeah," Kate said. "Moving on."

"So Boris and Nathan were flirting with Allie and Chloe, well, mostly Allie, and okay, we might have been trying to cut in on their action some, and yeah, maybe we were doing a little trash talking."

"Sounds like Tuesday." Jim, deadpan.

Luke looked from him to Kate. "Easy for you to say."

Dan laughed and Kate rolled her eyes and Jim grinned. "Fair enough."

"But then these four guys, weirdly buff, kinda like the dad on *The Incredibles*, who like I say were trying to make a little of their own time with the girls, decided to step in."

"The girls ask for help?"

"With Boris and Nathan? Are you kidding me?"

"So that would be a no."

"Besides, everyone knows about that shotgun Bernie has behind the bar. The business end of that tends to calm everyone right the fuck down." This from Mark.

"Everybody local."

They all looked at Peter. "Everybody local knows about the shotgun, and the baseball bat. These guys, not so much."

"Yeah, but it's Alaska. They're in Alaska. In the Park." Peter shook his head.

"Suicide by Alaska," Kate said. "Wouldn't be the first time."

Luke sort of laughed and sort of sighed. "So anyway, one of them gets up and comes over and says to Allie, 'This darkie bothering you, darling?'" He saw Kate's expression and held up a hand. "I swear to god, verbatim that's what he said. And then she said not at all, and then he said maybe she should stick with her own kind.

"So as you might expect that didn't go over well, and then the guy says 'Why don't you all go back to where you came from?' and Boris, who as you know is not the sharpest tool in the box says, 'You mean Niniltna?'"

"Or maybe he was being a smartass," Peter said. "With Boris you never know."

"So they got into it, and then his buddies come over to lend their aid, and Nathan leaped to his brother's defense, and..." Luke shrugged.

"And you just had to jump in."

Luke grinned. So did Peter, and so did Mark. The Grosdidier brothers were a year each apart in age and similar in dark good looks and quick tempers. They had been a byword for bad behavior around the Park from puberty on but Kate had been inclined to believe that there had never been any malice in it. So had Emaa, who had collared the four and sent them off to the tenth ranked school in the nation to become physician assistants on the Niniltna Native Association's dime, with the proviso that they return to the Park upon graduation to offer their services to their own. Word had filtered back from Oregon that Portland would never be the same, but four diplomas from the Oregon Health and Sciences University were framed and hung from the wall in an eye-level row where no one who walked into the Grosdidier Clinic could miss them. A doctor in Ahtna supervised operations over telemedicine but for the most part they were left on their own. In one fell stroke Emaa had changed the Park ne'er-do-wells into four men ready, willing, and able to set bones, prevent disease, and save the lives of Park rats and Park visitors and anyone else who wandered into their orbit.

But the devil riding their shoulders was not to be discouraged and they still liked to mix it up if they could find a good reason. Four strangers picking on two Park rats for no reason other than sheer meanness would have appeared like a gift from heaven.

And they were now qualified to patch each other up afterward. Win-win.

"It wasn't much of a fight." Peter looked at the backs of his hands.

"Until one of the assholes pulled a gun."

"What kind of gun?" Jim.

"Nine mil automatic, looked like. Back holster."

No one was surprised or even upset. As Jim had previously pointed out, in Alaska you could carry concealed anywhere, including on any regional airline. Carrying concealed into a bar wasn't a stretch.

"What happened?"

Peter laughed. "Bernie pulled out his shotgun and racked one in. At that distance he could have taken down all four of them with one round and they knew it."

"And after that we, ah, escorted them from the premises. They weren't what you might call aerodynamic."

"And after that Bernie gave us free beer," Luke said. "Good times."

Next to him Jim felt Kate vibrate like a tuning fork. "Where did they go when they, ah, left the premises?"

Peter shrugged. "Wasn't paying attention."

Mark cocked his head. "I heard some ATVs start up outside. Might have been theirs."

"I heard that, too," Luke said. "Seemed like they moved off to the east."

"Toward the river?"

"Yeah."

The four of them met up with Van and Johnny in front of the Riverside Cafe and by mutual assent they moved the consult out of the chill wind inside to the last booth in the corner.

"The Grosdidiers confirm the Ballutas' story about the cap," Jim said. "All four of the enemy were wearing them."

"Plus they had a gun," Kate said.

Johnny raised an eyebrow. "Who hasn't?"

"They pulled theirs."

"And?"

"And Bernie pulled his and his was bigger and they allowed themselves to be escorted from the building."

"I'll bet."

Conversation paused while Laurel brought their coffee drinks and an order of fries for Johnny, who applied half the salt shaker and dug in. She winked at him and he watched her walk away mid-chew until Van elbowed him in the side.

"Anything?" Kate said.

Van gave Johnny a last glare and turned back to business. "I found Special Agent Mason. He's Airbnbing Alice Kasak's cabin. Jo Dunaway is with him. Alice said they told her they were on vacation."

"Here in the Park."

Van looked at Johnny. "I'm sure I just said that."

"You did." He looked at Kate. "What?"

It was mid-September, well after Labor Day. All the visitors had gone home, bouncing from pothole to pothole in their SUVs and RVs, coolers full of silvers, covered with the bug bites of summer. Alice Kasak's cabin was a very nice one-bedroom with a wood stove and picture windows overlooking the river. It was a couple of doors down from Old Sam's cabin, which was in the process of being turned into a museum slash library. Both were within easy walking distance of everything else in Niniltna.

Including the airstrip. "Van, did you hear talk of anyone else still hanging around the Park?"

Van looked puzzled. "You mean other than hunters?"

"Dan?"

"'Tis the season, Kate," Dan said.

She held up a hand. "I know, I just—a large group of people who might not be hunters?"

Van looked mystified. "No, I—"

Kate's phone dinged at her. "Tyler." She tapped the text icon, read, and tapped again. She took so long about it that everyone else began to get restless. Finally she looked up, and at her expression Johnny dropped the fry he'd been about to put in his mouth. "What? What's wrong, Kate?" He made a move like he wanted to get up and come around to her side of the table. "Kate?"

Mutt's head popped up over the edge of the table, beneath which she had been gnawing on the pork chop bone that had been delivered with the fries.

"Where's the cap?"

"What?"

Her face lacked all expression, mobile mouth still, eyes blank and drained of life. "Where's the cap, Jim?" Her voice was thin.

He fumbled it out on the table and she picked it up and pointed at the logo. "J649. January sixth."

It took them all a minute or two to catch up. Van paled. "As in January sixth, 2020?"

Kate nodded.

"J6ers," Johnny said. "Oh hell no."

"Fuck." Jim said it from the heart.

"What's the 49?" Van said.

Kate swallowed. "Alaska, the forty-ninth state. The Arizona chapter is J648."

A numb silence. Van said dismally, "I suppose Hawaii's J650?"

"Hawaii doesn't have a chapter." Still that thin, reedy voice.

"Why didn't you Google it?" Johnny said. "I mean, geez, Kate, if I've—"

"I did. They don't show up on the first page and I never look further." She managed a smile although it betokened the very last thing from humor any of them could imagine. "I'll try to remember that from now on."

Dan was the last to catch on and when he did he lost all color in his face, so that his freckles stood out like rust spots. When he got his breath back he said, choosing his words very carefully, "Are you telling me we have a white supremacist group in the Park?"

Kate turned her phone toward them. "They even have their own page on the Southern Poverty Law Center website."

Van was already busy on her phone. "They're mentioned on the FBI website, too."

They sat in stunned silence. Finally Dan said, almost pleadingly, "One ball cap does not a white supremacist group make."

Kate spoke gently, almost pityingly. "A truck full of guys who might have been wearing caps just like this one run Bobby off the road north of my homestead. Then we find out that you have been fielding complaints from people who have been accosted on trails in the Park by men who sound suspiciously paramilitary, telling the hikers they're on private property.

"Then there's a fight in the Roadhouse featuring four guys wearing these same caps and they get their tails well and truly waxed by a bunch of guys who aren't even close to the right color. The next morning the Roadhouse burns down. Cause and effect? Sure feels like it.

"Then the midair, later we find with a spare body under the wreckage, shot gangland style. Then Paddy Murphy murdered on his own claim, right after he sold it to Frank Barr Senior."

"You think they're BB LLC?"

"I don't know how they're associated with the J649ers but it's ideal for their purposes. Isolated on a large tract of land, way off the road, all the room in the world to build and train."

"Train for what?"

This, too, they already knew but Kate said it anyway. "Armageddon. The next January sixth. The next migrant caravan from Honduras. Take your pick."

They digested this. Van said, "Why show their hand by running Bobby off the road and picking fights at the Roadhouse and then burning it down? Wouldn't it draw the wrong kind of attention? It sure as hell drew ours."

Kate could feel Jim's eyes on her. "What else? What else, Kate?"

She slid out of the booth. "Let's go see if Mason and Dunaway are receiving visitors."

"Let's just hope they haven't slipped into something more comfortable yet," Dan said in a mutter, and followed her.

"Ew," Van said, and she and Johnny left.

Jim sat where he was for a long moment, staring at Mutt, who was staring back at him and clearly wondering why they had yet to join the parade. "I hate it when she does that," he said.

"Wuff."

"She doesn't have to prove she's smarter than the rest of us put together. We already know it."

"Wuff."

He sighed. "Okay. Let's go."

"Wuff."

The door of Alice Kasak's cabin opened at the first knock, almost as if it had been expected. FBI Special Agent James G. Mason stood there. He still had his shoes on. He looked at the crowd of five—six if you included the dog and only a fool wouldn't—assembled on the doorstep. "A full-on Park rat delegation. To what do I owe the, ah, honor?"

Kate didn't look friendly. "What is BB LLC?"

She didn't sound it, either.

Twenty-six

THURSDAY, SEPTEMBER, 15
Niniltna

ALICE HAD STRATEGICALLY PLACED A PICNIC table between the cabin and the edge of the river bank, on an inviting patch of mowed weeds next to a brick grill charred with use. There was enough room for everyone at the table, including Jo Dunaway, who had her phone out and the voice memo app running. Kate was about to reach for it when Mason removed it gently from her hand. He turned the app off and slid it into his shirt pocket. Jo Dunaway, a zaftig, forty-ish woman with a riot of short blonde curls going silver, pretended to pout but didn't protest. Her memory, honed by twenty years of rooting out where all the bodies were buried in Alaska for the *Anchorage News* was probably up to the task of memorizing everything that was said on its own. Mason had to know that and still he allowed her to witness the conversation. Interesting, Kate thought. "I called your office."

"Ah." The 'ah' was a verbal tic, deployed deliberately in conversation as emphasis or as a delaying tactic while Mason thought over what he wanted to say next. He could also shade it with a dozen different meanings. This time it clearly invited further comment.

Kate obliged. "You've been promoted. Special Agent in Charge. Grand Pooh-Bah and Lord High Everything Else over the entire state. Congratulations."

"Thank you. And you are?" Mason said to Dan.

"Dan O'Brian, chief ranger of this park."

"Ah. And you are Van, and you're Johnny. We have, ah, met before."

"I'm also the owner and proprietor of *Kanuyaq Currents*, a weekly newspaper here in Niniltna."

"The *Kanuyaq Currents*, ah, yes. I'm afraid I'm unfamiliar."

Van tried hard not to blush. "We're new."

Mason didn't offer up a patronizing smile, a point in his favor. "Kate. Jim."

"Mason. BB LLC. Who or what are they?"

"BB, ah, LLC, yes." Mason fussed with the zipper of his vest. "May I ask how, ah, they have come to your attention?"

"They bought Demetri's lodge."

"Ah yes, Demetri, ah, Totemoff. I heard he had passed. I'm sorry for your loss."

"He wasn't our only loss, but thanks. BB LLC?"

Jim had always admired Kate's sledgehammer interrogative technique.

To his credit Mason didn't look noticeably flattened. He cast a fleeting glance at Dunaway, who wasn't giving anything away, which probably meant that she hadn't accompanied

Mason to the Park solely for recreational purposes. "Yes. Ah. Well." He folded his hands on the table in front of him and assumed the expression of a professor before a class filled with promising but heretofore wholly uninformed students. "BB LLC is the construct of a pair of twin brothers, Cisco and Ranger Barre, originally from Midland, Texas."

At this Jim stirred. Kate looked at him but he shook his head.

"Their father was a roughneck on oil rigs, their mother a homemaker. They were not prosperous, at one time making their home in a chicken coop donated for the purpose by a neighbor. The mother was and is a devout evangelical Christian and she raised the boys in that faith. Later, when her sons achieved financial success, she veered off the moderate rails of the Southern Baptist Church to found a church of her own, the One True God Church of Yahweh. She took the Old Testament as its guide. Homosexuals are an abomination, gay marriage is a sin, abortion is murder, et, ah, cetera."

"They eat bacon?" This from Dan.

Mason looked at him. Dan's grin faded. "They worship the thirteenth tribe, the lost tribe of Israel, and profess to be their direct descendants. All others are unclean, in particular those people who do not look like them."

Jim could hardly bear to look at Kate. The thought that people like that had moved into her own backyard and befouled it to the point of murder was affecting her at some level between fury and despair and it was there for anyone with eyes to see.

"The boys, meanwhile, were busy making their fortune in

petroleum, first in wildcatting and then in fracking, and they did well enough that they were able to sell their business ten years after they founded it for four billion dollars."

"Holy shit." Dan again. "Four billion? In ten years? We're all in the wrong business."

"They were evidently more gifted in the area of profit and loss statements than was their father. One is, ah, given to understand that the time spent in the chicken coop was motivational." At times Mason sounded like the elderly senior partner in a family law firm. Not unlike Mr. Smith, in fact. "They have since been investing in land and in conservative politics. They founded an online magazine called *The Ark* with the help of a former White House director of the Office of Public Relations and it has achieved a considerable conservative subscriber base in five years.

"In the twelve years since Citizens United, the brothers have donated more than $100 million to right-wing candidates whose views are so radical they have lost their primaries seventy percent of the time. It is said they consider it money well spent, if only to alert the larger population to the danger of pedophilia and bestiality being legalized in America."

"Wh—what?" Dan's mouth dropped open and stayed that way.

"They have, not unnaturally, attracted the attention of people of similar mind. My agency believes that they funded one and possibly more of the groups that attacked the capitol on January sixth, which the brothers believe was a righteous effort to restore the nation to the correct path. They, ah, have created a nonprofit specifically to provide for the defense of those arrested on charges arising from that day."

"Are they funding the organizations directly?"

Mason looked at Kate. "Not that we can prove yet, no." He cleared his throat. "At the instigation of their mother, they have been, ah, looking for property where they can live off the grid, something large enough to support a considerable, ah, population. They found that property when Alina Totemoff put the lodge up for sale following her husband's death."

Kate already knew the answer but she asked the question anyway. "How did they stumble upon this particular piece of property?"

"A local realtor by the name of Art Gorst Jr."

Because of course. "And by any chance do we know who referred the brothers to Gorst Junior?"

"A law firm in Chicago which represents BB LLC—"

She said it with him. "Cullen and Associates."

"Ah, yes." Mason paused and fussed with the zipper again. "BB LLC are now actively engaged in seeking out other private properties adjacent to the lodge, we understand in hopes of inducing the federal government to vacate its ownership of the lands in between in order to increase their holding."

"What the hell?" Johnny said. "They're building their own state within a state?"

"My ass those motherfuckers will do any such thing." Dan's face was brick red now. "These assholes are acting like they didn't just buy Demetri's lodge, they got title to the entire southeastern corner of the fucking Park!"

Mason's shoulders rose and fell on a sigh. "They have powerful friends in Congress, and they are making friends in Juneau, particularly representatives from the more conservative areas of Alaska."

Jim immediately thought of the Mat-Su Valley. One august Valley representative had recently accused Alaska Native women living off the road system of deliberately getting pregnant so they could get a free trip to Anchorage for an abortion and score a Costco run at the same time. He was one of the first Alaskans to join the Tea Party. He was also a lifetime member of the Oath Keepers and had been quoted in the press as saying "Hitler had the right idea, he just didn't go far enough." And he was more than happy to share his opinion that the 2020 election had been stolen. What was even scarier was that he was returned to office every two years with a clear majority of his district's votes, and that there were a lot of similar communities in Alaska. Almost all of them were rural, and almost all of them were on the road system.

"In the meantime, they are building fences around the lodge, curtailing access to traditional hiking and hunting trails, and"—he nodded at Dan—"have harassed people visiting the area on foot, snow machine, ATV, snowshoe, and ski with guards and attack dogs." He glanced at Mutt, who was following the conversation intently at the end of the table, ears straight up and yellow eyes intent. A faint smile might have crossed his face. He unfolded his hands and sat up. "And there you, ah, have it."

"They've got a large security force out there?"

"The, ah, evidence suggests they do."

"Are they using drones?"

Special Agent Newly in Charge James G. Mason went so still he appeared frozen in place. No one else said anything for a long moment. No one else appeared to be breathing for that time, either.

"Are they, Mason? Because that midair occurred pretty close to the lodge."

She saw an expression cross his face. It was there and gone again so fast she couldn't identify it. Later, she would realize what it had been, but only later.

"It's possible. BB LLC is sparing no expense to protect their privacy."

He was being awfully generous with information, Jim thought.

Kate said the quiet part out loud. "Why are you telling us all this?"

Mason spread his hands. "You, ah, asked."

"I don't remember the FBI ever being so forthcoming in the past. And you sure are read into BB LLC's file. Almost as if you were expecting to be tested on it."

Mason looked at Jim and seemed to have an internal debate without himself. In the end he made no answer.

Kate regarded him for a long moment, unsmiling. "Why were your people out at Paddy Murphy's mining claim on Labor Day?"

The staid persona slipped for a moment. "I beg your pardon?"

"Van and George Perry flew out to look at the site where the midair came down. They overflew Paddy's strip. There was a Caravan parked on it and some government issue types standing around. She took down the tail number. It's registered to the Department of Justice."

Mason's look at Van was less friendly this time, and next to her Johnny bristled.

The agent recovered his sangfroid. "I'm afraid Van must have been, ah, mistaken."

Van opened her mouth to protest and closed it again at a look from Kate. "Have you identified the extra body found in the wreckage of the midair?"

Something moved behind his eyes. "I'm afraid not."

She wanted to ask him if they'd identified the gun that had been used to murder him but she didn't want to get her clients in trouble. "Any suspects yet in the Paddy Murphy murder?"

"Again, no."

She sat back. "Your organization doesn't seem to be firing on all four cylinders, does it?"

His reply was a tad defensive. "The state caught the Murphy murder."

"The murder was committed in a federal park."

"Yes, but on private property grandfathered within that park."

"A case could be made."

"Perhaps." He got to his feet. "Now if you'll excuse us, we'll get back to our vacation."

Kate watched the two of them walk back to the cabin. "Jo Dunaway didn't say a single word." Van looked up at Kate. "Not one single word."

"Interesting, wasn't it? Silence is not that woman's middle name."

Jim touched Kate's arm, holding her back while the rest of them left. "How did you know he was here in the Park?"

"I didn't know. I suspected."

"How did you suspect?"

She looked out at the river, whose surface was made leaden by glacial silt. The water had risen with the recent rainfall, engulfing the sandbars before boiling swiftly southward. Now and then a splash betrayed the presence of a silver salmon late to the spawning party upstream.

It was pretty to look at but not an answer. "Kate?"

She looked up at him. "Honestly? I don't know. Something's not right here."

"There's a lot not right here."

"Yes, but that's not what I meant." Her shoulders moved as if she were trying to shrug something off. Perhaps a premonition. "Let's go find the others."

They gathered back at the airstrip, standing between the 206 and the 172. "Van, are you sure you got the tail number of that Caravan right?"

"I'm sure."

"So he lied."

"He obfuscated," Jim said with all the authority that comes from decades of being lied to on the job. "He didn't say the FBI wasn't there, he said Van must be mistaken."

"And why was he so forthcoming about BB LLC?" Kate was thinking out loud. "That has not been my experience with the feds." She looked at Dan. "Sorry. No offense."

He waved a dismissive hand. "None taken. Well?"

"Well, what?"

"What do we do next?"

Kate looked at Jim, who looked at the sun which was well over the yardarm. "I'd like to do a flyover of the lodge."

Yeah," said Dan. "I was headed out there myself when those idiot campers started that fire at Chistona Glacier. And then, you know, press of other business. I kept putting it off."

"I don't think you should go out there alone, Dan."

"Two men have already been killed," Jim said, backing Kate up. "Let's not make it three."

Dan spluttered but it wasn't like he could say with any truth that people didn't shoot at the NPS.

"Let's spend the day gathering as much information as we can," Kate was thinking of Tyler, "and then we'll make a trip out there together tomorrow. Around lunchtime. Nobody attacks anybody at lunchtime. And if Jim and I come in with you maybe they won't shoot at us."

"I don't like this," Johnny said. "What do you expect to do out there?"

"Just a friendly visit to drop in on the new neighbors. Who could object to that?"

Johnny's expression said he'd like to be the first.

"Johnny. Too much shit has gone down in the Park this summer, and this is where we live. If these people are shitting in our nest, we need to know what we're up against. If Jim's kids built them a church, what else are they building?"

"No law says they can't build on their own property. Not like we have building covenants in the Park."

Kate looked at Van. "No law at all. But—" She stopped, and shook her head. "We still need to go look."

"Fine," Van said. "Great. Perfect. But let me just quote you back to yourself, okay? They've already killed two people."

"That we know of," Johnny said.

Van nodded. "That we know of. We'd take it kindly if you didn't make it three, four, and five."

Kate felt a reluctant smile tug at the corners of her mouth. "We'll see what we can do." She looked at Dan. "You're coming back with us to the homestead, right?"

'Nah."

"Dan—"

"Knock it off, Shugak. You're starting to sound like my mother. I'm sleeping in my own bed tonight, not all tangled up in an army blanket on your couch with that character"—he nodded at Mutt—"waking me up with a tongue bath." He looked at Kate and his expression softened. "Quit worrying. Unless somebody targets the Step with a HIMARS I'll be fine. And I'm pretty sure Mr. Smith isn't that well armed."

Twenty-seven

THURSDAY, SEPTEMBER 15
Niniltna

JOHNNY AND VAN REMAINED IN NINILTNA to visit with friends. "We'll find a bunk here for the night and catch a ride back with someone tomorrow." They were making a point. So noted. Kate made no protest.

Dan helped loose the tiedowns on the Stationair, closed the doors and swept his hand over the locks behind Jim, Kate, and Mutt, and stood watching as the Cessna taxied and took off. He waited until they were out of sight before climbing into his 172. He checked the fuel gauges. Three quarters full. Good for about six hundred miles, maybe a little under.

He looked up and stared through the windshield in the direction of Demetri's lodge. It was a hundred thirty miles strip to strip, takeoff to touchdown. He knew because he'd flown it before, when Demetri was the owner and Dan had an open invitation to visit anytime. Demetri had been no dummy. At cruising speed Dan could make it point to point in under an hour.

He looked at the sky. Partly cloudy with plenty of blue showing through. He looked at the wind sock at the end of the runway. First third extended, wind three or four miles an hour right out of the Gulf. No wonder it had warmed up.

He tapped the sunrise/sunset app on his phone. Sunrise was at 7:53 p.m. that evening. The current time was 4:47 p.m. Almost three hours to play.

Be conservative, say a full hour Niniltna to the lodge.

Make two or three circles of the property, snap a few shots with his cell phone camera, say fifteen minutes.

Then fly back to the Step, which was further than Niniltna, say 150 miles, an hour and half in the air.

Two hours forty-five minutes total.

He looked again at the sky. Still plenty of blue showing through. Meant daylight would last long enough to light his way home.

A knock on the window made him jump. He turned his head to see George Perry grinning at him. 'You okay in there, O'Brian?"

He shoved the door open. "Yeah, fine, no worries."

"Only you been sitting here a while, I wondered if you needed a push."

"Up yours, Perry."

George laughed. "Hey, you hear anything about Paddy Murphy? Have they found out yet who killed him? Was it a claim jumper?"

Dan remembered what Mason had said.

Any suspects yet in the Paddy Murphy murder?

Again, no.

"Not that I heard."

George grunted. "Feckless jackasses couldn't detect their way out of a paper bag. They should hire Kate."

"Or get Jim to unretire, couldn't agree more. See ya, George."

"Fly safe, Dan." George jogged off back across the runway to his hangar. Now there was a guy who'd figured out how to make a buck out of the Suulutaq Mine. And amazingly, he was still here, instead of having cashed in his winnings and spent them on a coffee plantation in Hawaii.

He looked at the sky again. Yep. Still plenty of blue.

Well. If he was going to do it he'd better get to it before he had to set 'er down on a runway halfway up a mountain in the dark.

He got out to do the walkaround. Fifteen minutes later he was in the air, heading southeast.

Five minutes after that Jim heard Kate's voice over the headphones. "Have we got enough fuel to turn around, get to Demetri's lodge, do a flyby, and make it home again?"

Unknowingly, Jim ran the same kind and number of mental calculations Dan had just minutes before. "Sure, I topped off the tanks before we left. Sunset isn't until eight-ish today and it's clear enough that we can get in an extra half hour of flying time before we have to find a strip with lights." He was already pulling the Cessna into a wide bank, drawing a half-circle in the sky above the silver ribbon of the Kanuyaq River. Mutt, jolted off her seat in the rear, gave a reproving woof. Kate reached back to give her a reassuring scratch and she subsided.

They leveled out on a bearing 180 degrees from the previous one. The Quilaks loomed large on the horizon. He checked the instruments and the sky, throttled back a little, and dropped his hands to let his feet do the flying. "Why not wait until tomorrow like we planned?" He looked at her, admiring the way the slanting sun turned her olive skin a dark gold. He still couldn't believe he got to go home to her every day and sleep with her every night.

And then he woke up to the strained expression in her eyes. "What?" He took a quick look around, checking for traffic. Empty skies all around the clock face. "What is it?"

"For one thing, I don't think Dan went home."

"You think he went out to Demetri's?"

"You know what he's like, Jim. There is no one who believes more in the mission of the National Park Service. This is a guy who has been the chief ranger of the Park for, what, twelve years? Thirteen? He's never even bought a piece of land where he could have built a house because it would have been acreage that could have gone to the Park. Instead he lives full-time, year-round up on the Step in crappy government housing, where the conditions are so bad in the winter you can't fly and the road is so bad year-round you can't drive. Who does that? Only Dan."

He thought about it as the Cessna hummed onward. "What do you think he's going to do when he gets there?"

She settled back in her seat. "The same thing we're going to do when we get there. Descend and take some photos so we'll have some idea of what the hell the Barre brothers are up to."

"Don't we know?"

"But we haven't seen."

"We met one of them, you know."

She turned to look at him, eyebrows up.

"Cisco Barre. On July first. The guy with all the kids and the vanity plates." Who acted like you were invisible, he thought, only because you probably were. To him. As soon as he realized Mason was talking about Cisco Barre, he knew everything he needed to know about BB LLC. He'd met their kind on the job too many times before, guys like Father Smith who brought their families into the Alaska Bush in the sure and certain knowledge they could do anything they wanted because no one was watching.

The Cessna ate up more miles. "You don't think Mason is in the Park on vacation, do you."

She snorted.

"What was that you asked Van, if there were any large groups in the Park other than hunters? You think Mason has a task force with him?"

"I think if he had probable cause he would already have kicked down their doors."

Jim thought out loud, playing devil's advocate. "There are two unsolved murders within easy distance of the lodge."

"Proximity alone won't get him a warrant."

"No."

She leaned over to look at the airspeed indicator.

"Kate." He hesitated. "What are you afraid of? You think they're going to shoot him out of the air or something?"

Out of the corner of his eye he saw her jaw tense. "How many security guards have you met in your life?"

"More lately."

She laughed. It was short and it wasn't exactly filled with humor, but it was a laugh. "I met my first when I did that job for RPetCo up on the Slope. They're all either wannabe cops or retired military, usually retired because they couldn't handle the regimentation and went looking for an easier way to make a living with a gun. Short of going to work for a drug cartel, a private security force is going to be their best bet at a paycheck. They take a job where 'protect your employer' is the mantra and the interpretation of how to get that done is too often left to them. And with these guys there's the religious angle."

"You think they have to be believers before they're hired?"

"They at least have to be open to it."

"And willing to back it up with a nine mil."

"They're out in the middle of nowhere, they don't think anyone's watching, and if we're right they've already gotten away with it twice. So yes."

"If that's true, Kate, I don't know what we're going out there to do other than provide them with another target."

"One guy in one plane is one thing. "Two planes, three people? Too many witnesses. Especially now."

"Why…" He was silent for a moment. When he spoke again his voice was hard, even stern. "Kate. Do you think these people had something to do with the midair?"

"I don't know." It sounded as if her answer had been wrenched from her by force. "I don't know, Jim. But I think Mason might." She got out her phone and brought up her contacts list. She found the one she wanted and pushed back her headset. "Tony? Kate Shugak. Help me out here. I'm looking for a group in Ahtna who have been there at least a few days. Government-issue haircuts, they aren't friendly, they aren't doing the usual tourist things, and they might have their own aircraft. What? Seriously? Your whole lodge?"

The rambunctious Italian was boisterous and bombastic even on the phone. "It's the second time they've booked me out this year. It's a godsend, Kate, after the last two years. Covid damn near shut us down, empty rooms, empty tables. If Stan hadn't figured out takeout and home delivery, no question we would have been out of business." Stan being the dour Russian chef who was Tony's partner in life as well as the lodge. "We might have been anyway except these guys showed up."

"They rented the whole lodge? How many of them are there?" He talked, voluble as always, and she listened. "Thanks, Tony, I owe you."

She hung up. "The Ahtna Lodge is currently enjoying the patronage of a week-long joint law enforcement exercise. There's twenty-five of them and they've rented all the rooms and the public areas and the restaurant. They've asked that their rooms not be cleaned until they leave and that the restaurant serve only them. And they flew in in an unmarked Caravan and their own helicopter."

Jim whistled. "Which agencies?"

"Funnily enough, they didn't say. They were there the first week of June, too, he says." She looked out the window. They were coming up on Niniltna. She called another number. "Mason? Kate Shugak. Your team in Ahtna? You should activate them. Dan O'Brian, a federal employee, was fired on in his federally owned and identified aircraft by personnel on the ground at the Barre brothers' lodge. Yes. Yes, I'm sure. Mason, you know me. We've worked together. Why are you here if not for this? Get on your goddam horse and go." She hung up.

"Kate. You just lied to an FBI agent."

"I hope so."

So did Jim. He reached for the throttle.

Twenty-eight

THURSDAY, SEPTEMBER 15
The Park, Demetri's lodge

THE LODGE SAT ON A BLUFF OVERLOOKING the Steller River, which rose in the Steller Glacier in the Quilaks to the east and emptied into Prince William Sound to the south. It was broad and shallow and gray with silt, and home to one of the most reliable red salmon runs in the area, in part because it wasn't on the road system and it had no competition from other lodges or settlements nearby. If you wanted to fish the Steller, usually it was from this lodge.

Other attractions included the equally healthy population of moose and caribou in the foothills and Dall sheep and mountain goats in the Quilaks, one of the few places where the sheep and goats shared the same territory. It didn't hurt that every game bird deified on a Federal Duck Stamp migrated north in their flocks to nest and breed on the river's delta. It was a sportsman's paradise and Demetri had not run it on the cheap. There had been much speculation among Park rats as to how much Alina had got for the property.

It was, in a Park where it was hard to find a bad view, a staggeringly beautiful location. It was also easily approached from the air, which Dan found a relief as his imagination had been providing him all sorts of scenarios all the way from Niniltna. These were people who liked their privacy and given what he now knew of them, he could well understand why. He was rather expecting a defense setup on the order of Minas Tirith.

He came in from the west, on a direct heading for the main building, giving them plenty of time to see and hear him coming. He stayed high enough not to be obnoxious but low enough to miss no detail.

The lodge was a large structure, with green shingles and rough siding painted brown. It was surrounded by many outbuildings, something large enough for a shop, a dozen cabins, a greenhouse, and others whose use was unidentifiable from their exteriors. The lodge building had a broad staircase leading to a double door flanked by picture windows. The second floor was lined with smaller windows, curtained, probably bedrooms. On one side was a massive fire pit surrounded by a concrete bench. There was a small dock with one slip on the river's edge, reached by a set of wooden steps that zigzagged down the face of the bank.

So far it looked pretty much like the last time he'd seen it. Then, as the 172 approached the west side of the Steller, over the roof of the lodge he saw the single white spire. So that was where Herbie's kids had been paid so handsomely to build their church.

En route he had told himself that he had until the river's edge to change his mind. Turn around, go home, plenty of light for a runway paint job, fry a steak, have a beer, sleep in his own bed. Get up the next morning and do the job he did best and knew he did well.

The spire made the decision for him. The sun on its westerly journey cast the shadow of the 172 on the gilt waters of the Steller River and he couldn't have changed direction then if someone had held a gun to his head. He had to see what other changes there were, and how far they extended. Into his Park? His growl, had he but known it, sounded a lot like Mutt's.

The lodge had a deck and there were people on it, shading their eyes with their hands as they looked up at him. He waggled his wings because why not, a friendly gesture recognized by anyone who had ever flown a small plane, and certainly every Park rat living. And then he made a shallow turn, enough so they could see the NPS logo on the side, before banking again and flying over the roof of the lodge.

The large flat area behind the lodge had once been covered with evergreens and aspens, both clustering at the sides of a dirt airstrip about three thousand feet long. There weren't even stumps remaining to show where the trees had been and the runway had doubled in size. He tried to think back to the map in his office. How far and in which directions did this particular homestead run? Was the far end of the new runway on Park land? Because that would be reason enough for him to introduce them to the might and majesty of the authority of the National Park Service, by god.

The little white church stood back from the edge of the runway closest to the outbuildings. There was even a bell in the steeple. Opposite it stood a series of large square buildings. Behind them was what looked like a bunkhouse—he counted windows rapidly—that probably slept thirty. Next to it was what appeared to be a mess hall. Everything looked very new.

The Poly kids hadn't built all of this. Which begged the question, why have the kids build the church? He was going to ask the kids that shortly and he wasn't putting up with any NDA bullshit when he did, either.

He overflew and came back for a second look. This time he had his phone out, snapping photos. There were more people outside now, between the buildings and on the airstrip, most of them in desert camo fatigues—seriously? desert camo? in Alaska?—and every one of them had their arms up in the air, crossing them back and forth, waving him off. Yeah, he'd already seen the black crosses at the ends of the strip, thanks.

He flew out over the river and turned back. One last pass and he'd haul ass.

He came over the lodge and the tip of his right wing clipped the drone hanging just beyond it.

"Fuck." He pulled back on the yoke, grabbing for altitude. A flash from the ground, another, several in a group.

It couldn't be. Muzzle flash? Seriously? They were shooting at him. Someone was actually shooting at him.

It took a moment to register. When it did, he wasn't afraid;

he was indignant. "What the fuck? This doesn't happen to me! This happens to the other guys!"

The 172 shuddered. The engine began to run rough and a spray of oil hit his windshield.

Yeah. They were definitely shooting at him. And at least one of them had hit his basic means of transportation.

If he walked away from this one he was coming back with an RPG with thermobaric warheads. Put these assholes into orbit. He'd never laid hands on an RPG before in his life but he was feeling very motivated to learn.

His radio crackled. "Dan? Dan!"

They saw it all as they came in from across the river.

They saw the drone carry away at least the starboard green light. The rest of the wing looked intact.

They saw the muzzle flashes of the rifles.

They saw the jerk of the 172 when one of the rounds hit.

They saw the small stream of smoke from beneath the cowling.

"Dan? Dan!" Jim swung the Cessna around and came as close to the 172 as he dared without risking the Park's second midair in a month. He rolled out about fifty feet off Dan's left wing. "Can you see him?"

"Yes, the cockpit's clear, no smoke."

"Can he see us?"

"Yes, I— Yes, yes, he waved!"

The radio came to life. "Hey, guys. Good to see you. Kinda busy here."

The lodge's airstrip was receding rapidly behind them.

"Dan, you've got to get that bucket down on the ground. Paddy Murphy's strip isn't far. Follow me in."

"Soundsh good."

She looked at Jim. He'd heard the slowing of speech and slight slur on the words, too. "Can you climb? Just a little? Just enough?"

"I can try."

They watched as the 172 grabbed for air. It gave up at two hundred feet and started to lose altitude again.

"That's it."

"It's okay, only a few miles to go. Stay on me."

"You got 'at right."

Kate felt herself straining against the seatbelt, as if she could pull the 206 through the air faster than it was already going. Mutt nosed her shoulder with a soft whine.

They'd passed Dan completely now. The sun was still up in the sky, still plenty of light to get both of them safely on the ground. Come on, come on.

"There! There's the strip." She pointed.

"I see it. Dan? I have the strip in sight. Follow me in. I'll do a touch-and-go and get out of your way. Okay?"

"M'kay. Sooner better."

"Just get on the ground, get stopped, and bail. We'll be right behind you."

"Rogsher that."

"He's injured."

"I know."

Jim set that Cessna down on the extreme end of the strip, tail up, just slow enough to stay down, and at the end goosed it and took off again. They climbed and turned and ran back down the runway at fifty feet, in time to see the 172 bounce three times, drop and catch its right wing and do a textbook ground loop. It didn't quite cartwheel but the wing hitting the ground pulled the craft around to nose into the brush at the edge.

Jim made the fastest one-eighty of his life and put the Cessna back down with a thump and a bump but it did the job. They came to a halt across from the 172. Kate had the door open before they stopped rolling. "Kate! Wait! It could catch—"

Fire exploded from the right wing of the downed craft as the fuel caught some spark and went up. Kate could feel the heat on her face and kept running.

"Kate, stop! Goddammit, wait!"

The left door of the 172 swung wide, hanging lopsided from its hinges. There was no one in the cockpit.

"Hey."

She spun around and saw Dan on the ground ten feet away.

Mutt got to him first. She sniffed him all over with an anxious whine.

He put a shaky hand on her head. "Hey, girl."

Kate came running up and flung herself to her knees on his other side. "Are you shot? Is anything broken? Where are you hurt?"

He grinned at Kate with a bloody mouth. "Hey, look at you, all concerned like you care." He raised his head to squint at Jim, who had come up to stand behind her. "Cutting in on your ackshon, buddy."

"Big talk from a man who can't even get his own airplane down in one piece." But Jim's voice was rough.

Dan laughed and choked. "You know what they say. Any landing you walk away from."

His eyes closed and his head lolled to one side.

"Is he—"

Kate checked the pulse in his neck. "No. Lost consciousness." She ran her hands over his arms and legs and spine and pulled back a hand covered in blood. "Shit. He caught one in his right thigh." She finished patting him down. "I don't feel anything broken. He's got one hell of a goose egg over his left ear."

An open pocket knife appeared over her shoulder. She used it to split Dan's pant leg open. "Oh. That's a lot of blood."

A bottle of alcohol and a square of gauze. She took both and swabbed the wound. A sigh of relief. "A graze, I think."

A handful of gauze squares this time, followed by a roll of lime-green elastic bandage. She applied the gauze to the wound and secured it with the bandage. "Lime green? Really?"

"If you're going to be wounded you want some contrast with all the blood. Speaking of which where's the blood on his mouth coming from?"

"Might have bit his tongue when he crashed or knocked into something when he was getting out. I'm guessing he was in a hurry."

"Wasn't a crash, it was a controlled flight into terrain." Jim was admittedly a little light-headed with relief.

"Whatever. Let's get him into the plane while he won't feel it. We can call the clinic from the air, get the boys to meet us at the strip."

Overhead came the rumble of a powerful engine. They looked up to see a large unmarked helicopter on a southeast heading.

"Better late than never." Kate slid her hands beneath Dan's knees. "Come on."

Twenty-nine

SEPTEMBER, FOLLOWING
The Park

NONE OF THE PARK RATS MOST NEARLY concerned with the events leading up to what happened at the lodge that early evening in September saw them unfold in person. However, many of the people on the ground commemorated the event on their phones. Videos were uploaded live to Gab and Rumble and Telegram and a host of closed Facebook pages, and of course it was all over Twitter. It took the blink of an eye for much of it to migrate into everyone's feed.

News broke almost immediately of the ownership of the lodge, which caused a minor frenzy on Fox News. Sean Hannity and Glenn Beck tried to get either of the Barre brothers as on-air guests. When that failed, they instead produced people who said they'd met the brothers once. Hannity found a guy who'd played football with them in high school. "They missed a lot of practices. They were either working or in church, you know?"

All requests for comment or interviews were referred to *The Ark*. An answering service took names and numbers and promised callbacks in a soothing voice – callbacks that never materialized.

When it became known that shots had been fired on a government employee, interest perked back up, only to die outside the hospital room where Dan was recovering from his injuries. No one was allowed in, not even the television cameras, which at first astonished and then affronted the media organizations involved. Who did this guy think he was?

Mainstream media mostly scratched their heads over reporting a story where nobody died except an old miner and an unidentified male, although the fact that this was frontier Alaska and as close to the Wild Wild West as they were ever going to get in real life made them work it as long and as hard as they could. It wasn't very long because in this internet age everyone had ADD and when the number of clicks started to fall the media turned with relief to breaking news of a US Congressman sexting with a fifteen-year-old Instagram influencer who was more than happy to go on camera anytime, anywhere.

The *Kanuyaq Currents* considerably increased its readership when Van wrote an eyewitness account of the finding of Paddy Murphy's body in conjunction with the on-camera arrest of one of BB LLC's private guards, whom she identified as a member of BB LLC's security force. He'd been ID'd as Tatum Anderson, and she included video she'd shot that day on her phone. There was no mistaking him for anyone else. He'd been found by the task force on his knees, ankles crossed, hands behind his head, his sidearm on the ground where he'd thrown it. "Great survival instincts on that guy," Jim had said, not at all admiringly.

On Park Air Bobby Clark did helpful recaps and posted video clips on his YouTube channel, close captioned, with graphics, careful to point out the difference between the good guys and the bad guys. It took three days for him to come to the attention of the FBI, who immediately issued a takedown writ, but by then anyone who was interested had already viewed and downloaded everything they wanted to.

Johnny put together a supercut video, which Kate saw on the *Kanuyaq Currents* website. It opened with footage of the helicopter descending to the airstrip right in front of the little white church. "I read somewhere that before they took it down that clip alone doubled donations to the Christian Coalition."

Jim, over whose shoulder she was watching, grunted. "'Tis an ill wind, unfortunately."

The bunkhouse and the three cabins nearest it had burned down due, it was reported, to a fire started by muzzle flash. Jim snorted when he heard that. "Somebody fell over a Coleman lantern, more like." The conflagration had been caught on video and was immediately uploaded with captions like "Your tax dollar at work."

Some of the video that had been taken by the invading force had been released and Johnny had intercut it with the ones shot by the invaded. Heavily armed men in body armor dropped out of the helo like they were fast-roping into Fallujah, to face camo-clad men who mostly threw themselves flat on the ground and hid their heads in their arms. There was actual footage of one of the BB LLC guards tripping over the strap of his own rifle and falling flat on his face while trying to run away.

"Where was he running to?"

"The inside of a bear, be my guess."

A dozen of the defending force were wounded, two seriously enough to merit a Lifeflight to Anchorage.

The head of the task force appeared on a Zoom interview the following day, broadcast from inside the compound's armory, and gave a long talk about the threat of domestic terrorism and the defense of democracy and how the FBI and the Department of Justice did it better than anyone else and how this raid was just another example. Anyone interested in attending or who logged on to watch after the fact saw the amount and kind of weaponry on display, enough for Lithuania to keep the Russians on their side of the border for a year, and were convinced that the FBI had all the just cause they needed.

A reporter asked if the Barre brothers were in custody. The brothers and their families were away from the lodge at the time, the head of the task force said. He was a whipcord-thin man in a dark suit and a skinny tie. He had a reedy voice that diminished the force of his answers. Were they still in the country? They were but not under indictment. But were they under investigation for the creation and support of what appeared to be a private army? The task force leader smiled mysteriously and said he had no further comment at this time.

And then the *National Geographic* photographer, who it turned out had survived his dunking in the Kanuyaq, and who was also a reporter and recognized an opportunity when he saw one, uploaded some choice snippets of video filmed by his drone. "He must have had a spare," Van told Kate. "Considering his first one has to be buried in glacial silt offshore of Double Eagle by now."

On his float down the river from Ahtna to the Kanuyaq River delta the drone had recorded many interesting things. One of them proved to be footage of four guys in desert camo bringing a skiff across the Kanuyaq. There were ATVs on one side and actual trucks on the other, parked in rudimentary lots bulldozed for the purpose. Both had been constructed on Park land, a federal offense. Further, it so happened that his drone had just enough range to spot the tracks, one leading from the east side of the river to the lodge and the other from the west side of the river to the road that led to the Roadhouse. It made Bernie's insurance agency perk up and it certainly improved the pre-orders for the *NatGeo* guy's documentary.

A brief release from the FBI some days later made reference to the many drones available to BB LLC's security force, accompanied by a guarded announcement that information had been received that one of those drones might have caused the midair collision that took nine lives in the Park on Labor Day. The matter was under investigation and the interrogation of witnesses was ongoing, and the NTSB was contributing their expertise to the case.

None of this was of much comfort to Kate. "They're going to get away with it. They've got all the money and they can hire all the lawyers, starting with Cullen and Associates and Mr. Fucking Smith, which is, I think, his legal name. And the Barre brothers will skate and they'll just start over somewhere else."

"But not here. Might be the best we can ask for."

"They killed Paddy Murphy, Jim, or they ordered it done."

"Why, if he'd already sold his property to Barr Senior?"

"I don't know."

"Me, either." He shook his head. "I am so very glad I am not one of the ones who has to sort out this mess."

"And they had to have had something to do with the unidentified dead guy. What happened? Who killed him? Who moved his body into the wreckage? Why?"

"I think we'll find out. Maybe not soon, but we will know one day."

"When?"

Jim nodded at the screen. "I don't think that bunch has any kind of unit loyalty. I'd bet most of them are already talking so fast the poor Feebs can barely keep up."

He proved to be correct in at least one instance. Tatum Anderson lawyered up immediately following his arrest and offered to make a deal. He fingered Albert Bragg, who turned out to be the young guy who in Anderson's company had accosted them—or tried to—at the airstrip that day. Bragg of course fingered Anderson right back, and hinted that he had other secrets he could tell if they'd give him a better deal than Anderson's.

"Which one do you think is lying?"

"I'm sure they're both lying about something but if it was one of the two my money would be on the kid. He didn't strike me as a true believer, or the most stable personality."

He got up and put his arms around her. "It's late. Let's go to bed."

Her smile was rueful. "Tomorrow will be better?"

He leered. "Tomorrow's always better when I wake up in a bed with you in it, baby."

She laughed and succumbed to his manly charms.

Mutt watched approvingly from in front of the fireplace. Outside the wind blew and the rain splatted against the windows, but inside there was warmth and a soft quilt and roommates who were behaving sensibly for a change.

Thirty

THE DOOR BELL CLANGED AND AUNTIE VI erupted into the room. She looked around, spotted them, and fixed Kate with a fierce eye. "Ha!"

"Oh lord." Kate only hoped she hadn't said it out loud.

But the eye moved on to Bernie. "You think my food not good enough for you? You come here to eat instead?"

Bernie cringed but wisely did not try to defend himself, especially when Laurel appeared laden with burgers and fries. After she set down their plates she leaned in and lowered her voice. "Matt says The Powers That Be are authorizing the next Covid booster tomorrow. Get down to the clinic after lunch and he says he'll give you yours early."

Over her shoulder Kate saw Matt looking at them from his stool at the counter. He gave a brief nod. Auntie Vi was standing next to him, tapping her foot while she waited for Laurel to return and take her order. "Do the aunties know?"

Laurel snorted. "The aunties got theirs this morning."

"Which means they'll be putting the word out."

Laurel's nod was emphatic. "Much as any Park rat's life is worth to disobey an auntie order, and don't they all know it."

Alaska was a red state full of anti-masking vaccine deniers but from the beginning of the Covid pandemic the aunties had come down hard and unanimously in favor of Park rats getting their shots as soon as they were available. It was a good thing for the health of the Park rats that they were more afraid of the aunties than they were of the most recent plague.

The buns were crisp and golden, the burgers oozing juices, and the fries crunchy on the outside and soft on the inside. "Heaven in your mouth," Jim said thickly.

The bell over the door clanged. "You swallow your food before you talk," Auntie Vi said. "Your mother not teach you any better, you?"

Now, it was a strange thing, but when they wanted to the aunties could speak perfect English, all the verbs in their correct conjugation, all the modifiers in front of the right nouns. Usually that happened in one of two cases; either non-family, most likely Outsiders, were present and they wanted to put on a show, or when family was present and the aunties were so pissed off at them they wanted to be clearly understood. Since Auntie Vi was talking Bush, as they called it among themselves, Kate and Jim and Bernie deduced that they were off the hook. For the moment.

Auntie Vi returned to their booth, snagging a chair from a table along the way, and plumped herself down next to Bernie. She glared at Kate. "You find out who do this thing?"

"Yes, Auntie."

"They in jail?"

"On their way."

"Good. They wipe out this boy. Now he want to build a bar in Niniltna."

Kate cocked her head. Auntie Vi's reaction to the idea was less incendiary than expected.

"Not a bar, Auntie Vi," Bernie said timidly. "A brewery."

"Ha! All the same, them."

Annie Mike came in, nodded at Auntie Vi, and went to the counter to put in her order. Jim said, "Auntie Vi, could you move your chair to one side, please?" and got up to move an empty table so that it butted up against the table in the booth. Annie Mike, as plump and serene as Auntie Vi was skinny and volatile, settled down comfortably and included everyone in her radiant smile. It never failed to make anyone in range feel better about life, the universe, and everything.

But this was taking on the aspect of an ad hoc committee meeting and Kate was unsurprised when Auntie Joy was next in the door, her round face wreathed in smiles and her delightful chuckle making hearts lift wherever it was heard. Between the combined benevolences of Auntie Joy and, let's face it, the person who was becoming Auntie Annie right before their eyes, Auntie Vi's acerbity was softened to an endurable volume, which eased the tension on so many levels.

Kate looked around the table and knew with absolute certainty that the spirits of past aunties were with them, standing at their shoulders. Auntie Edna scowling. Auntie

Balasha saying nothing but hearing everything. Emaa, too, larger than life even in death. Emaa, Kate's grandmother and the leader of her tribe, whose bottom line was ever and always would be, "How does this benefit our people?"

The new postmaster came in. Out from behind the half door he looked even taller and wider and even more like he'd starred in *The Unit*. He headed straight for the counter without looking around and gave his order to Laurel in a low voice. A mug of coffee appeared in front of him and he curled his hands around it and bent his head as if he were taking communion. No one said hi. Martin Shugak actually slid down one stool. Jackson drank coffee and appeared not to notice.

Everyone's food came at the same time, which was pretty crafty of Laurel, and—Kate craned her neck to see through the pass-through—Arabella Kvasnikof, who was slinging the burgers today, lucky for all of them because she was by far and away Laurel's best short-order cook. Kate tucked in with a will. There was little talk as they ate because Covid was not so long ago that it was still a rare pleasure to eat a meal you hadn't cooked yourself that you didn't have to clean up after, in the company of other people, in a place that wasn't your own home.

Kate finished first and got up to use the bathroom. When she came out the postmaster was waiting. "They tried to recruit me."

It took her a moment. "Oh. You mean the J6ers?"

He nodded. "My last week in. Several of us were

approached." He looked away and back, jaw tight. "Not my thing at all."

"Good to know. So, that's why you—"

"Tried to warn you. Those folks don't like people who look like you."

"I noticed."

He nodded again. "I'm sorry."

"What for?"

He looked away again, thinking. "I could have tried harder, talked to more people. I'm not the most social guy."

"I noticed that, too," Kate said again with a straight face.

"Yeah, well." He looked back at her, a glint in his eye. "I like it here. I'm in the Park for the long haul. I'll try harder."

"Good decision. You stick it out one winter and you're pretty much in. We don't bite."

Miracle of miracles, he gave her a small but perceptible smile.

When she returned to the table the dishes were being efficiently disappeared by Laurel. They were immediately replaced by fresh coffee and derivatives thereof all around. After which she drew up a chair. Kate looked at her, surprised. Laurel smiled at her.

"Roadhouse gone," Auntie Vi said.

Let the meeting come to order.

"No place to quilt."

Auntie Joy nodded.

"No place for crazy climbers to raise their Middle Finger to Angqaq."

Bernie looked like he might cry.

"No place for you"—her thumb jerked at Kate—"to jump all over him"—thumb jerked at Jim—"and embarrass your elders like Dawson Darling!"

Laurel smothered a laugh with a cough. Kate gave her a dirty look but only half-heartedly. What could she say? It was only the truth.

Auntie Vi turned to Bernie. "Alcohol is the worm in the Bush apple. All the time we fight bootleggers who sell to our children. Now—pah! Drugs! This oxygens, this fenneldill. Everywhere, in the schools, in our homes, on the streets." She pointed. "On the mountain!"

She looked accusingly at Laurel.

"I didn't crash that plane up there, Auntie." But her defense was without heat. She knew this wasn't about her.

Auntie Joy patted her arm. "You and Matt save childrens. You good girl, Laurel."

"Ugliness." Auntie Joy's voice was sad. "All is ugliness."

Auntie Annie was more stern and more specific. "Addiction. Overdose. Death. This must stop."

Bernie looked more miserable than ever.

"You a good boy, too, Bernie."

He looked up, surprised, and maybe a little suspicious. Kate didn't blame him. Auntie Vi never offered random compliments.

"You don't let people drive drunk. You don't serve underage. You don't serve pregnant girls. You welcome everyone—even crazy tourists from Outside!" She shook her head at such madness. "In Park, if people get drunk, they get drunk in one place. Your place."

"Mostly," Auntie Joy said.

Auntie Vi nodded. "Mostly."

She nodded at Laurel, who took up the tale. "You all know that this building used to be a cannery?"

"Whitney-Fidalgo," Auntie Annie said.

"They built it to last and it almost doesn't smell like fish anymore." She shrugged. "Even if it does, it's part of our history. It's two, maybe three times the space I needed, but they would only sell me the entire building, and their new Japanese owner was shifting from land-based canneries to sea-going processors so they let it go cheap." She leaned forward. She looked excited, Kate thought. "I've been wanting to expand out onto the dock anyway. If I'd had outside seating I might have been able to stay open for service during Covid, and who knows, when the next bug shows up I might have to."

It would not be fair to say that Bernie's eyes were starting out of his head but he did look just this side of hypnotized.

"I did some looking online. You'll want to check my figures to be sure, Bernie, but I think there is more than enough floor space for a small brewery on the other side of this building. Plenty of room for an apartment if you don't mind living over the shop. The main problem will be water, but the Niniltna Native Association is coming in for a big chunk of change from that infrastructure bill they passed in DC. Their first priority is to upgrade the village's existing water and sewer."

Most of which was put in by the Kanuyaq Mining Company back in 1908, Kate thought.

"Good water would be very important. I thought I'd have to truck it in from somewhere, and have a tank for storage." Bernie was recovering his power of speech.

"We do this, we do it right." Auntie Annie was even beginning to talk like the other aunties. She tapped the table. "You continue best practices in barkeeping. You don't open until noon."

"Eleven o'clock."

"You want to compete with Laurel for lunch?"

Well, when you put it like that. "Open at noon. Closing time two a.m."

"Midnight."

"One a.m. Just on Fridays and Saturdays?"

"Midnight."

Bernie threw in the towel. "Midnight it is. What about the ABC? Will they transfer my license?"

The ABC was the dread Alcohol Beverage Control Board, a state agency which allocated licenses to sell beer and wine and hard liquor on a per capita basis. They could be extremely persnickety in said allocation, by statute due to the population of the area in which the license would be used but realistically also influenced by which way the political winds were blowing between the community in question and the legislature in Juneau.

Auntie Vi snorted. "Buddy Halvorsen do what he is told."

Buddy being the chair of the said board. Well, then.

"Last thing," Auntie Vi said, glaring at Bernie and ratcheting up the fierce, which didn't need ratcheting.

"Yes, Auntie?"

"Name is the Roadhouse."

For a moment Kate thought Bernie might burst into tears. He pulled himself together and managed a wavering smile. "Roadhouse it is." And then he leaned forward and gave her a kiss on the cheek. The balls on the guy.

"Congratulations, Bernie." Dan smacked Bernie on the back, and when had he shown up? He looked almost like new, although he had lost a little weight and was walking with a cane. Wrecking a plane would do that to you. "It's a bar."

Auntie Vi gave the table a stern rap, demanding their attention. She got it, too. "First night. Potlatch, for everyone we lost in the pandemic."

Kate was watching Bernie and it was clear that a wake was not the way he wanted to start his new business, but he knew better than to say so. "Whatever you say, Auntie Vi."

She looked at Laurel. "You make food. We help."

Laurel nodded. "It shall be as you say, Auntie."

Wasn't it always?

"Only bad part is we have to learn to like beer." Auntie Vi didn't look happy about it, either.

Bernie, looking years and years younger, laughed out loud, probably the first time he'd done so since the Roadhouse burned down. "If they transfer my license entirely I'll be able to sell hard liquor too, Auntie. I'll still be able to make you your Irish coffee."

In spite of herself Auntie Vi brightened at the news. Auntie Joy clapped her hands and gave her infectious chuckle. Auntie Annie smiled benignly upon them all.

Movement caught the corner of Kate's eye. Van was standing there, holding her phone up, recording this momentous meeting for posterity, and for clips to post on *Kanuyaq Currents*.

"Martin." Dan beckoned. "C'mere a minute. I want to talk to you."

Martin looked panicked. "Why? I haven't done anything!" He thought, and said in a smaller voice, "Lately."

"You're not in trouble." Today, everyone heard, though it remained unspoken. "Your cousin Howie might be."

Martin, who had begun to relax, tensed up again. "I don't have anything to do with Howie. I can't. It's a condition of my parole. Judge Singh said."

"Yeah, yeah, but he's going to get Willard in trouble, too, and we don't want that, do we?"

The two of them adjourned to the counter.

Laurel was right, and the aunties were, too. The Park rats needed a place to assemble, visit, talk business, gossip, enjoy each other's company, and, yes, disagree and quarrel and fall in love and fall out of it again, and fight and feud and generally celebrate the extended family that included everyone within the Park's boundaries and maybe a little beyond.

Even, she thought, people who thought they could carve off a part of the Park for their own and live however they wanted. But then there would always be people wanting to live in a place where they had to answer to no authority but their own. Even they needed a Roadhouse. If only, once there, to be shown the error of their ways by the Balluta brothers and the Grosdidier brothers.

Their mistake for anyone to think they could get away with it here. Whatever "it" was. Because there was always an "it."

She looked at Dan. He was still speaking earnestly to Martin, no doubt attempting to enlist the other man in his feud against that little weasel, Howie Katelnikof. Martin, surprisingly, appeared to be holding his own. Kate surprised herself by thinking, And good for him.

Business done, chairs scraped across the floor as the aunties rose to their feet and departed.

The bell on the door jingled and Bobby Clark walked in, holding the door for Dinah and Katya, who sashayed in like she owned the joint. The silence stopped all three of them in their tracks.

"What?" Bobby said. He saw Kate and frowned at her uncharacteristic muteness. "What?"

Jim got up to hold Auntie Joy's chair. "You snooze, you lose, Clark." He flashed his shark's grin into Bobby's gathering wrath.

Back in her office Van synced the video to her laptop and edited it down to its essentials before posting it on the *Currents* website and social media. She cut a much shorter video for their TikTok account and posted it, too. Nobody under twenty looked at Facebook anymore.

She laced her fingers behind her head and stared out the window at the street outside it. Park rats were texting furiously on their phones, stopping pickups window to window to talk back and forth, clumping together in groups of two and three, trotting up the hill to the post office and the Niniltna Native Association headquarters.

And the word went forth, she thought.

Her phone was already lighting up with texts, people wanting to know if she'd heard the news and when it would be online for them to read.

She picked up her phone and texted Johnny, who was back in school in Fairbanks.

Check out the Currents page.

A few minutes later her phone dinged.

Nice. But not unexpected.

She texted back.

Only here. Forget what I said about microaggressions.

A pause.

I already had.

Thirty-one

THE FOLLOWING WEEK THE AUNTIES PUT out the call and the Park rats responded as one. Classes at Niniltna High School and Herbie's were cancelled, the Bingleys closed the store, Dan shut down the Step, fishermen stopped working on their boats, and hunters let their annual moose hang for another day or two before cutting and grinding and weighing and wrapping. Never anything any of them minded doing and something that might even enhance the tenderness of the winter's meat, but still. Even the weather fell obediently into line as that month proved to be the clearest and driest October in Park record.

Park rats congregated before the Riverside Cafe in their hundreds. With so many hands the demoing of the interior down to the studs took half a day. The biggest problem the volunteer work force had was getting in each other's way.

Bernie's insurance company was delighted when the Ballutas and the Grosdidiers joyfully identified four of the men arrested at the lodge as the four who had run into the brothers' fists with their faces, repeatedly. One of them ratted out the other three for a lighter sentence and confessed to the arson, and Bernie was shortly thereafter in possession of a check that designated itself as a claim honored in full.

With that fat amount in hand Jim huddled with Phil Mason and came up with a list of materials which went into a bulk order to SBS in Anchorage. Jim found a transportation company that wasn't afraid of unpaved roads—so long as it hadn't snowed yet—and a series of semis delivered the goods, stacked in several tarped piles along the Niniltna road.

They weren't there long enough for anyone to complain they blocked traffic. The electrical engineer drove in from Ahtna in an RV handmade from a Conex, the back half of which opened into his own personal shop. It even had steps that let down, and he lost no time in assembling his students into a lean, mean, wire-hauling machine. They worked side by side with the plumber, Harrison Ford, and yes that really was his name although for obvious reasons he preferred Sonny, whose students ran pipe while Sonny drove the excavator digging the trench across the street to connect the new sewer system into the equally new septic tank, set into a yawning pit equidistant from the buildings around it and the river. Once the tank was in place and the pipe laid and connected he filled in the pit around the vent pipes as the rest of the Park rats temporarily downed tools to watch in admiring silence. "There is something mesmerizing about watching people work heavy equipment," Ruthe Bauer said. "Not to mention sexy."

DANA STABENOW

Kate, standing next to her, saw several young men standing nearby perk up their ears—Ruthe was an elder, she should know—and foresaw a heavy equipment operations workshop in Herbie's not-too-distant future. She decided not to tell Jim. Let it be a surprise for him.

Since effluent and solids produced by breweries were not necessarily healthy for septic systems a filtration system was also installed, which took a lot of finicky adjusting and added to the kind and amount of already colorful language required of any construction crew. The members of Herbie's student body were learning many useful new skills.

While the wiring and plumbing were being attended to inside, the carpentry class, aided by their contingent of enthusiastic and variously experienced helpers, replaced the roof and the walls, blew insulation, added solar panels to the roof and siding to the exterior walls, all of this in good time to move inside and put up Sheetrock when the wiring and plumbing were done. A concrete floor was next and while it cured they mudded and taped and then moved next door to wreak improvements on the Riverside Cafe, including new wiring, new plumbing, new drywall, new flooring, and new paint. Matt and his brothers surprised Laurel with a new counter, made of oak planks rescued from a derelict wooden scow Matt had found downriver. Fitted and fastened together, sanded, and waxed to a creamy shine, shaped to fit the space, it made the old-fashioned porcelain dishware of the Riverside Cafe look almost elegant. "A wedding present," Luke said, and lined up with the rest of his brothers for the enthusiastic embrace and kisses bestowed on them by Laurel, when she stopped crying.

A week later they were spraying paint on the brewery's walls, a white the color of eggshells, light but not too bright, and it was dry when more semis rolled up with the many and sundry parts required to produce a pint of lager: mills and mashes and filtration systems and tanks and pumps and valves and kegs and whatever. "A microbrewery, you said."

Bernie, standing next to Kate with a grin whose wattage probably registered from orbit, said, "A microbrewery. Fifteen barrels. Enough for today."

She gave him a suspicious look. "And tomorrow?"

He didn't answer but his grin, impossibly, widened.

Under his supervision the bits and pieces, large and small, most made of gleaming copper and shining stainless steel, were fitted together inside the large white space to form a functional whole. Or so everyone hoped but Bernie seemed sure. "It's like putting the Legos together," one of the plumbing apprentices said. They should know.

Once the components of the brewery were in place the carpenters were back at work, building a wall between the brewery and the front half of the building. The bottom half was wood and the top half Plexiglas. Next came a bar which ran most of the length of the room, followed shortly by upholstered booths on either side of the door. Tables and chairs to fill up the center would come later, as would a jukebox, although Bernie added a small stage just in case someone showed up with a guitar. Because why not?

Phil and the gang cut a pass-through between the brewery and the cafe, as Laurel would be filling the food orders that came in from Bernie's side. Bernie told Kate privately that he'd never been so happy to be rid of something in his life as he was the kitchen at the Roadhouse. Finding a good cook and kitchen helpers who didn't disappear during fish camp was at best problematic and at worst a fucking nightmare. Eduardo, a taciturn forty-something who had materialized in the Park five years before and the only one of Bernie's kitchen helpers who had stuck, was moving to the Riverside as chef.

"What about cabins? Are you going to build some?"

He shrugged. "No need. We're right downtown. If I take someone's keys, someone else can walk them home or let them use their couch."

No cabins might also contribute to a significant reduction in the percentage of adultery per capita. Kate wasn't sure Park rats would think that was altogether a good thing.

After construction was complete the next job for the apprentice carpenters was four one-bedroom apartments on the second floor, the first one of which would be Eduardo's. For the moment he was staying at Auntie Vi's bed-and-breakfast and there was a slight but perceptible tussle ongoing over Auntie Vi's kitchen, so the sooner he moved into his own quarters the better. Bernie was moving into a second. The others would acquire renters as needed.

More flooring, more paint, light fixtures, glassware, appliances, and the thing was mostly done. Clear, clean water from the aptly named Clear Creek was trickling into the tank installed below the floor and the last semi showed up with a load of grain for the bins, and there were still ten days of October left.

Okay, then.

Laurel threw down with the aunties over having her wedding before the potlatch. Laughter before tears, she told them, and wouldn't budge. By a miracle, they did. So beneath a new ceiling festooned with new light fixtures, between walls still smelling of new paint, standing on a concrete floor stained, according to the paint's manufacturer, a Desert Amber, Laurel Meganack and Matt Grosdidier were pronounced husband and wife by the Right Reverend Anne Flanagan. Every Park rat from five years old up was there to bear witness, each and every one of them determined to show to advantage, freshly bathed, resplendent in Carhartts brushed clean of salmon scales and Xtratufs washed clean of moose guts. It was a sight to behold and one likely never to be repeated.

No less than the bride, who wore a cream-colored gown with an off-the-shoulder neckline and a handkerchief hem. She looked like Grace Kelly, only prettier and happier. Matt looked terrified, but that may have been because he was wearing his first suit and tie ever over his old Timberlines. His brothers had hidden his new dress shoes.

Bobby Clark was the DJ, playing classic rock with a few hip-hop numbers thrown in as a sop to anyone born after 2000, beer and wine and pop in ice-filled coolers in every corner, and tables trembling beneath a potluck supper to which everyone had contributed something, from mac and cheese to mooseburger meatloaf to smoke fish. The wedding cake was a sheet cake that took up most of its own table and Laurel and Matt cut and served it and did not smear each other's face with frosting. The party went on until dawn, although the bride and groom disappeared soon after the cake cutting. Officially no one knew where to, but it was easy enough to guess, and Sergei Moonin had seen them take off on a four-wheeler in a vaguely easterly direction anyway. There was some discussion among the younger Park rats of following them up to the cabin at Canyon Hot Springs. Or there was until they noticed Kate Shugak standing behind them, listening to the conversation with an expression of polite interest.

The happy couple was back three days later, though, in time for the potlatch held in remembrance of those they had lost over the past two years. The losses weren't all from Covid. One of the Kvasnikof sons had drowned off the Kanuyaq River delta, one of the Kashevarof daughters had died in a car crash on the way to Anchorage, an Ollestad had died of old age alone in his cabin and been found ten days later, and there had been a stillbirth. There were others. The wheel of time turned for them all.

They began with a moment of silence for the people who had died in the midair. They weren't Park rats but the victims had died on Park ground and their passing commanded acknowledgement and respect.

The Covid deaths were the worst. In spite of the aunties' firm hand the Park had still had its share of Covid deniers and as a result the Park suffered the average national loss of one percent of the population. Twenty people, including Demetri Totemoff and Balasha Shugak. Every Park rat was related to or knew someone who had died. The pandemic had hurt them all whether they'd caught the bug themselves or not.

They added Paddy Murphy to the roll call of the dead. They did not include the tenth body found in the wreckage of the midair, because he still had no name.

There were piles of gifts, jewelry beaded and silver, grass baskets, ivory carvings, gift certificates to Walmart and Costco, bundles of towels, blankets, 198-count packages of diapers in all sizes, cases of canned milk and Spam, boxes of pilot bread. No one left empty-handed. Howie Katelnikof was caught passing cases of canned salmon out the back door to Willard, who was loading them into their pickup, but after Auntie Vi tore him a new one someone was detailed to fetch them back and no more was said. Howie was definitely a little weasel but he was their little weasel and he was Willard's caretaker. Unless he actually hurt someone in the process of one of his many petty crimes they would be ignored. It was a pity he knew that.

Dan had cornered him about hunting with a drone. Howie denied it. Willard confessed. A box of shells matching the one Van had found on Murphy's airstrip was discovered in their house. On the strength of such "evidence," Dan confiscated the drone, although Kate wasn't sure he had the authority to do that. And Amazon was still only a click away, as Dan was bitterly aware.

The aunties came down hard on the length of speeches and most of the time on the mic was given over to friends and family members. There were many tears but there was laughter, too.

When the speeches ended and before the karaoke began, Kate found herself standing next to Anne Flanagan. "Hey, Right Rev."

"Kate."

They were standing against the wall opposite the bar of the new Roadhouse. Bernie had left the light on on the other side of the glass and the stainless steel vessels shone proudly. "Never thought I'd live to see the day the aunties would let someone open a bar in Niniltna."

"Neither did I."

Anne looked at her. "You were against it?"

Kate shook her head. "It's a new solution for a new day. I think it's the only way Auntie Vi and the rest could think of to have any kind of control. And there's the added bonus that the village is still so small that it'll be a long time before the Alcohol Beverage Control Board issues a license to anyone else."

"And Bernie's a good guy."

Kate nodded. "Mostly. When he sticks to bartending."

"His wife ever come back?"

"Not this time."

Anne shook her head, more in sorrow than in anger. Anne never did do anger all that well. "What's this kerfuffle everyone is talking about?"

Anne had been Outside the previous month, officiating at her mother's third wedding. "At Demetri's lodge? Some crazy ass billionaires bought it after he died and proceeded to build a compound staffed by a private army, and not a very good one, either. Dan O'Brian went out to say hi and they put up a drone and it clipped his wing and then one of them started shooting at him and then a bunch more thought that was a fine idea and then the FBI got involved."

"Some kind of white supremacist group, was my understanding."

"Some kind," Kate said. "The first thing they did was build a church. Second thing they built was an armory."

"Christofascists."

"Say what?"

"What you get when you bastardize Christianity with white supremacy. I heard one of their drones might have caused the midair."

"I heard that, too."

"An awful thing. Their poor families."

Kate thought of Barr Jr. and his sister sitting in her home, dry-eyed, mourning put on hold until they found out what really happened to their father. She thought she knew, now. She hoped to be able to tell them soon.

Anne's attention was claimed by a lapsed parishioner who

needed spiritual guidance and to Kate's inchoate fury in the next moment she had been maneuvered into sitting between Auntie Vi and Auntie Joy. She felt marginally better about it when she saw that Annie was sitting on the other side of Joy, but then Laurel brought them all plates of food, the first to be served. That had been her job. She stared at the plate in her hands and looked up to see Jim struggling not to laugh. Next to him Bobby was laughing outright, loud enough to be heard by the newly dead.

Her expression must have given everyone a pretty clear indication of what she was feeling because she was elbowed from both sides simultaneously.

"Something wrong with the food, hey?" Auntie Vi said, scowling.

"You eat, you feel better," Auntie Joy said with her usual beaming smile.

Emaa was standing right in back of her, jerking the string tied to the wrist of the hand bringing a forkful of mac and cheese to her mouth. She chewed and swallowed but she couldn't taste a thing.

From the back of the crowd, her cousin Axenia, here from Anchorage for the occasion, was giving her the look of death. Kate had essentially given her Kate's seat on the Niniltna Native Corporation's board of directors but evidently she wanted to be an auntie, too. She would never believe that Kate would have gladly surrendered the honor to her cousin, and even now was scheming of ways she could. It would have to be subtly handled...

Auntie Vi elbowed her again, staring pointedly at her plate, whose laden state demonstrated a lack of her usual robust appetite and was an overt insult to all those fine Park cooks who had contributed a dish to the meal. She dug in, her taste buds slowly reviving.

This wasn't over.

Bobby broadcast the whole thing on Park Air, roping in special on-air guests from Auntie Vi to Keith and Oscar, who got in a hefty plug for In Praise of Cooks dot com. Dinah recorded it all on video, later cut into a twenty-minute documentary she titled "Park Rats at Play," with the subtitle "the best little community in America." She let Van put it up on *Kanuyaq Currents*, where it was much admired and shared, mostly to prove to out-of-state friends and family that Park rats didn't live in igloos after all.

Kate was standing at Bobby's shoulder late that evening when the crowd began to thin and he had signed off. "What do we hear on the lock-'em-all-up front?" he said.

"The Barre brothers, neither of whom were home at the time and who declare ignorance of all illegal activities, have lawyered up. I don't think the FBI is ever going to be able to charge them with anything. But the guards, that's a different story. There were twenty-four of them and their captain apprehended at the lodge. After that first guy fingered the one who killed Paddy Murphy a few others saw the way the wind was blowing and they flipped, too, and pretty soon it looked like a pancake feed at a Lions Club fundraiser."

He laughed.

"Yeah, if two people hadn't been murdered it would be hilarious." Bobby stopped laughing. "Since nobody died the four guys who burned down the Roadhouse fessed right up, but really the group as a whole wasn't notable for good character. Three were dishonorable discharges, seven or eight of them failed the entrance examination at various police academies, six of them had felony warrants out on them and were returned to their respective states, and I understand two were subsequently identified as being present at the January sixth Capitol insurrection."

"From what I hear of the Barre brothers that would have come as an automatic recommendation for employment. What about the guy who shot Paddy?"

She shook her head. "No priors. From what I hear, he was just a kid looking for a cause."

"He found one, all right. Who was shooting at Dan?"

"Several of them, although everyone is pointing the finger at everyone else. The ballistic forensics alone will take months, if not years."

He gave her an odd look.

"What?"

"What did it feel like, up in the air that afternoon?"

He was a pilot himself, and she understood what he was asking and why. "For a few minutes there it felt like I was in the air with the Blue Angels, only under fire. We weren't fifty feet off Dan's port wing. I could see him sweating. It's not an experience I care to repeat."

"Did anybody shoot at you?"

"I don't think so. If they did, they missed."

"Been there, done that."

He was a veteran who had served under fire. "It occurs to me you're one of the few Park rats who really understand what Dan went through. You should see if he wants to talk about it."

He didn't say anything and she realized he already had. Bobby was the head of a loosely organized group of veterans who had made the Park their home. Once a month Dinah brought Katya out to the homestead and they stayed the night, to give Bobby's group some space to gather and vent. Once a year they partied hard on the anniversary of the second battle of Fallujah. Of course he would talk to Dan.

"Thanks," she said softly. His returning smile was at less than its full strength. "What?"

Bobby was one of those people who never aged but today he looked every one of his years and more. "Those guys who ran me off the road. Even the Barre brothers and their paid militia. They're just a symptom, you know? Maybe someday people in this country will be able to look at each other and not see the enemy, but not today and not anytime soon." He saw Kate's expression. "Oh, we'll be fine, here in the Park. We've figured out how to get along, more or less. And when we forget the aunties remind us." He waved a hand at the room. "Like this."

He looked at Katya, asleep on Dinah's lap.

"But what about her? What happens when she wants to leave?"

Thirty-two

OCTOBER
Anchorage

A WEEK LATER JIM FLEW KATE INTO Anchorage to meet up with Kurt, who had snagged a large corporate client about to go on a hiring spree and who needed someone to vet potential employees. They snugged down the Stationair at Lake Hood and liberated the Forester from the townhouse garage. Jim dropped Kate and Mutt at Kurt's office and set off on a comprehensive reconnaissance of every hardware store, lumber yard, and airplane parts shop between Anchorage and Wasilla. Herbie's Polytechnic was an inexhaustible maw for raw material and the tools needed to beat it into something useful for human use. The supply side shortages and shipping problems exacerbated by Covid and Vladimir Putin's ill-advised If-It's-Tuesday-This-Must-Be-Donetsk tour of Ukraine made ordering anything from the Park inadvisable. Any purchase was far more likely to arrive at its destination if claimed and bought in person and sent to the school's storage unit on Muldoon while one was standing guard over it, preferably armed. As this point he was wishing he'd bought a Herc, because the SUV with wings was proving barely adequate to the task.

He pulled into the Home Depot parking lot on Tudor and paused with his hand on the keys. A Herc. Not necessarily a bad idea. He'd actually flown one years ago in Bering. If that could be called flying. Still, he got it down in one piece and walked away, which was a good landing by any pilot's definition. Most recently Dan's.

Kate and Mutt arrived at the office to find that this time there was no one else waiting for an audience. It looked absolutely the same as it had the last time she'd been there, all damage from the fire repaired and old furniture replaced. She couldn't smell even a trace of smoke.

From behind her desk Ms. Fancyboy, looking entirely unruffled by the alarums and excursions of the previous month, fixed Kate with her usual paralyzing eye. "Ms. Shugak."

"Ms. Fancyboy. Is he in?"

"He is." She surprised Kate with a wintry smile. "He's expecting you. Go right in."

Kate waited a moment, to make sure Ms. Fancyboy really wasn't going to escort her the five feet from her desk to Kurt's door, before sidling past. Mutt followed, keeping Kate between her and Ms. Fancyboy. Once inside with the door closed safely behind her she said, "Agrifina smiled at me. I thought her face was going to break."

"Hey."

"Sorry."

"She believes in formality in business affairs. Nothing wrong with that, and that attitude has sealed the deal with more than one walk-in client."

"I said I was sorry. Geeze."

Kurt's face broke into a grin. "S'okay. She's a strange one but she's all mine."

Mutt barked once. "I beg your pardon, was I ignoring your serene and majestic highness? My bad." Kurt fished out the beef jerky and successfully negotiated another temporary truce for his eardrums.

"Tell me about this new client."

"New clients, plural." Kurt puffed out his chest. "Both corporate. The first one brought in a second. And guess who else?"

"A third? Who?"

"Ikiak Air."

"You're kidding."

"Nope. Barr Junior himself waltzed in here on Monday and said he was expanding the business along the ideas his father had had and he wanted to make sure he was running a clean house. He wanted all their employees vetted and he wants a forensic analysis of the books going as far back as they have been in existence."

"I expect you didn't tell him Tyler has already made a start on that."

NOT THE ONES DEAD

"I expect I did not, and we will definitely be billing Barr Junior for those hours."

"Pirate," Kate said without heat.

Kurt deflated his chest. "I expect you heard. Barr Junior bought Demetri's lodge."

"You're kidding," Kate said again. "I heard it was back on the market, but…"

And very quietly and unobtrusively, too. It had been listed by a Remax office in Boise. Dan had had George fly him out to the lodge and found it stripped and deserted. "They took everything, according to Ranger Dan," Kurt said. "Even the bell out of the church steeple."

The Barre brothers had baled on the Park. Sounded like they were going to be Idaho's problem now. Pity. If they wanted wide-open space and the kind of strongman leadership they appeared to favor she was sure Vladimir Putin would sell them a chunk of Siberia. Although that might be a little too close to Alaska for Kate. "Tyler good?"

"So far as I know." Kurt pulled out a couple of files. "Let me introduce you to our new revenue generators."

An hour later Kate and Mutt debouched from the elevator, frightening a balding, middle-aged man with his chins spilling over the collar of his J. Crew polo, and walked outside into a day where the skies were turning increasingly gray and the air was cold enough to bite. Winter was coming. A black SUV was waiting at the curb and Kate walked around to the back to match the license number with the one displayed on her phone, and opened the hatch. "Dale?"

"Kate?"

She stood back to let Mutt jump up and got into the backseat. The people at her destination made her wait on the street side of security. Five minutes later the elevator opened on Special Agent in Charge James G. Mason. He came through security. "Ms. Shugak."

"Agent Mason. Who was the tenth body?"

They stared at each other, unblinking. He broke first, stepping past her to open the outside door. "Let me buy you a cup of coffee." She felt a light touch on her back. "This way."

Mutt growled, just once, just loud enough to be heard.

The touch vanished. "How does she do that? She wasn't even watching."

After a walk of several blocks, necessarily brisk in the bitter air, they seated themselves in the corner of a sweltering Starbucks over steaming cups of drip coffee. Kate stirred a packet of raw sugar into hers, tasted it, emptied a second packet into it, and stirred some more. A second test with some half-and-half proved satisfactory. She sat back in her chair and looked at him. "Is your office bugged?"

"No." Then he shrugged. "I don't think so."

"Then why here?"

"There, it would have been on the official record. I would have had to take notes. Here, it's an informal conversation between friends."

She watched her hand twirl her coffee cup in circles. "Who was the tenth body?"

"It has yet to be officially identified."

"I am aware." Kate put a calming hand on Mutt's head as her ears had gone ever so slightly back at the tone of Mason's voice. "That doesn't mean you don't know who he is." She looked up to meet his eyes. "And have always known."

He have a faint smile. "What is it you think you know, Kate?"

She leaned back in her chair and looked around the room. It was darker in the corner where their table was than in the rest of the shop, and since it was mid-afternoon it was sparse of customers. A tired-looking young woman in worn gray sweats, a knot of brown hair skewered with a bitten pencil, hunched over a thick book open to what even at a distance looked like a very gory illustration of an open wound on a human body. Her lips moved as she read, and when she felt the need to mark a passage she pulled out the pencil. Inevitably her hair fell down which, revealed, did not look as if it had been washed since Mother's Day. A few underlinings, a marginal notation, and her hair was screwed back into a bun resecured by the pencil.

A few tables beyond her a hipster blinked through a pair of black Wayfarers at a phone the size of a pad. His hair, although much shorter than the woman's, looked as if it hadn't been washed since Russian New Year's. His long, sharp nose, his spiky hair, and the light reflected back from the screen made him look uncannily like a hedgehog.

Neither of them were paying Mason and Kate and not even Mutt the least attention, even if they could be seen through the gloom. Behind the bar the barista, a plump young woman fresh out of high school, was more interested in restocking the cups and napkins and half-and-half than she was in Mason and Kate, but she did give Mutt a long, interested look, which in Kate's book made her smarter than the other two put together.

She looked back at Mason. All the evidence she had to support her theory was circumstantial and speculative. Any ADA worthy of the title would laugh her out of their office practically before she started talking.

But she wasn't making a case here. She was verifying information for her own satisfaction and because she'd been hired to do a job. Her clients were owed the truth. Whether she could prove it or not, she was determined to find out what had happened in the air that day, and why. "Got time for a story?"

This time his eyebrow went up, infinitesimally. "Sure."

She moved her cup in a gentle circle, watching the coffee inside swirl around. "There are a lot of stray details that don't mean much by themselves, but taken together form a convincing context."

"You sound like you're testifying before Congress."

"Maybe in front of a grand jury." But she didn't sound amused and his attempt at humor fell hard enough they both heard it thud on the table between them. "A lot of odd things happened in the Park this summer and fall. A lot of strangers moving through. They're always on their way to somewhere else. Take, for example, the four guys in the Republican red SuperCrew that ran Bobby Clark off the Niniltna road near my house. He is quite certain that if he hadn't had the forethought to bring his HK along with him, and display it in a, shall we say, aggressive manner, that they were prepared to work him over. Maybe more than that."

"Interesting."

"He certainly thought so."

"He have a description?"

"'Four wannabe military in camo fatigues too clean ever to have come anywhere near the real thing.'"

"A direct quote, I'm guessing."

"Yes."

"And he would know?"

"He's a vet. Served under fire, wounded in action."

"So he would know. When was this, exactly?"

"June."

"What else?"

She took him through the oddities her brain trust had laid out one by one. He listened, his face a mask.

"And then there was that Caravan at Paddy Murphy's airstrip on the day of the midair. Where we found evidence of a campsite." She was watching him carefully and saw the repressed wince. "He was one of yours, wasn't he?"

Nothing.

"Yeah," she said. "He was keeping those yahoos at the lodge under surveillance. You'd been tipped, maybe about the new owners, about their private army. You'd been planning for something like this. It's why you had that team on standby in Ahtna, at least twice that I know of, once in June, and again in September. And we found out that the Caravan was registered to the DOJ."

He couldn't hide his flinch. "I'd really like an intro to your hacker."

"It wasn't a hacker, it was a nosy reporter who spotted the tail number and traced it back."

"Vanessa Cox."

"And then I was hired by Barr Senior's kids to find out what happened. Eighty-seven or not, they didn't believe in the NTSB's finding of pilot error. Correctly, as it happens. Barr Senior was engaged in buying up remote properties, and the Barre brothers were in competition with him at least in the Park. It was even more interesting that BB LLC was represented by a law firm in Chicago, Cullen and Associates. As you know, we had the advantage of prior interaction with a fellow client of their law firm." She saw realization dawn and gave him a thin smile. "Yeah. The Chicago mob. I owe you for the intro and I don't mean that in a good way. They tried waving me off."

"The office fire?"

She nodded. "And a phone call. After that all we had to do was follow the breadcrumbs."

He drank coffee and avoided her eyes.

"You should know I don't really give a shit about your man. Fortunes of war. I don't think you do much, either, because wouldn't that be awkward." He flushed but he was smart enough not to say anything. "I am seriously pissed off about Paddy Murphy, however."

He set his jaw.

"I'm betting your man saw him go down, and watched his killers dispose of his body."

Still nothing.

"Probably how they caught him at it. He had a drone, didn't he?"

Mason looked out the window.

"You were relieved when I said that maybe a drone had caused the midair, a drone put in the air by those idiots at the lodge. Because you were afraid it was his drone that caused the midair, weren't you? Your agent's. The guy you had surveilling them. One of the planes swerved to avoid the drone and collided with the other plane. I think your people were there that day to pull him out and landed in the middle of the result. I couldn't figure out how you did it but after I saw the helo arriving in all its Operation Iraqi Freedom glory I figured you beat the NTSB to the crash site. You were looking for any remains of the drone, which I'm guessing is some fancy dandy DARPA model, which if anyone else found it would give away your game. You left his body to muddy the waters, to make people ask questions, to cause them to look around. People like me." Kate took a long breath and let it out slowly. "Really shitty thing to do, Mason. Hide the body in the wreckage."

She waited while he thought. She was willing to wait however long it took.

When he spoke it was slowly, with care for every syllable.

"Hypothetically speaking? If any of this were true, it is possible that the raid could have been carried out by a part of the federal organization in question that is not based in Alaska." His jaw set. "Hypothetically speaking, such a group could have bypassed the control of the local agency entirely, answering only to an authority in DC."

She thought back to the footage she had seen in Johnny's supercut, the skinny guy with the reedy voice preening all over the screen. "Jesus, Mason, why didn't you just kick in the door when they first showed up on the radar?"

He was stung into speech then. "Storm the place? Like Waco? Like Ruby Ridge? You have heard of them?"

"I've even heard of Wounded Knee. So." She reshuffled her ideas. "You were pissed off that you weren't tapped to run this operation, and that's why you leaked the news of the extra body. You knew it would motivate someone to sniff around. Maybe even me. Because I couldn't help but notice that when I needed information, there you were, right in Niniltna. On vacation."

He raised his head and she almost recoiled at the fury she saw in his eyes. "They ran this operation out of DC, based on information passed to them by some CI they had embedded with the J649s. They completely bypassed the local office when they sent that idiotic task force up to Ahtna, not once but twice, on the off chance they'd acquire probable cause to kick down the door. In the process they stumbled and bumbled around and got one of their own killed and very probably one of your own as well. As sure as I'm sitting here they caused that midair although I'll never be able to prove it because they went galumphing in in a panic and tampered with the goddamn evidence. Yes, I outed them, the clumsy, clueless fuckers. It's not like any of them knew where Alaska was before they stepped off the plane."

His fury lasted long enough for her to feel ever so slightly scorched. It faded slowly and only somewhat from his eyes, and he sat back. "As much as I could, anyway, and still keep my job." This was said more with resignation than with defiance, as if he knew how specious that reasoning was. He added, "Hypothetically speaking, of course."

"Oh, of course." She thought back, running down the timeline of events: Demetri's death, the sale of the lodge, the encounters with the low-rent Brink's guards passing for security, the midair, both murders. "Do they know? That you're the leaker? Is this why you've been named agent in charge in Alaska? Is this assignment your punishment?"

"I asked for Alaska," he said shortly. "I like it here. And I believe I can be useful. Current evidence notwithstanding." He paused. "What are you going to do now?"

She looked out the window, at the fading blush of alpenglow on the Chugach Mountains. "The Barr kids asked me to find out what happened to their dad." She smiled at his expression. "I did. Their parent, his business partner, and seven other people died in a midair collision caused by a drone deployed by the federal government. I have a duty to tell them so."

"You have no proof."

"No."

"They won't be able to take any action."

She shook her head. "You know the first thing I tell people who come here? Cheechakos? Never pick a fight with an Alaskan. Never call her a name, never tell a story making fun of them, never hit on his wife. You know why? Because six months later you'll be working for him or she'll be working for you or you'll be working together."

She stood up. "Same goes for manipulating people to do something that was your job in the first place. Take that advice to heart if you ever want local help on a case again."

Epilogue

OCTOBER
The Park

THEY WERE HOME THE NEXT DAY, THE SUV with wings snugged into the hangar and Kate making bread in the kitchen.

"You always make bread when you're pissed off."

She sprinkled more flour on the counter and kneaded it into the dough with unnecessary force. "There are worse ways to work off aggravation."

She was concentrating fully on the task at hand, her expression closed and guarded. He retired to the living room, where he built a fire and sat down once again with Graeber and Wengrow, who had been neglected of late due to the press of other business. Assimilating a total upending of the history of humanity was easier on the nerves than tiptoeing around a pissed-off Kate Shugak.

He looked up from the tale of Kandiaronk, the Wendat who came to dinner with Baron de la Hontan in Montreal and stayed to verbally annihilate European society and mores. You had to respect a guy who could eat his host's salt while saying things like, "I find it hard to see how you could be much more miserable than you already are."

He looked over the top of his book to see only the top of Kate's head through the pass-through. Loud smacks indicated she was still taking her mad out on the bread. He went back to the book.

Six o'clock rolled around before he risked another look, mostly because aromatic rumors of dinner were wafting over to the couch. This time she was at the stove. Something was sizzling. "It was my turn to cook dinner."

"Yeah, well, I was here and you were all engrossed in your doorstop there."

She sounded grumpy, which was an improvement over homicidal. He looked over at Mutt, sprawled in front of the fireplace, also holding a watching brief from a safe distance. She flicked her ears at him.

He marked his place and got up to prowl around into the kitchen, where he stopped just behind Kate, all the better to slide his arms around her waist and pull her in tight. Into her ear he said, "Have I ever told you what happens to me when I watch you cooking?"

He fully expected an elbow to the gut so he was agreeably surprised, not to mention relieved, when she replied with a smile in her voice. "Or watch me walk, or talk, or—"

"Breathe." He spun her around and kissed her.

"Whew," she said when he raised his head, and to his

satisfaction he saw that a lovely color had run up beneath the olive skin. "Shall I pause dinner?"

"Let's not be hasty." He kissed her again, a quick one this time. She laughed, that low rasp of sound that always grated so pleasurably across every single one of his nerve endings. "I'll set the table."

It was a cold, clear night beneath a sheen of stars slowly being eclipsed by a rising moon, which itself was soon to be eclipsed by the northern lights if the aurora forecast was to be believed. When the table had been cleared and the dishwasher loaded Kate said, "I'm going to go sit on the rock for a while."

He considered his response carefully and made it as neutral as possible. "Want some company?"

His heart turned over at the smile in her eyes. "Always."

They bundled up and Jim remembered to grab the cushion from the closet. The rock in question, perched at the top of the cliff overlooking the creek named for Kate's mother, had had its top worn smooth by two generations of Shugak backsides but it was still hard and cold. He hopped up first and gathered her into the nest made by his crossed legs. She leaned against him with what he could have sworn was a sigh of contentment and he wrapped his arms around her and leaned his chin on her head. Behind them the silver radiance from the rising moon grew. Ahead of them a delicate line of green light threaded itself across the northern horizon.

"You've been awfully quiet since you came back from

talking to Barr Junior and his sister. They say what they're going to do?"

For a moment he thought he might have broken the spell. Then she stirred but more to snuggle in closer than to draw away. "People with money are different."

"They have more money than you and me."

There was a smile in her voice. "You channel Hemingway again, you'll find yourself at the bottom of this cliff we're on the edge of."

He chuckled.

She sighed. "Will they sue? I doubt it. Be more their style to have their lawyer contact the FBI's lawyer and broker a deal."

"Yeah, but there's no proof of anything. We're only guessing."

Kate thought of Mason. *Yes, I outed them, those clumsy, clueless fuckers.* "I have a feeling the DOJ will settle."

"With an NDA."

"Undoubtedly."

"Wonder how Barr Senior would have felt about that?"

"Fine, so long as the check was big enough. The bottom line is how people like Barr Senior keep score. And, hey, his son is expanding the business. He will be all over a cash infusion about now."

"What about the families of the victims in the Beaver?"

"The didn't hire me, the Barrs did."

In her own way, Kate was as hard-assed as any Barr Jr. or Sr. ever thought of being. "Tough on their families."

She wouldn't tell him about the four anonymous calls that

had been made from a burner phone whose location had been masked by the ever helpful Tyler, to four different numbers, one in Kodiak, one in Seattle, one in Las Vegas, and one in Taiwan. Wait and see what happened, if anything. "Very."

"And you."

She went still. He wondered if she was surprised that he had noticed. He waited.

"You know why I like my job?" she said eventually. "It's because usually, not always but most of the time, I get a perp walk. This time I don't get one. It feels so—"

"Frustrating?"

"I was going to say anticlimactic, but frustrating works, too." She sounded glum.

"Like I said before. You got those chuckleheads out of the Park and you found out what actually happened so your clients don't have to spend the rest of their lives thinking their father killed himself and eight other people because he was too goddamn stubborn to let go of the stick. Maybe you didn't get a parade but you did good."

She wasn't satisfied by his words, but she was comforted, a little.

"One thing I don't understand. Why did they hire the kids to build the church?"

"I asked Mason that. The CO told them that Mother Barre insisted on building the church and the boys didn't want to take the crews off from the other construction so they looked around and found Herbie's. Might have thought it would build some rep with the locals, too."

Jim thought back to that sunny day in front of Bingley's, and of the thin, angry woman glaring at them from inside the camper van. "Huh. Well. At least they paid them in cash. I can't believe they just walked away. The construction costs alone must have been astronomical." Nowadays he knew far more than he ever wanted to about those.

"They don't like publicity. And they can write the loss off."

"What? How?"

Kate gave a soundless laugh. "They're a nonprofit."

"You are fucking kidding me."

"According to Mason there were a lot of hinky nonprofits that got through the screening process at the IRS during the past administration. For a hefty fee, I'm sure."

The line of green light in the north was widening. Soon it separated from the horizon and formed a band that began to kink and bend. The band spread into sheets and then pillars. One shifted into red and formed its own sheets and pillars. The stars shone through them like diamonds embedded in the firmament.

"I keep thinking about the Barre brothers," he said. A thin green line spiraled up overhead. "About all of them, the election deniers and the politicians who are trying like hell to keep everyone who doesn't look like them from voting, and the folks who seem determined to elect a dictator so long as he's as white as you can get without bleach.

"They've been so angry for so long and they don't seem to be doing anything but get angrier. I mean, your own private army? What's that about? Who did they think they were going to march on, Niniltna? I don't get it. I don't see what it gets them."

A second green thread joined the first and began to widen. He rubbed his chin over her head again, taking comfort in the texture of her hair, in the warmth of her body against his. What could be wrong with this world if he still had these things?

Kate remembered what Anne Flanagan had said about Christofascists. "I think I understand them pretty well."

"Let's hear it then, because I would welcome any argument that these people aren't just ordinary, everyday batshit crazy."

"People who look like them have had it all their own way on this continent since the first European stepped on shore. They're not stupid. They can add. They can read the demographics and they can see that they are about to be in the minority. They're terrified of what might happen to their children, because they know exactly how badly their ancestors behaved toward ours. And so they have engaged in this fruitless, hopeless quest to roll back the clock, and they can't, and deep down they know they can't, and it only makes them more scared, which makes them more angry, and then we get the craziest ones of all forming groups like the J649s to defend themselves against the great replacement."

"What's the solution?"

"A practical one?" The aurora increased in intensity and movement overhead, engaged in their own dance. "I don't know, but we'd better find one quick. You heard Bobby. He's terrified for his daughter. He doesn't want her to get shot for sleeping while black in her own bed."

"Are we done then?"

"As a nation? We might be. Ruthe says no law says the American empire lasts forever. She's right. No empire ever has." She sighed. "But maybe not. We survived our first civil war. No law says we won't survive our second."

"Jesus, Shugak. And on that cheery thought." His chest rose and fell beneath her head. "You know what I find scariest about all this?"

"What?"

"The drones."

"How so?"

"I'm pilot in command every time I climb into the left seat. I'm careful, I follow the rules, I watch for traffic, and I know the stats say how safe flying is. And then I think about all those drones. Willard, the *NatGeo* guy, the spook, those morons at the lodge. For crissake, who didn't have one in the air that day? The idea that some jackass like Howie Katelnikof, that little weasel, someone with no time on the stick and no idea of what's safe and what isn't being able to put a drone in the air and run it into me is… disconcerting."

"Also terrifying, and thanks for that."

"Anyone can buy a drone off Amazon or buy them in bulk like the Barre brothers. Pretty soon we won't need rifles to fight a war, we'll just send in a drone with a bomb."

"Pretty sure we're doing that now."

"All the more reason to be afraid, be very afraid."

"'No one in space can hear you scream.'"

He huffed out a laugh. "Or at altitude." But some of the tension he was feeling drained away.

Mutt drifted out of the gloom like a very hairy ghost and took up station at their feet. In the distance a wolf howled. Her ears flicked but otherwise she didn't move. She had chosen. She was home for good.

He raised his eyes to the heavens and watched the aurora dance. He might even have heard them singing. "Well. As long as we've got aunties, I think the Park is as safe a place to live as anywhere is these days."

She snorted. "We got people drinking downtown now. That'll end well."

She sounded so much like Auntie Vi in that moment that he almost laughed. "Don't you get it, Kate?"

"Get what?"

"You're an auntie now."

The lights danced higher in the sky, green and red and icy white, and she sighed again, but not at them. "Damn you, Emaa."

And there it came, that familiar three notes descending, that lovely, poignant call of the golden-crowned sparrow, welling up out of the dusk and filling the night air with memories of the gruff old woman who had raised her and bullied her and—

Loved her.

And still did.

And beneath that lovely trill of sound did Kate hear an undertone of laughter?

Nothing spooky about hearing the spring-is-here bird sound off in October, Jim thought. He quelled the involuntary shiver that ran up his spine. "It's not all bad. I mean, hey."

"What?"

"Look at me." He grinned at the lights.

"I'm sleeping with an auntie."

Notes and Acknowledgments

THE TITLE OF THIS NOVEL WAS INSPIRED BY Robert Frost's poem, "Out, Out—", specifically the line reading "And they, since they/Were not the one dead, turned to their affairs." The world always moves on, and so does the Park.

My thanks to my insurance agent, Nancy Field, who clarified what happens when an insured property is destroyed by arson. They'll pay, but a lot quicker if the property owner has an ironclad alibi.

My thanks to Gary Porter for estimating how many hours Jim has. I do so love getting the details right.

My thanks to Patrice and Rick Krant for inspiring the Lego test. I have no idea if it would really work but I recommend vocational schools everywhere give it a try.

The idea for this book is an easy trace back to its origin. I was weeding my rock garden one day when I heard a buzz and looked up to see a drone hovering overhead. It hung there for about thirty seconds, long enough for me to go get my

DANA STABENOW

gun and shoot it down, should I feel so moved. And then I thought, I can't do that, because what if there was a plane flying overhead and I missed the drone and hit the plane? I could kill somebody. And then I thought, whoa.

Shortly thereafter I read Simon Winchester's *Land*, which includes the story of a couple of billionaire brothers who have bought up much of eastern Idaho and western Montana and are busy building compounds and fences and refusing the locals access to the same trails they've been hunting and fishing and hiking on for centuries. So I thought, What if somebody tried that in the Park? And then I thought, park lands come under federal jurisdiction. Enter the FBI, which views domestic terrorism as the biggest threat to the nation today. That was easy.

But before anything else I read *Our Towns* by James and Deborah Fallows. Their book reinforced something I have always believed: that if you want real change, if you want real progress on any front, you start at the local level and work up. It's not glamorous, and a lot of the time it's not fun, and sometimes you just want to tell everyone to shut up and do things your way, but local is where everything begins. Kate's Park and Emaa and her aunties and Jim's board are the result of a lifetime spent watching Alaska Native women rise to leadership positions in every single Alaska Native organization from village tribes to the regional corporations, as well as in local and state governance, and most recently to Congress.

It's not a new story that people come to Alaska to start over. Many do so anonymously and want to keep it that way.

When I was working at Galbraith Lake on the TransAlaska Pipeline in 1976 I saw a reporter with a video camera come in one door of the mess hall and several workers immediately get up and leave by another. Alaska's a big place. You can always find someplace here to hide, even today. Just not from Kate Shugak.

The book Jim is reading is *The Dawn of Everything* by David Graeber and David Wengrow. The book Kate is reading is *The Galaxy, and the Ground Within* by Becky Chambers. They are very good books and you should read them, too.

Lastly, a hat tip to Nala, Scooter, and Trouble, who by their actions offer inspiration for Mutt's behavior, although Mutt would like it clearly understood that she is the boss dog of this pack.

ABOUT THE AUTHOR

DANA STABENOW was born in Anchorage, Alaska and raised on a 75-foot fishing tender. She knew there was a warmer, drier job out there somewhere and found it in writing. Her first book in the bestselling Kate Shugak series, *A Cold Day for Murder*, received an Edgar Award from the Mystery Writers of America.

Follow Dana at www.stabenow.com.